The One TRUE Me and You

The One TRUE Me and You

A Novel

Remi K. England

W

WEDNESDAY BOOKS

NEW YORK

First published in the United States by Wednesday Books, an imprint of St. Martin's Publishing Group

THE ONE TRUE ME AND YOU. Copyright © 2022 by Megan N. England. All rights reserved. Printed in the United States of America. For information, address St. Martin's Publishing Group, 120 Broadway, New York, NY 10271.

www.wednesdaybooks.com

Designed by Devan Norman

Library of Congress Cataloging-in-Publication Data

Names: England, Remi K., author.
Title: The one true me and you : a novel / Remi K. England.
Description: First edition. | New York : Wednesday Books, 2022.
Identifiers: LCCN 2021043366 | ISBN 9781250814869 (hardcover) | ISBN 9781250814876 (ebook)
Subjects: CYAC: Fans (Persons)—Fiction. | Congresses and conventions—Fiction. | Beauty contests—Fiction. | Gender identity—Fiction. | Lesbians—Fiction. | Dating (Social customs)—Fiction. | LCGFT: Novels.
Classification: LCC PZ7.1.E5368 On 2022 | DDC [Fic]—dc23
LC record available at https://lccn.loc.gov/2021043366

Our books may be purchased in bulk for promotional, educational, or business use. Please contact your local bookseller or the Macmillan Corporate and Premium Sales Department at 1-800-221-7945, extension 5442, or by email at MacmillanSpecialMarkets@macmillan.com.

First Edition: 2022

10 9 8 7 6 5 4 3 2 1

For everyone who's found themselves in fandom.

And for teen me.
Our struggle paved the way for the world in these pages.
We are happy. We are okay. We are powerful.
We are loved.

Part I

FRIDAY

Chapter One

TEAGAN

I secretly hate tiaras.

They're itchy, for one. The cheap ones have little scalp-killing claws that clutch your head like a praying mantis about to devour a sad, struggling fly (me). The slightly less cheap ones either strangle your brain within an inch of its life or fall off, taking twenty pins and half your hair with it. And the real ones? The worst. Heavy, and expensive, whispering in your ear like: *Don't screw this up. Aww, you want a scholarship? That's cute. Now walk down these steep-ass stairs in four-inch heels and don't look down, or everyone will think you're a mess. Got it?*

I don't got it. But I'll take a quick glance at the stairs over falling out of this bus, thanks.

The group moms have their hands full orchestrating the chaos of fifty-one competitors arriving simultaneously. Most of the girls are too busy meeting up with their roommates, hugging their pageant besties, or whining about the humidity to listen to the politely veiled orders, much less notice me. I've seen a few of the girls on the East Coast pageant circuit, but it's mostly a sea of unfamiliar faces from all over the country.

There's really only one face I'm desperate to see, though. I glance down at my phone to see if she's texted . . . but no. Texts from my aunt and dad to make sure I got here safe and messages of support from my friends in the local pageant system back home, mostly. And of course, marching orders from my pageant coach, Rhonda. Scheduled check-ins, reminders about being discreet, and a demand for a phone call immediately after registration. I can never afford to pay her expenses to be with me at out-of-state pageants, though some girls certainly do that. It never stops her from reaching out in nearly psychic moments of scolding and reassurance, and I always find myself looking around to see if there's some kind of spy drone buzzing overhead, watching my every move. I text back: **Yes ma'am, orders received. *salute***

"Teagan!"

My head whips around at the sound of my name, and a giddy, honest smile breaks through my practiced facade. *There* she is. I turn just in time to catch Jess as she throws herself into my arms. The Florida air is like hot dog breath, moist and smelly, and I'm overly conscious of how damp I am after being outside for a whopping thirty seconds. Jess doesn't seem to notice or care, thankfully.

"I missed you so much!" she says into my thick, near-black hair, her hug nearly cracking my ribs. I tighten my arms around her and squeeze, not trusting my voice to produce actual words. We talk online almost every day, and on the phone a few times per month, but it's just not the same. We only see each other in person at pageants for the most part, whenever our regions overlap for competition. The five-hour drive from central Virginia to western Pennsylvania is just long enough to make it impossible, except for our annual summer vacation extravaganza. She pulls back to look me over, brushing her hands over my shirt and Miss Virginia sash to straighten out the wrinkles she caused.

"I scoped out our room already," she says, flashing me her hotel key, bright-white plastic against warm-brown skin. "Solid view of a brick wall across the way. No judges spying from the pool deck this time."

"Thank God," I reply. "I needed something to go right. You know who's right next door to us? *North Carolina*. She'll be on my ass all weekend. In a bad way, obviously."

Jess winces. "Ouch, bad luck. I think Oregon said she was rooming with her, though, so at least we'll have friendly forces on the front lines. Have you met? You might like her, actually," she says with a significant eyebrow waggle.

I roll my eyes and lower my voice.

"I don't date pageant girls. Period. Been there, done that, never doing it again, thanks. Can we go register now? I'd like to have time to actually hang out with you before the first rehearsal." I pause and glance down at the fair, Irish skin of my arms then up at the sun. "Also, I'm pretty sure I'm going to turn into a tomato if I stay out here."

Jess looks for a moment like she doesn't want to let it drop, but the bellhop interrupts, one hand on the cart piled high with my garment bags and cheap luggage. I peel off a five-dollar bill and tell him my room number with a thank-you, suppressing a cringe as the money disappears into his pocket and he rolls the cart away. The first of many expenses I forgot about when budgeting for this trip. I'll have to be really careful this weekend.

Now's not the time to obsess over worries, though. Now's the time to focus on the best friend right in front of me and make the most of our brief freedom before the demanding pageant schedule takes over. I let the pure joy of the moment take hold: I'm finally here, at a national pageant, with a good chance of winning and my best friend by my side. What more could I ask for?

I hook my arm through Jess's and tug her toward the enormous glass front doors of the hotel. Two attendants pull them open for us as we approach, but Miss North Carolina bursts through before we get there, her glittering high heels clicking aggressively through the tiled foyer.

"Oh *my* God. Wait until you see the freak show inside!" she calls to her groupies in her long, southern drawl. She breezes by without sparing either of us so much as a glance. "It's like a nerd convention in there, y'all!"

Jess and I exchange the kind of glance we've perfected over years on the pageant circuit: small, charming smiles, twinkling eyes, and an eyebrow so barely raised that an outsider would never know. To anyone else, it reads as two polished young women sharing a moment of humor. To us, it means *are you serious right now?*

Miss NC may own the evening gown portion of every competition, but the first sniff the judges get of that attitude will knock her out of the top fifteen for sure. Along with the strict guidelines set forth in the pageant application (never married, never given birth, having good health and "moral character," all totally unsubtle discrimination), they also expect you to live up to the organization's *values* at all times. Meaning, don't be an awful human being.

Some people have a hard time with that part.

North Carolina, though, she's a master manipulator. The judges have never managed to catch her at any of the pageants I've seen her at. Or if they did, she somehow southern charmed her way out of it. All that shiny, blond hair must have a hypnotic effect.

On the other side of the entrance, the foyer opens up into a massive lobby with soaring pillars, glittering chandeliers, and velvety red armchairs in cozy groups. Floor-to-ceiling windows let the Florida sunshine spill over the room and its occupants, though the overactive air conditioner keeps it frigid. The people behind the front desk look like they could be pageant contestants themselves, with their polished smiles and well-fitted suits. It's nice—a reasonably priced hotel that takes itself as seriously as a five-star. A bit gaudy in its attempts to look fancy, but nice all the same.

And then I look past the glam to the groups of people milling about.

Oh.

No.

Everywhere I look, I see badges, T-shirts, and accessories themed after one thing: *The Great Game.* My all-time favorite show, the latest in a long string of modern-day Sherlock Holmes remakes. My ultimate nerdy indulgence. Better than *Elementary,* better than the BBC one, even better than the one they kicked off last year on one of the big US networks. *The Great Game* is objectively amazing, and I'll fight anyone who tries to argue. I read the fanfic, I draw the fan art, I've watched the episodes a dozen times each, and it's *everywhere.* I knew GreatCon was happening this weekend—how did I not put it together that it was happening in *Orlando?* At *this* hotel?

That's not even the worst part.

All throughout the lobby, there are amazingly hot fandom folks, laughing in groups and hanging all over each other. Brightly dyed hair, piercings everywhere, tattoos on arms and chests—the chests, wow—and all of them part of the fandom I love. I admit, I have a type, and it's just about *everyone in this lobby,* dear God. Every chaperone at this pageant must be able to *feel* the waves of gay pouring off me right now.

There's no way I'm going to make it through this weekend. I don't stand a chance.

Jess coughs delicately. "Tea, I can see your lady boner from here. Put it away and get your smile back on before a judge sees you drooling," she says, shifting to block me from the view of the pageant check-in table. "You're here for one thing: to win some scholarship money. And to see the look on North Carolina's face when you do it. And to help your charity. Okay, three things, whatever."

She pauses, raising a perfectly sculpted eyebrow. "But none of those things include hitting up some fan convention where any judge can see you geeking out over a TV show and hitting on fangirls. You know I love and support you, but the only person I'm willing to lose this pageant to is you, so I'm gonna need you to get it together, Miss Virginia. You have a real shot this year."

A real shot. Ideally, my last shot. I *can* keep competing once I go to college, if I have to. But every year I compete is a year I have to deny myself. I can't be out and proud, can't date openly. If I win this year, though, that's it—the Miss Cosmic Teen USA pageant awards $25,000 to the first-place winner. Combined with the scholarship money I've cobbled together winning local and state titles, I'll have enough to cover all four years of college.

I can finally be free.

I take a slow, deep breath in through my nose and fix my gaze on the ceiling. She's right. I know. I love fandom, and as soon as I can, I'll support it publicly until my last breath.

For now, though, obsessing over femslash fan fiction isn't exactly the sort of good, wholesome, all-American, pageant-acceptable hobby I can talk about during my stage interview. And the whole lesbian thing definitely wouldn't help. Sure, there was a gay Miss America contestant back in 2016, but she came out *after* winning the state title and didn't even get to the top fifteen at the final pageant. Maybe those facts are totally unrelated, but maybe they aren't. I can't risk it. I just wasn't prepared—I never expected my two lives to collide like this, and definitely not on the most important weekend of my pageant career.

At my last meeting with Rhonda before leaving for Florida, she told me straight up that I'll have to nail everything if I even want a chance at Top Five. This is a whole new level of competition for me. My first—and hopefully last—national pageant.

I have to focus.

I tear my gaze away from the curvy waist of a girl in a tight shirt with *"I believe in Johnlock"* printed on the front, skip right over the two boys kissing in front of a cardboard cutout of the lead actors, and close it all away to do a posture check, feeling the alignment of my spine, the tension in my neck. There will be plenty of time to date cute fandom girls once I'm at my fully-paid-for college of choice. The college I'll never be able to afford any other way.

For now, I have a mission.

I lift my chin, adjust my tiara and sash, and turn the charm on full blast. I've been looking forward to this weekend for weeks, and I won't let this hiccup stand in my way.

With practiced pageant smiles and swinging hips, Jess and I glide up to the pageant sign-in table, radiating confidence and grace as we take our places in line. Some of the less experienced girls are dressed down and makeup free, stale from their long travel, but we know better. The judges are *always* watching, every single minute.

I introduce myself to the woman behind the table, accept my welcome packet, and sign my name on the dotted line.

Time to win this thing.

The game is on.

Chapter
Two

✳

KAYLEE

Their lips crashed together, hungry and impatient, a hot mingling of breathy groans. Finally. *John's tongue teased at Sherlock's bottom lip, ta—*

"Ugh, *damn it!*"

I slam my finger down on the backspace key until the entire paragraph disappears and flop back on my fluffy hotel pillow, hands pressed over my eyes. "I've used the word *lips* like a *hundred* times in the past three sentences. How do people write kissing? This is *infuriating.*"

I can practically hear Ami rolling her eyes at me from the other bed. "Why don't you ask the *you* of three weeks ago that posted that alternate universe firefighter thing? It was basically all kissing with an occasional fire truck thrown in for flavor. You clearly know how to write it."

I let my hands fall away from my eyes and sigh, staring in despair up at the weirdly textured ceiling. "That's the worst part—I've done it before. I know I can. So, what, have I completely lost my writing ability? Or maybe I've written every possible description of kissing there is and there's nothing new left to write."

"Or maybe you're distracted by being at *freaking GreatCon* and you need a break," Ami says, her face buried in the con program guide. "We're supposed to go meet the others for dinner soon anyway."

My stomach goes all fluttery, just like it does right before I hit POST on a new fic. Meeting Cakes and Lady for the first time in person *shouldn't* be a big deal. We basically live in one another's pockets as much as you can when you're over a thousand miles apart. Our nightly chats and video calls keep me sane when Ami's super-permissive parents go through one of their occasional we-should-be-more-strict-shouldn't-we phases and put her on lockdown.

And yet.

"I promised my readers a new chapter tonight. I can't go until I'm done revising it. Besides, this story could be the best one I've written if I could just focus. What if someone asks me about it at the panel tomorrow morning? And the judges for the contest might be looking at our back catalog and—"

Ami slams her program down with a huff, her deep-brown eyes glaring with the promise of a swift death. "Half your readers are probably *here*, Kay, and the rest will understand because they wish they were here. I'm sure the story you submitted is fantastic—not that you've let me read it. And they aren't going to go looking for your fanfic when what they're judging is an original Sherlock Holmes retelling that has nothing to do with TGG. Cut yourself some slack and let's *go*. I'm hungry."

I am, too, honestly, but my stomach is doing flips for a totally different reason. The second I leave this hotel room, I have to face the *other* reasons I came here this weekend. I have goals. Three of them. And they're terrifying.

1. Ask someone to use they/them pronouns for me for the first time.

2. Dress and cosplay in a way that's more gender-comfortable and see how it feels.

3. Kiss a girl for the first time.

I'm definitely going to do all three of these things by the end of the weekend.

I'm definitely hiding in my hotel posting a new chapter of this fic instead.

Ami tosses her program across the room and flops dramatically on the bed by my feet. "I'm going to lick your big toe if you don't get up in five seconds."

I recoil in horror, tucking my feet underneath me to protect their virtue.

"That's the most disgusting thing you've ever said, and also, I've been wearing these socks since 4:00 A.M., and they probably taste like sweaty Cheetos from the band room floor."

"The *most* disgusting? I feel like I have a pretty strong track record on disgusting and this isn't really—"

"*Please* just let me finish rereading this chapter. I'll post, we can go, it'll be great, promise. Five minutes."

"Five."

"Exactly."

"Four."

"What?"

"Three."

"Come on."

"Two."

"Please don't do this."

"One."

She comes at my feet with her tongue out, and my laptop nearly goes flying as I flinch away. My thumb manages to click the POST button in the process.

Well, so much for rereading the chapter one more time. It's out there now. Instant notification in my subscribers' inboxes.

Sigh.

"I can't believe you almost licked a sweaty band-room Cheeto," I say.

"I mean, not literally."

"Basically."

She wouldn't have done it for real. I think. You never can be too careful with Ami, though. Her determination takes her to weird places. She can't just be a gamer, she's the gamer who's played every single game that even mentions Sherlock Holmes. And she can't just *play* all those games, she's got to take coding classes and make one of her own. She's the brave one, always charging ahead to the next thing and dragging me kicking and screaming behind her. I wouldn't even be at the con this weekend if she hadn't spent two months laying out a detailed plan to convince me.

And now that we're here, there's no way she'll let me miss out. She pops up and bounces on the balls of her feet, the skirt of her custom magnifying glass–print dress swishing around her knees as she waits for me to get my ass up. My "working on a fic" excuse is gone. I cast around for a replacement. I just had a brilliant idea and I need to get it out? I have to prep for the fic authors' panel I'm on tomorrow morning? I feel a sudden bout of stress pooping coming on? My mom is calling?

My phone vibrates on the nightstand.

Actually that last one is true. Ugh. I groan and wave the

phone at Ami then flop back onto the pillow again with an arm over my eyes.

"Hello." Total deadpan.

"Hi, baby, just checking in. Everything's okay?"

"Just as fine as it was at lunchtime."

You know how you can hear people smile over the phone? Well, my mom does that, but with puffed-up, delicate-southern-lady indignation instead.

"Don't you sass me, missy. You are still under eighteen, and that means you're my responsibility. Don't make me regret letting you go to this . . . thing." She knows exactly what this *thing* is, but her passive-aggressive game has been carefully honed over years of small-town politics. "Have you talked to Mr. and Mrs. Choi this evening?"

I roll over so my face and phone are pressed into the pillow. "No, Ami's parents are staying at a different hotel and leaving us alone." Like I wish *you* would. The only reason they came at all was so they could sign for the hotel room. They're at Disney World all weekend, leaving us in perfect fandom bliss.

"No *what?*" Mom says significantly.

The pillow prevents me from rolling my eyes, but the intention is there.

"No, *ma'am*," I say through gritted teeth.

"Good girl," she says. "I'll leave you be for the rest of the night. I know you want to be rid of your poor old mom—"

Yes, please, lay on the guilt.

"—but I expect a phone call from you in the morning, young lady. Have fun tonight."

"Yeah."

Silence.

"*Yes, ma'am*," I correct.

"I love you, baby."

"Love you, too, Mom."

I stab the END CALL button before she can draw it out any further.

Good girl. Missy. Young lady. Every one of them feels like nails down the chalkboard of my brain. Why does every single word directed at me have to drip with gender expectations? My resolve hardens, and I finally roll my ass out of bed.

With quick, decisive movements, I pull a plaid button-down on over my TGG T-shirt and roll up the sleeves then head over to the mirror and pull my burgundy-dyed hair back. It's barely long enough to get a hair tie around, and the shorter pieces in the front fall forward. It makes it look like I have shorter hair than I actually do, and the dark color pops against my fair skin. I run my eyes over my form in the mirror, looking for anything else I can tweak, but I'm already makeup free and wearing my simplest jeans and sneakers. My eyes linger on the slight button gap in my shirt over my chest, and the faint stretch around my hips, but overall, I really like this look. It's comfortable, on multiple levels. Fairly neutral. If you squinted at me from across the room, I don't think you'd be able to make a gender assumption. Not that people *should*. Not that dresses and skirts can't be neutral. No clothing should come with gender assumptions. But when you've been forced into skirts and dresses your whole life despite the fact that wearing them makes you feel like an imposter . . . ugh.

Why am I trying to justify all this in my head?

Baby steps. I feel good. Comfortable. Ready to meet my friends in person for the first time, looking like myself.

I step back to the bed and slam my laptop closed. The words weren't really happening anyway. Ami was right—I was distracted. I can always move that bit I just deleted to the next chapter and start on it later. Maybe a brain break will help. An annoying voice in the back of my head scolds me that the whole point of checking in early instead of tonight was to have time to write in the hotel room, but if I force it right now, I'll only vomit garbage words all over the page. Realistically, I know that once we meet up with Cakes and Lady, there'll be very little time for writing. I'll just stay up after everyone else has gone to bed.

I take one last look in the mirror, breathe deep, then turn back to Ami.

"Okay. I'm ready. Let's go."

A furious bout of butterflies attacks my stomach as soon as we open the door to our room, and I feel like rolling my eyes at myself. I know Cakes and Lady better than almost anyone. We've video chatted so many times. We've exchanged like a hundred selfies. They know what I look like already. They may not have seen my whole body up close, but they've seen me, and I've seen them. It's fine. Everything is fine. I yank my shirt down, run a hand over my hair, and throw myself out the door before I lose my nerve.

Ami and I catch the elevator to the lobby and spend a severely awkward sixty seconds trapped with two aggressively peppy power moms who fill the elevator with their clashing perfumes. They chatter in sharp, high-pitched voices about judges for something or other and repeating rumors about people called *Daisy* and *Trixie* and other names that could either belong to young girls or small dogs. I catch Ami's eye and only barely keep from bursting out into an inappropriate giggle loop.

The fresh air of the lobby is like the sweet nectar of the gods when the doors finally slide open, and I take a long breath to clear my nose . . . only to choke on it when I process the scene around me.

Why is the hotel full of models?

No . . . not models. *Pageant girls.* Everywhere I look, it's bright-white smiles, sashes and tiaras, stylish clothes and perfect curves. Every girl is polished and perky, chattering happily and posing for selfies in front of a giant, glittery satin banner that reads MISS COSMIC TEEN SCHOLARSHIP COMPETITION. My chest floods with a single overpowering feeling.

Immediate and visceral fear.

My eyes automatically scan the crowd for a familiar face as I calculate the odds. Even if *she* is here, fandom folks and fake tropical plants both outnumber pageant contestants at least three to one. Hundreds of people are attending the con. The pageant has maybe fiftyish contestants at most. The chances of running into her can't be that high, can they?

Who am I kidding, of course they are. I share no less than four classes with Plainsborough's local teen beauty queen, and she's made it her personal mission in life to torment me. Just last week, she wrote *lesbian* on my locker in obnoxiously bright-pink lipstick. I mean, I'm not sure she's wrong, and it's not like it's an insult, but still. That's for me to figure out. That's my business. And does the term *lesbian* even apply if you're maybe, quite possibly . . . nonbinary? I don't need her in my head on this weekend of all weekends. This stuff is confusing enough.

But there are a million pageants. This is just one, three states away from home. There's no way she's here. People *like* her, sure, but not her specifically. I'm safe. Even if someone latches on to me, gives me hell, it'll stay here. It won't follow me home. Just like the rest of this weekend, it's temporary. It'll be fine.

Ami clutches my arm and leans in to whisper, "They were definitely not here when I came down to get lunch a few hours ago. Where the hell did this all come from?"

Those power moms in the elevator—they must have been

pageant moms. Two of them probably could have set up this entire registration area, complete with wafting drapes of lavender tulle and ribbon, in twenty minutes flat. In heels and pencil skirts. *While* schmoozing the judges. Every year they take over the entire town for their Miss Plainsborough Sweetheart festivities, somehow managing to alter traffic patterns, seize control of the local police, and sway every local business into sponsoring. They're unstoppable.

Intermingled with the glitterati are more familiar, comfortable faces. I don't recognize all of them, though some I've definitely seen as selfies posted on Scroll, but I recognize the *type*. These are my people. The kind of people I'd walk past at the mall and actually feel comfortable making eye contact with. People with amazing dye jobs, bodies of all shapes and sizes, bright eyes with open emotion. Nerdy T-shirts and fannish hand flapping everywhere—the one place in the world where I can easily meld into a crowd and have something to say.

Then I spot two faces in particular that are as familiar to me as Ami's, though we've never met in person.

Cakes and Lady. They're here. My fandom crew. My closest friends besides Ami.

I squeak in the back of my throat, excitement and nerves lighting a flare in my chest.

"There they are!"

Cakes spots me at the same time and lets out a shriek that turns a few heads in both crowds. Next thing I know, I have a nose full of formerly blond curls dyed fabulously purple and blue, pale arms wound around my neck, and a shoulder damp with happy tears. I clutch her shoulders like I'm drowning and fight back the rush of heat behind my eyes. We talk every day, every *single* day without exception, but this is already so much better. I hold her close with one arm and reach out to fist-bump

Lady with the other. Unbelievably, Lady's perfect eyeliner and dramatic lip color choices hold up just as well in person as they do in her selfies, and it's so great to—

I freeze, completely paralyzed at the sight over Lady's shoulder.

No. Nooo, no, no, no, you've *got* to be kidding me.

She *is* here. Miss Plainsborough Sweetheart. Miss Lipstick-on-My-Locker.

Miss North Carolina. And she's standing twenty feet away.

Cakes pulls back and holds me at arm's length. The silence grows awkward, but I can't make my breath move, and my muscles are locked tight under her hands. A surge of anger overrides the rest of my thoughts. Of *course*, something had to mess with this chance. My time away from home, away from my mom, away from my suffocating little town that prides itself on embracing every bad stereotype people have about the South. She's *here.*

"What's wrong?" Cakes asks, her earlier giddiness gone.

I hunch behind her taller frame and look over my shoulder, catching Ami's gaze. Judging by her horrified expression, I'm guessing she saw her, too. This is bad. So, *so*, bad.

Ami shuffles around so her back is to the pageant crowd and leans closer. "Behind us, Miss North Carolina. She goes to our school. She ignores me and pretty much everyone else, but she gives Kay hell all the time. If she sees us here, things at school will get even worse."

My eyes fix on Ami's con badge. More specifically, her Scroll name (ConsultingMi221b) printed in bold letters across the bottom. *Oh no.* "If she gets a look at my badge, she'll see my Scroll username. She'll be able to find all my fanfic. Oh my *God*, she'll probably print it out and tape it all over my locker and pass it around school so everyone can read it."

Acid boils in my stomach, forcing hot bile into my throat. "I have to go back to the room. Just bring me something back from dinner, okay? I need to work on the next chapter anyw—"

"No," Lady says, cutting me off with the fiercest glare I've ever seen from her. "I did not take a three-hour flight to Florida to have you hide in your room. I have exactly three days to spend with you all, and I'm going to use every goddamn minute, even if I have to put a leash on you and *drag* you everywhere."

Cakes waggles her eyebrows. "Kinky."

I choke on a laugh, and just like that, I feel normal again. I look around—*my* people. My weekend. My friends.

My hotel, assholes.

I'm not going to waste this.

I flip my con badge over so my Scroll name (KayfortheWinnet) is temporarily hidden. I could take it off altogether, but that would defeat one of the purposes of the weekend—to meet the people I talk to on Scroll all the time, to meet the people who read my fic. Call me egotistical, but I'd really love to associate some faces with those gushing reviews on the FicArchive. It means so much, knowing that people actually feel the things I'm trying to convey through my writing. When the emotion in my heart makes it onto the page, and it makes its way into other people's hearts, I feel more seen than I ever do in face-to-face interactions.

Besides, how will I accomplish my three big goals by hiding in my room?

This is my one chance.

I take in a deep breath, look around at my friends, and drum up a weak smile.

"Okay. Let's go to dinner."

Cakes's shoulders relax with relief, and she immediately loops an arm through mine, escorting me to the door and placing herself between me and Miss NC. "Oh my God, did you read the chapter Leslie posted last night? I'm *dying*. It's so good. I may not survive until the next update."

"*Me too*, if those two idiots don't kiss soon, I will reach through the screen and smack them."

Lady blocks for Ami, too, letting her shoulder-length tumble of black braids form a curtain between her and the pageant brats. "I've been too afraid to start that story. I know she always finishes her fics, but I have zero patience for works in progress, even if they update regularly."

"No, I get that!" Cakes says as we step out into the humid evening air. "It consumes my thoughts until the next update, then rinse and repeat. I don't wish that on anyone. If you have the willpower to resist, then good for you."

"Noooo," Ami protests, shooting a horrified glance my way. "Fic authors live for reader feedback! If a story doesn't get any love as its being posted, the author might get discouraged and quit. Then you'll never get to read it. Right, Kay?"

"Right," I agree, relieved that she spoke up. It's one of my huge pet peeves in fandom, but I never want to sound ungrateful toward readers, least of all my friends. But Ami knows how I feel. Once again, she's brave enough to speak up.

Lady's stricken expression is instant and hilarious. "But I *need* it! They can't quit!"

"Then comment early and often," Ami says with that same calm, cool tone she always uses to talk me off my ledges. She's the best.

The conversation builds as we walk to dinner in the humid Florida summer evening, words flowing as easily as if we were DMing rather than talking in person. It's an amazing feeling, light and simple, so different from trying to function around non-fandom people at home. No hiding necessary with these three. I can be wholly myself. Whoever that may be.

I slow my steps, look around at the glittering lights of Orlando in the fading sunlight, and grin.

Now the weekend can really start.

Chapter Three

*

TEAGAN

urn, two, three, arms *up* and *hips* and close!"

I miss the hip tilt completely but manage to get one foot in front of the other for the closing pose just before the choreographer turns in my direction. A maddening drip of sweat inches its way down my temple, daring me to break the pose and swipe at it under the ballroom's burning pseudo–stage lights. I really hate these group dance numbers. Following dance steps isn't one of my strong suits, even on the best of days. Even worse are the identical outfits they force us to wear for the opening, which invariably suck the worst of ass. No one thing looks good on every body type. It's impossible, even in a group like this where everyone is universally thin, fit, and generally conforms to American beauty standards. We still have different shapes, different curves and proportions.

I swear this year's outfit was designed to emphasize all my worst features. My legs are technically too muscular for classic pageant beauty, though they definitely help on the soccer field, and I've always thought my knees look weird. For the parts of the pageant I have control over, I work with Rhonda to choose clothes that make my strength and athletic build pop. This year, the group outfit is a crop top and a skirt that hits just above the knees. Tragic. Seeing myself in it for the first time nearly destroyed all my carefully cultivated confidence and poise, bringing out all the insecure feelings I've spent years trying to master. I can't wait to show off the clothes I chose for this competition— clothes I absolutely love, that make me feel like myself dialed up to eleven.

This outfit? It can get torched in the dumpster out back.

The choreographer wanders among the fifty-one girls assembled in the hotel ballroom, correcting posture here, adjusting a pose there. In front of me, the back of Miss Minnesota's neck flushes when she's told to tilt her arms at a slightly different angle because they'll look skinnier. Miss DC gets told to lift her chin higher so she doesn't get double chins. A gross unease unfurls in my chest, and I shift my hips, lift my chin, suck in my stomach. This woman is clearly old-school pageant trained and hasn't gotten the memo that we're supposedly trying to embrace differences now.

For some people, pageants make them feel worse about themselves. Most of those girls never make it past local or state competitions, which is good, because it breaks my heart seeing people suffer through something that makes them miserable. The constant comparisons can be rough, the diets and exercise regimens totally grueling, and it can definitely get into your head if you don't place well in competition. But at the same time, you need to have an enormous amount of confidence to walk out on that stage at all. I feel like the first few years of doing pageants are all about growing thick skin.

Before I lost my mom, I was a pretty outgoing and confident kid. After . . . I kind of collapsed in on myself. I got quiet and painfully awkward. My therapist helped me realize that I hated people looking at me, like all they could see was the giant wound. That's what I felt like—one giant, walking, bleeding injury that wouldn't heal. Getting into pageants helped me get comfortable in my own skin again and project on the outside what I wanted to feel on the inside. The whole fake-it-till-you-make-it thing really works sometimes. It's helped me rock interviews, connect with teachers, take on new challenges, and win my dad over when he wants to say no to something. It's helped me heal.

But this ridiculous pose in this awful outfit is almost enough to undo all that hard work and fluffy self-acceptance stuff. My arms are starting to shake from the exertion, and I can smell my own armpits. And the girl next to me. Pageants look shiny and polished, but so much of the reality is this: hairspray fumes, eyes watering from trying not to squint into the lights, and fifty-one unique mingling body odors. When will this eternal stink end?

Finally, the choreographer double claps. We all drop the pose as one, stretching sore arms and shifting to relieve the pressure in our high heel–abused feet.

"Please go straight back to your hotel rooms and hang up your opening number outfits before you sweat all over them. We'll do one last run-through right before the finals, but feel free to review the choreography on your own time in small groups."

Meaning, *We expect you to practice in your free time, or the judges will think you're lazy.* Acknowledged.

"Any questions? No? Okay, ladies, it's going to look fabulous! Thanks, y'all."

She hops off the front of the hastily assembled temp stage, her shiny blond ponytail swinging as she makes her way to confer with the pageant coordinators. I gasp a lungful of fresh air as soon as I'm free of the crowd and turn to find Jess, but she's already occupied, weaving through the crowd toward a trio of glamorous Black women with amazing style and serious eyebrow game. Ah, the family matriarch and her ladies-in-waiting have arrived. Jess will be busy for the rest of the night, laughing over salads and lemon water with her grandmother, mother, and older sister, a true pageant dynasty and the closest group of women I've ever known in my life.

A pang of jealousy stabs like a thin blade between my ribs. My family can never be at events like this. I always have to go it alone. My dad travels for work constantly so he can support us, though I see how much it eats him up inside every time he leaves. My grandma is my absolute champion and number one cheerleader, but her health isn't good, and she doesn't travel outside of New Mexico anymore, just dictates tragically long texts to my aunt and forces her to be the middleman. She also sends me a crisp fifty-dollar bill at the start of every pageant season to help with the costs.

I love them all fiercely, but I'll never stop wishing they could be here to support me in person like Jess's family.

I raise a hand to wave at the group of women—but my gaze is blocked by a perfect body that looks great in the assigned outfit, *of course*. Miss North Carolina smiles brightly.

"Hey, Teagan, so great to see you! Can we walk back to our rooms together? I'm *so* spacey, I've already forgotten my room number, but I know it's right next to yours," she says with a tinkling laugh, looping her arm through mine. I open my mouth to make an excuse, but she's already half dragged me out of the hall. Across the room, Jess spots me and winces, then smoothly covers it up. I shoot her a regretful smile. We'll find time to hang out later tonight. Maybe even rehearse this choreography like we're supposed to.

Miss North Carolina pulls me down the hall toward the elevators, while somehow making the whole thing look totally voluntary and mutual. Her manicured nails leave tiny half-moon marks when she finally releases her biting grip.

"I'm so excited you got to the finals this year, Teagan! You were totally robbed last year," she bubbles, her smile hard-edged and dangerous. "Everyone always says how nice you are and how much fun you are to hang out with—a regular Miss Congeniality. Congrats on your Miss Mid-Atlantic win last month, by the way!"

I plaster a polite smile on my face. I can be gracious. She's actually being pretty nice, I guess, though I can't shake the feeling that it's all a trap. The elevator arrives with a cheery *ding*, and we step on, careful to keep our heels far away from the elevator door tracks.

As soon as the doors close, she pounces.

"So, Teagan, it's such a shame that Priya from New Jersey didn't make it here. Do you know what's going on with her? I thought she would get the state-level win for sure, but then I saw she didn't even compete this year!"

I freeze. Definitely a trap. I hesitate just a fraction of a second too long, and North Carolina's lips quirk into a victorious smile. Damn it, *damn her.* I fight to keep the snarl off my face.

"Why would I know?"

Bad answer, overly aggressive. Ugh, what is wrong with me?

The victory smile grows. "Well, you know. I heard you two were close."

DANGER. DANGER. ABORT.

I glance at the illuminated numbers above the elevator door as they tick slowly upward. *Why* do we have to be on such a high floor? Too far for me to stay silent and ignore her probing. I forcibly steady my breathing, summon my poise, and shrug delicately, all casual indifference.

"We were just pageant friends. We ran into each other on the circuit pretty often, enough that we could hang out, but we never talked between pageants or anything."

NC lets her eyes widen in faux innocent surprise. *"Really?"* she drawls, her accent making the single word into two. "From what Miss Tennessee told me, y'all were nearly inseparable during the Miss Eastern Teen pageant last year. Was she wrong?"

I rack my brain. Who is Miss Tennessee this year? Which Tennessee pageant system sent winners to Miss Eastern? The pageant systems are so complicated, and I've competed so often, it's all mushed together in my mind. I have a vague memory of a girl with shiny copper hair. She walked in on something I really wish she hadn't seen, and I thought we'd covered it all up, but apparently not enough to save me from her giant mouth. The annoyance is a sharp prick in my mind, enough to provoke my temper.

"Hm, yeah, she must be mistaken. Funny, I don't even remember Miss Tennessee being at that pageant. Guess she didn't leave too much of an impression on me," I say coolly, the ultimate insult. "Sure, Priya and I hung out some, but I haven't spoken to her since."

Because she broke up with me at that pageant and we had a major falling-out, but NC doesn't need to know that.

"Oh, well, isn't that a shame," she replies with genuine disappointment. Hoping for better dirt on me, but I won't crack. It's going to take more than blatant attempted interrogation to make me spill. The elevator door finally slides open with a *ding*, freeing me from the eternal land of lemony floor polish and awkwardness. We step out onto the fourteenth floor and pass the oh-so-temping snack machine on our way down the hall toward our rooms.

I was too focused on finding the right room last time I was up here to really take in my surroundings, but now it's clear that the hotel hasn't separated the pageant and GreatCon guests at all. Probably not smart; anyone could look at these two groups and tell the overlap isn't going to work out well for anyone involved.

I've seen the pictures on Scroll. *The Great Game* conventions can get seriously wild, with parties late into the night and marathon watch-alongs with all the screaming you might expect. At pageants, we have to be in bed by curfew, and the group moms patrol the hallways at night to make sure we don't sneak out and besmirch the Miss Cosmic Teen name. Some pageant chaperones take it super seriously and do stuff like put tape over the door seam so they'll know if you leave. Major spy tactics.

Hopefully they won't be pulling any of that this weekend. I usually manage to sneak out for at least a little bit at every pageant, just to go somewhere I can breathe and not feel watched by judges or competitors. And okay, occasionally to meet up with Priya, before she broke up with me. Now that I know the con is here, there's no way I'll be able to resist my post-curfew wanderlust.

Miss NC leads me down the hall to the left of the elevator, past several doors decorated with crime scene caution tape, shippy artwork, and Scroll usernames. I want so badly to knock on their doors, to ask them to take me to Cosplay Karaoke with them tonight, but they'd probably laugh me and my gaudy Miss Virginia sash right back out the door. If I manage to make it to any con events this weekend, it'll have to be incognito.

Besides, we have our own events to worry about. Tonight: designer PJ mini pageant.

Ugh.

Supposedly it's a time for us to relax, meet all the other pageant participants, and have a little goofy fun in our pajamas. In reality, the PJs are provided by a designer company that sees this as both free advertising and a free photo shoot opportunity. A few of the judges will undoubtedly be in stealth attendance, so we even have to keep our makeup, heels, and sashes on. With our PJs. Ridiculous. At least they gave us an option for yoga pants–length bottoms instead of forcing us to choose the ass-hugging shorts.

We reach our rooms, number 1410 for me and 1408 for her, and I stand back as NC pulls her key card from inside her bra and unlocks the door.

"Ha, silly me," she says with an exaggerated giggle, "the room number was written on my key card the whole time! Oh, well, it was fun catching up with you anyway, Teagan."

My cheeks ache with the effort of forcing a smile. "Same. Good luck this weekend."

I'm so lucky to have Jess as a roommate. Not only is she my best friend, but she's one of those people who inspire everyone around her with her passion and dedication. I hope being in her orbit this weekend will keep me distracted from the room full of TGG fans right next door. They have a giant winking picture of Marc Ferro, one of the lead actors, taped up in the middle of their door surrounded by their Scroll names: Cakesforall, LadyFurious, ConsultingMi221b, and KayfortheWinnet. All the names sound vaguely familiar, but especially the last one—maybe someone I used to follow on Scroll before I abandoned it? Or a fic author I read? Their door calls to me way more than my own, with its little glitter crown cutouts and state names.

"Total freaks, right?" Miss NC says, noticing my distraction.

"I hope we don't run into them this weekend. I heard some of the moms complained to the hotel about the room arrangements. They claimed they couldn't do anything because this convention thing booked the hotel first, but I don't see why that matters. They should make them all move to a different floor."

I clamp my teeth down on my tongue to keep from saying the first thing that pops into my head: *How about we move* you *to a different* universe, *asshole?* I give myself a full two seconds to master my composure as I swipe my card in the door and wait for the little green light to blink. "I'm sure it's a hard thing to change once everyone's already checked into their rooms. They aren't going to bother us. It's like we live on two different planets, right?"

The lies taste sour on my tongue.

NC laughs her overly loud, completely fake cackle as she opens her door. "You're *so* right. It must be hard for them, being around all these gorgeous, smart, successful girls that are, like . . . everything they'll never be. Maybe I should feel sorry for them instead."

It takes everything in me to hold back a bark of laughter. It's like she learned everything she knows about being a teenager from '90s jocks-vs.-nerds movies. North Carolina takes everything toxic from pageants and none of the good. Honestly? I think they're the ones who should feel sorry for her.

I slip into my room without replying and smile when I see Jess's semiorganized pile of reusable drink containers, organic snacks, and eco-friendly cosmetics. She is everything that's good and right about the pageant world, and my heart hurts with how much I've missed her. I cross over to my luggage and dig out the small, wrapped gift box I brought from home: beeswax candles and goat milk soap from my local farmer's market. It's not much, but hopefully she'll appreciate that I supported small farmers and feel that I was thinking of her and missing her. Pageant friends are the best friends.

But pageant enemies are the worst enemies, too. North Carolina's laugh pierces through the wall between our rooms, and my shoulders tense.

I need to be on my guard.

Chapter Four

KAYLEE

I. Look. Awesome.

My low-key John Watson cosplay turned out even better than I thought it would. The cream-colored, cable-knit sweater is too hot for Florida, especially on this ninety-degree evening, but it hugs my body exactly how I like: boob-minimizing, curve-maximizing, and long enough to make my shortness look more well proportioned. The pants almost didn't button, but hey, it worked out.

Screw all those beauty queens running around in their matching skimpy lacy pajamas—I'm the real hot one here. My hair is even the right shape and length for the cosplay with the majority of it pulled back, though the burgundy color doesn't match. There's no way I'm dyeing it blond to match the character, though. I would for sure screw it up and end up with hair the color of dehydration pee. My lip and eyebrow rings aren't exactly canon, either, but I love them and don't want to take them out. People will deal.

I tug the hem of the sweater down one last time then turn

away from the full-length mirror and hold my arms away from my body for inspection. "Well? What do y'all think?"

Ami saw it when I first tried it all on back home, so she just shoots me a thumbs-up and goes back to reading through Scroll on her phone. Lady pulls me in for a quick selfie, since she's cosplaying a simplified version of Sherlock Holmes to-night, then posts it to Scroll immediately (#cuties #my cosplay #greatcon #my friends are hot #ilu Kay). Cakes runs her eyes down my body then raises an eyebrow and grins.

"I think it's working for you," she says with a wink. I blush and strike a pose, projecting a bluster of confidence I don't en-tirely feel. Cakes is definitely more of a lady-preferring bisexual, and though she and I are clear on the whole "just friends" thing after some very frank conversations, her gaze still makes my skin feel warm. I don't really know whether I'm bi or pan or gay or what, but I can definitely appreciate when a girl is gorgeous and enjoy her attention in return.

"Are we ready, then?" Ami asks. She's our taskmaster for the weekend, making sure we actually get to all our panels and events on time. Someone has to do it, and it sure as hell won't be me. I'll be too much of an anxious mess over the writing contest and my panel tomorrow to keep anything else straight. Fortunately, we have bullet journaling master, color-coded high-lighter queen, and keeper of the ten thousand phone alarms Ami on our side.

"Ah, yes, we need to get there before someone steals my song!" Lady says.

I glace at my phone. 8:45 P.M. Don't want to be the one to break it to her, but "Shut Up and Dance" was probably the first song someone got up to sing when the party started. It's be-come a fandom anthem, despite it being like a decade old, with countless fanvids set to it. Maybe she'll get lucky, though. I grab a water bottle out of the fridge on our way out the door then jog to catch up with Cakes where she trails after Ami and Lady. She loops her arm through mine and gives me a little elbow hug then speaks in a low voice.

"So, how are you feeling about your checklist, now that you're here?"

I nearly brush the question off with a quick "we'll see" and change the subject, but I press my lips together instead and watch the dizzying pattern of the carpet under my sneakers. It's some kind of abstract gray squiggle pattern, impossible to follow a single strand as it disappears beneath me. Cakes guides me without fail, giving me the space to think about a real answer. I love that about her. She presses when I need it, when I'm avoiding things, but never makes me rush to fill silence with bullshit. The elevator dings (when did we get here?), and I stare out the glass back wall onto the main floor far below. The lights gleam off the tile floor, and even from fourteen floors up, I can see bunches of people clustered around potted palm trees or sipping drinks at the bar. There are so many people here. So many possibilities.

If I'm brave enough.

"I'm not gonna lie," I say finally, glancing at Cakes from the corner of my eye. "I'm terrified. I'm afraid I'll chicken out, and then I'll never know."

She bumps my shoulder with hers as the elevator glides ever downward. "It's never too late. There will always be more chances. I won't let you chicken out, though. If that's what you want, of course. If you don't feel safe here—"

"No," I cut her off, too sharply, then soften. "No, that's definitely not it. I haven't been here that long, but I already feel safer and more myself than I have . . . maybe ever, actually. I feel like I can trust that most people here are at least somewhat educated about LGBTQ+ stuff, and there's a culture of asking for pronouns and never assuming things, which is just . . . so different."

Cakes grins as she catches me eying a teal-haired girl hanging out near the elevators as the car bumps to a gentle stop on the ground floor.

"I do get what you mean," she says. "Even though my school is pretty chill, this is a whole new level of . . . I guess *casual acceptance*, and I could definitely get used to it."

As usual, I have to beat down a bit of jealousy at that. I wish my high school were more like Cakes's school. Or honestly, like *most* schools. Cakes is part of a huge LGBTQ+ student group that's really active on campus, and they have supportive administration, librarians who keep the school stocked with intersectional queer books of all kinds, and teachers who respect pronouns. My small private school has . . . not even one of those things. Our librarian is great, and she does her best to slip me things she thinks I'll like, but she barely has enough funds to keep the basics in the library, and her job is constantly on the line. At least she tries.

And because we have uniforms, and we're not allowed to put pins or patches or anything on our bags, it's super hard to find your people. It's honestly a miracle Ami and I found each other. I know there have to be more queer kids and tons of other fandom nerds, but I just have no idea how to find them without opening myself up to even more of Madison's garbage. If my school were more like the one Cakes goes to, where people wear fandom shirts to class and scream about their favorite ships at lunch . . . well, I'd probably have myself figured out by now, wouldn't I?

"So, what if," Cakes says, raising her eyebrows to lighten the mood, "the actress who plays Gwen Lestrade showed up at the con?"

My cheeks burn.

"Then the whole list thing would be a moot point because I'd be *dead*," I say, clutching at my heart. "I would swoon off a balcony somewhere and become yet another tragic victim of the Lestrade Effect."

Cakes busts out laughing, and I grin, fixing my gaze on Ami's swinging black ponytail ahead of us. My heart leaps again with the knowledge that we're actually all here, together in person for the first time. Dinner was fantastic, and the four of us have hardly stopped talking since we first saw each other. Ahead of us, Ami and Lady have their heads bent together, chattering happily about some new video game that just came out as they lead us through the lobby and into a bland maze of hallways.

On our way to the convention hub, we walk past an enormous ballroom with the doors flung wide open. Inside, all I see is pastel—dozens of pageant girls in varying styles of night wear and heels with their ever-present sashes. In one corner, girls pose for a camera in front of a solid-white backdrop, laughing and preening for the cameraman. Others stand together in groups, nursing bottles of water and chattering. Older men and pageant moms ring the periphery of the room, watching intently over their wineglasses, studying their every move.

Gross. You could *never* pay me enough to prance around in my shorts in front of a bunch of old men. What could possibly make someone want to do this?

Cakes nudges me in the side, drawing me back to earth once we pass the ballroom.

"Have you heard anything about the publishing contest yet?"

"Not yet," I say, trying my best to keep my nervousness (and dinner) down. "Only that they received my submission and it made it past the initial screening round, so it's getting passed on to the editor. It's not really a big deal," I say, more to myself than to her. "Getting published in a Sherlock Holmes retelling collection isn't anything that will make me a writing career."

"Not by itself, no," Cakes says, her voice oddly intense, "but you're a great writer, Kay, and this could really mean something. Your first paid writing job! And who knows, maybe the editor will like you and can put you in touch with someone to read your original writing, too."

Something in my chest tries to float to the top, but I squash it down hard. "That's not really how it works. And I don't think my original writing is any good. I'm only good at fanfic. Writing's not really a 'viable career option,' anyway," I say, parroting my mom's words.

"You only say that because you don't have people leaving tons of comments and likes on your original writing every day like you do with your fic. I bet they're equally good. Different, but both amazing. You have talent, and you deserve to do something with it." She purses her lips, and I know what's coming. "I wish you'd let me read your original stuff. Or anyone at all. Then we could tell you how great it is."

My cheeks heat from all the praise, but I can't shake the feeling that it's all lies, that she's only saying it to be a supportive friend. One day someone will tell me the truth—that I'm just a silly teenager who likes to smash fictional characters' faces together, and not very well. I live for those comments and likes notification emails from the Archive. Each one is like a tiny cry of *Hey, you're not a total failure!* As long as I never show my original writing to anyone, there's at least a chance people might like it as much as my fic. It *might* be decent. There *might* be hope.

Letting go of that possibility to face the reality is honestly horrifying. I wouldn't have even entered this contest if Ami hadn't bulldozed me into it. She convinced me it was the perfect baby

step: not fanfic, but not 100 percent original, either, since it uses
the original Sherlock Holmes stories as source material. Now I
kind of regret submitting, if it means this sick nervous feeling is
going to follow me all weekend.

I'm supposed to be spending this summer picking out col-
leges and majors and all that other stuff straight-A rising seniors
do, but I just can't make myself get excited about it. Writing is
the only thing I love to do, and majoring in business or com-
munications just feels . . . pointless. I briefly thought about con-
tinuing with band and majoring in music, but I just don't love
my clarinet the way I love writing, and it wouldn't really satisfy
my mom's need for "something practical," either. I can't major
in creative writing without submitting a portfolio of original
work, though.

So that's the deal. If my story gets accepted into the anthology, if I win this contest . . . then I'll let others read my original
writing. I'll put together that portfolio.

And maybe let myself hope.

"What about you?" I ask Cakes, deflecting the attention away
from the soul-crushing topic of the future I'm supposed to decide on in the next six months. "You never told me what happened with the fancy French dessert you were trying to make
for your baking portfolio."

Cakes makes a fancy gesture, as if displaying her gorgeous
creation. "It looked perfect for the photos. They'll never know
that the cream between the layers was unspeakably horrible. It
totally split and curdled. I don't know what I did wrong."

She lets her hands fall back to her sides, and her whole de-
meanor falls along with them. It's like someone flipped her internal light switch. "I'm starting to think this whole culinary
school thing is a bad idea. Baking is a tough business."

"Yeah, a tough business you're amazing at. Why do you think

all the cake pops you brought us are already gone? I almost didn't want to eat mine because it was so pretty. But it was delicious, so I *did* eat it. And its friends. And *their* friends." I bump my shoulder against hers. "This is your dream, and you're good at it."

"Hm, that sounds familiar," she says, looking up from her dejected posture with a raised eyebrow and a grin.

Well, that was a trap.

It's still somewhat light outside, despite being nearly nine o'clock at night, and the pool next to the hotel annex is still filled with more humans than water. The muffled, pounding rhythms of the music throb deep in my chest before the annex even comes into view, packed with jumping bodies. The party's barely been going for twenty minutes, but you'd never be able to tell with the energy in the room. I've been to plenty of conventions before, but they were always the big, commercial conventions that were clearly hoping to cash in on our fannish love. Huge convention centers, major celebrity guests charging the mandated forty-five dollars for a signature, huge crowds creeping on professional cosplayers . . . they were their own fun kind of chaos, but honestly? Nothing beats the spirit of this small, fan-run con. It feels like it's *for* us in a totally different way.

Ami pulls the door open, and we're blasted with a wall of sound. A girl with blue-, purple-, and pink-striped hair stands onstage, belting out a catchy love song with a throbbing beat under a flurry of dazzling, multicolored lights. The lyrics are *so* perfect for *The Great Game*, as one would expect at Cosplay Karaoke, I suppose. There's not a pageant girl in sight, wiggling around in their skimpy clothes and being perfect, polished dancers—just tons of brilliantly happy fandom people having an un-self-consciously great time. It's amazing.

Ami and Lady, being the more outgoing of the four of us,

take me and Cakes by the hands and drag us directly to the center of the writhing mass of bodies. Lady disappears immediately to go sign herself up for the karaoke queue, leaving the rest of us to find a rhythm and start dancing.

And it's . . . awkward as hell. Normally I wouldn't go anywhere near a social event involving dancing unless there was a free buffet and a nice, quiet corner to sit in. This feels like a weekend to try something new, though. Lots of somethings, actually. My friends are here, and in this place where everyone is so wholly and completely themselves, it feels like I can risk something.

At home, I'm such a freak. Obsessed with queer fan fiction. Locked in my room all the time with sore wrists from excessive typing. Most of my social interaction comes in digital form. But right here, right now, I'm having a hard time figuring out why any of those are *bad* things.

So what if I spend most of my time writing? That's a valuable skill. And so what if most of my friends are online? Better than trying to force a fake friendship with the jerk next to me in calculus just because he happens to be in proximity. Why settle for that when I can have a real connection with someone I care about?

Why settle for that when I can be accepted for who I am, right here and now?

The opening notes of "Shut Up and Dance" break through my introspection. My head whips up . . . and there's Lady, onstage, working the crowd into a frenzy of excitement. I guess the song hadn't already been done, and they must have let her skip the queue, because the crowd screams in approval. The whole room seems to jump up and down as one, the energy rising higher and higher, and we all shriek our support for Lady as she bursts into the opening lines of the song. Her voice is strong and husky, deeply resonant and melodic, and her dark skin glows under the rainbow of stage lights. She's fantastic, and the crowd eats it up, shouting the chorus along with her.

Cakes grabs my right hand, and Ami grabs my left, and with our hands joined, we throw our heads back and sing, letting everything spill out into the humid night air and blend with the voices of the beautiful people around us.

I feel electric.

I feel like I'm home.

Chapter Five

*

TEAGAN

I run my room key through the reader, holding my breath as the mechanism whirs and the light winks green. *Please be empty, please be empty . . .*

The door swings open to reveal a dark room, heavy with silence. Thank God. Jess has a meetup this evening with some of the other science-genius types in the pageant, and I'm taking advantage of the gap in my schedule. I love Jess to death, but she would definitely try to talk me out of what I'm about to do, exactly *because* she's such a good friend. It's a terrible idea. And I'm definitely doing it.

I whip my overly expensive pajama top over my head and chuck it into my suitcase, scrabbling frantically for the plain clothes I hid at the bottom of the bag. Rhonda would tear my ears off if she knew I'd brought anything so casual, but I always feel the need to sneak away at these things, and it's hard to blend into the crowd in high fashion and glittering stilettos.

And here, with the TGG convention so close and tempting? I have to at least take a peek. It's pageant suicide if I'm caught, but after having all those eyes on my body at the pajama party, I need to disappear into a crowd and be faceless for a bit.

With my ears straining for any sign of activity in the hallway, I pull on a plain black tank top and wiggle into my best skinny jeans. A purple zip-up hoodie provides some necessary camouflage, despite the heat, and practical sneakers finish off my lightning-quick transformation. Undercover judges actually exist at these things, and I need to be as inconspicuous as possible.

A few quick tugs, and my suitcase looks untouched, exactly how it did when I last came into the room. I'd love to do something with my hair to make it look a bit more casual, but brushing out the carefully crafted waves and getting my hair to do something human again afterward would take more time than I have. I'll have to roll with it. Maybe I can pull it back once I get there and don't need it to hide my face anymore.

I shove my ID, debit card, and phone into my back pocket and press my eye to the peephole, watching for any flicker of movement around the elevator. The last thing I need is for Miss North Carolina herself to catch me on her way back to her room. I hold my breath, asking myself one last time: *Definitely doing this?*

The hallways are still.

Definitely doing this.

I open the door, peek my head around the corner, look left, right . . . and dart down the hall toward the stairs, light on the balls of my feet. The elevator dings behind me, and I throw myself into the stairwell, my breath burning more with panic rather than exertion, never thinking for even a second about seeing who it is. The stairwell echoes with my footsteps as I run down the staircase as quickly as possible. There's probably no hope of making it back by curfew, but the sooner I get down there, the sooner I can get back. I don't want Jess to worry too much.

On the ground floor, I repeat my superspy lookout technique again then duck down an unoccupied back hallway that echoes my tiny, not-quite-silent scuffing sneaker sounds back to me. I did some quick googling on my phone right before the PJ party and found the convention website, and apparently a cosplay karaoke and dance party is happening tonight in the annex. It's the perfect event for me: big crowd of people, dark room, loud music, someone onstage to focus on—the ideal place to blend in. I'll get a tiny taste of the con, and no one will be the wiser. Right?

Outside, it's nearly full dark, but the humidity still hangs thick in the air. Harsh fluorescent lights illuminate the still-busy pool area, stark and bright next to the deep shadows and flashes of glowing color I spot through the hotel annex's windowed door. I pause for a moment with my hand on the door, drawing sticky, chlorinated air into my lungs. Am I really ready for this?

Maybe the better question is: How could I possibly pass this up?

I pull the door open, and a blast of air-conditioning greets me, along with the heavy strains of a slow song, something sad by Adele that gives everyone feelings. The whole room is piled into one giant group hug, arms thrown around each other's shoulders and swaying to the music, belting out the lyrics. I saw a fanvid set to this song once and bawled my eyes out for twenty minutes straight then immediately watched it three more times. I'm sure all these people have done the same.

The worst thing about this, though, is that I've walked in at the literal most awkward moment possible. How can I insert myself into this scene without walking up and forcing myself on some group of people I don't know, wrapping my arms around them like *Oh, yeah, sure, I totally belong here.*

Not gonna happen.

I stand there for a lost moment, my hands clasped tightly in front of me like I'm waiting for results onstage, my posture awkwardly proper in this room full of loose, swaying bodies. I watch them all, people I share something in common with but who feel so far away. They all know each other or have had a chance to introduce themselves, at least, enough to share this experience.

I blink back a sudden hot surge of tears and take a step back toward the door. This was a terrible idea. I could never belong here. I don't know what I was expecting.

I whirl around and raise my hands to push the glass door open then freeze.

Miss North Carolina is *right outside,* laughing with four other girls and one of the chaperones near the entrance to the pool.

I jerk away from the window and press my back against the wall. Curfew is in fifteen minutes! What are they doing out here? It's almost pitch-black in this room, so they probably can't see me from out there, but the second I open this door, I'll draw attention to myself and step out into much better lighting.

No, I can't. There's no way.

In the background, the song shifts to something much happier and more upbeat. Before I can change my mind, I pull together all my pageant-earned confidence, turn, and plunge into the crowd, weaving my way through the gyrating bodies to the middle of the dance floor where the other pageant girls will never see me. With a deep breath, I squeeze my eyes shut and let the music take me, raising my arms above my head with all the others.

And I let go. Completely.

No one seems to notice that I'm here alone. In fact, several people whoop at my dancing, and eventually they part to make room for me in their circle of dancers. *This* is the kind of dancing I love—natural, free-flowing, the beat pulsing in my chest and guiding my hips. Nothing like that choreographed disaster they force us into for the opening number.

A true, honest smile breaks onto my face for the first time in hours, and I really turn it on, jumping and giggling and *finally* looking around the circle at the others. They're *stunning*, laughing and talking and dancing all at the same time, all together. Two of the girls dance close, every curve molded together, and it's so hot, I can't stand it. I want that so bad.

And maybe . . . well, this is the only time I'll ever see these people in my life, so what harm could it do to *try*?

I take a deep breath, gather my courage, turn to my left—

—and am nearly knocked off my feet when a white girl about my age gets shoved into our circle by her friends. I catch her around the waist and steady her, concerned and ready to jump in on her behalf . . . when I notice she's laughing uncontrollably.

"All I said was I wouldn't *stop watching the show* if Violock became canon, not that I'd *like* it," she shouts back to her friends, to a chorus of boisterous *nope*s in reply. Then she turns in my arms and lays her hands on my shoulders, totally open and uninhibited, caught up in the comfortable high of being in this safe place full of people like us.

"I am *so sorry* for that," she says between giggles that won't quit. "Are you okay?"

I need to reply, need to say *something*, but my voice stays firmly lodged in my throat as my brain tries to figure out which Teagan I'm supposed to be in this moment. This is my first chance to talk to someone in my biggest fandom face-to-face, someone *really* pretty, and . . . brain? Tongue? Vocal cords, just do . . . something? I must make some kind of face, because the girl's amused expression falls a fraction as she backpedals. "Wait. You don't ship Violet and Sherlock, do you? I'm sorry, I shouldn't have assumed. Rude, right?"

I feel her tense and start to draw back a bit, so I say *screw it* and lay it all out there, looking at her from under my lashes and lowering my voice. "Of course not. Johnlock aside, Violet is clearly a giant lesbian. I'm more into the fem pairings. Violet and Irene, ride or die."

She hesitates then smiles a bit, lifting one hand off my shoulder to brush a bit of burgundy hair out of her dark-lined eyes. "Good. That's . . . good. I'm Kay."

"Teagan," I reply. My hands, still on the curves of her waist from when I caught her, hum with potential energy. I've just met this girl—I should get my hands off. But then, she's still got one of her hands on my shoulder. Maybe, with a bit of that confidence I'm supposed to have, I can just . . .

"Do you want to dance?" I ask, the words falling straight from thought to air with no intervention on my part. I let my lips curl into a hesitant smile, dart my tongue out to wet my suddenly parched lips. Her eyes follow the motion, and she nods, flicking her gaze back up to mine.

"Yeah. Okay."

In slow motion, she lets her other hand fall off my shoulder but shifts half a step closer. She's gorgeous, with close-cropped, deep-red hair, black eyebrow and lip rings, and perfect eyeliner that makes her eyes pop. Her hips are soft and round and made for my hands, her mouth a natural resting place for the quirk of a smile, and I'm *really* letting this moment linger into awkwardness. Time to move.

I draw back and unzip my hoodie to give my hands an excuse to finally leave her waist, letting it fall open to reveal the black tank top beneath. There's no mistaking the way Kay's eyes dart down, then away just as quickly, almost guiltily. Definitely into girls, then. Good. I relax, let the music calm my nerves and drive my body. We begin to move, slowly at first, a bit hesitantly, but the sway of her hips unlocks something inside me. I move on instinct, letting the thrum of the bass fill my chest and pool in my stomach. Every scant touch of hands and accidental arm bump is like a jolt of electricity—but none more so than when she scoots closer, and our breasts and hips brush together for the first time. Kay sucks at her lip ring for a moment, a move I find utterly irresistible, then speaks, breaking through my total fog of lust.

"Is this your first convention?"

A jolt of fear turns my stomach—does she know I don't belong here? But there's no need; she already thinks I'm here for the con, obviously. No need to convince her. I just have to keep up the act. "Um, yeah. I've always wanted to go, but they're usually too far away, or my dad won't let me."

Kay grins and dances closer so she can talk in my ear. "So you managed to convince him this year?"

Absolutely not. How can I cover my ass and make this plausible at the same time?

"Sort of. I don't have a badge for the con, so I can't go to any panels. Some friends of the family were coming to Orlando for something else anyway, so they're supposed to be watching me like hawks all weekend. I managed to sneak away for a bit." Perfect. I feel bad throwing my awesome dad under the bus, but he'd forgive me.

She frowns, and a chill shoots up my arm as she moves a curl over my shoulder, her fingers brushing skin where my open hoodie has slipped down. "Why do they watch you so closely? You must be my age, at least—seventeen-ish?"

"Yeah, seventeen. It's, uh . . ." I trail off. How far do I really want to go with this? How bold do I want to be? But for the first time, I'm feeling like I'm actually in a safe space, a place where I can come out within minutes of meeting someone and know how it'll be received. It's the TGG fandom—half the people here are probably queer anyway. Including Kay, if I'm reading things right. I already tested the waters, admitting my TGG pairing is Virene. Her eyes, so soft and sincere, beg the truth from me, and it spills from my lips before I've consciously made the decision.

"He's afraid I'll come home with a girlfriend and he'll have to stop ignoring the fact that I'm gay," I say with an eye roll, to diminish a bit of the pain of honesty. It's not the whole truth—my dad is actually fine with it. It's the pageant chaperones (apparently my fake family friends for the weekend) who aren't. And most of my extended family. And the rest of the world. I can see the headlines now: LESBIAN BEAUTY QUEEN STRIPPED OF ALL TITLES AND WINNINGS, AN UTTER MESS.

Kay's features crumple with pain, her lovely mouth drawn down at the corners and her eyes bright with empathy. Without a word, she pulls me into a hug, her arms wrapped around my neck and threaded into my mess of dark waves. She smells sweet and warm, and it takes everything I have to not turn my head into the curve of her neck and breathe her in.

"I'm so sorry you have to deal with that," she says, pulling back to move to the music again but leaving her arms on my shoulders. "That's one of the things I love about cons like this. I never have to worry about being completely myself. Even if . . ."

She pauses, bites that damn lip ring again, and looks up at me. "Even if I'm not entirely sure about everything yet."

I think I get what she means, but if ever there was a night

for pushing my luck, this is it. I catch her eye, smile, and guide her to turn around. A new song kicks on, even faster and harder than the one previous, and I lean forward to murmur in her ear.

"I think this is the perfect place to figure things out."

The beat drops, and I pull her closer, my hands on her hips, with her entire back molded to my front. I rock and sway and press into her, feeling her body lean back harder against mine, a hundred bodies around us surging with the music, and for the first time in five years, I feel true, stinging doubt.

Is winning a pageant really worth giving this up?

Chapter Six

KAYLEE

My y heart feels like it's about to beat out of my chest with the exertion of the dancing, and to be completely honest? I have never felt this alive in my life. My skin burns and tingles, my breath rasps in my chest, and my muscles are sore in such a satisfying way. I never knew dancing could be so much fun. I've never felt comfortable enough to try. Now, with Teagan's body flush against mine, her breath in my ear, and a pool of heat glowing in my stomach?

I'm definitely a fan.

This is working for me. I'm with a girl, and we're dancing, and there's this *tension* that I've never felt to the same degree when I've been around a guy. My chest is a pounding mess of giddy and terrified and triumphant, heating my blood to the boiling point. I'm a bit closer to my answer, I think. It's *working*.

Teagan seems to be feeling the same. She pulls away reluctantly when I turn around to face her, sweat trickling uncomfortably down my temple. I spot Cakes, Lady, and Ami over her shoulder, a few people away in another circle of dancers. I should probably get back to them, though my feet are intent on keeping me right here.

"Want to take a break?" Teagan asks, gesturing to the refreshments table in the back corner. She smiles, but her eyes are wary, like she expects me to turn her away. I've only just met her, but letting her down seems unthinkable. She seems . . . alone, like me, and we spend so much of our time wishing we had people IRL to click with. Now, in this place, we finally do, and it's worth a bit of the effort I never bother putting into human interaction back home.

"Yes, *please*," I say between gasping breaths. "Give me water. I embrace death."

She snorts and takes my hand gently, guiding me through the crowd to the cluster of tables loaded down with sweating water bottles and granola bars. I snag two waters and pass one to Teagan then find a blank bit of wall to lean against. Teagan tips her head back and takes a long pull from the bottle, a tiny drop of water escaping the corner of her mouth. A drop of condensation curls around my wrist in a cool, sharp trail, a stinging reminder that I have my own bottle to drink. I tear my gaze away from the movement of her throat, crack the seal on my bottle, and let the water soothe my parched mouth.

"How are you enjoying your first con?" I ask her, practically shouting to be heard over the music. I'm terrible at making conversation, but hopefully that's innocuous enough to get the talking started.

"What?" she shouts back, then scoots closer, leans in next to my ear. "Is there somewhere quieter we can go? I can barely hear myself think this close to the speakers."

My eyes automatically find Cakes, Lady, and Ami again. They won't mind, will they? I manage to catch Ami's eye and wave then point to where I'm heading. She nods, grinning as I turn back to Teagan. Pretty sure this new girl isn't a murderer trying to get me alone, but better to be safe and let my friends know where I'm going. Hopefully Ami is proud of me actually putting myself out there for once.

"Actually, there's a perfect place right next door," I say. "Follow me."

I tug the edge of her hoodie sleeve and guide her toward a heavy black door surrounded by rainbow streamers. A sign on the door reads INTROVERT BREAK ROOM in bold letters, with OPEN 9:00 A.M. TO MIDNIGHT FRIDAY–SUNDAY scrawled in Sharpie underneath. I pull the door open and beckon Teagan in with a flourish and a half bow, which she accepts with a perfect hoodie curtsy.

The door clicks shut behind us, sealing all but the deep bass vibrations away. We pass through a short foyer then through another glass door into a room decorated in calming blues with life-size silhouettes of all the major TGG characters along one wall. People with con badges sit alone or in small groups, talking quietly, working on craft projects, typing on laptops, or scrolling on phones, many with headphones on.

"What is this?" Teagan asks in a low voice, picking up on the tone of the room.

"A lot of people get overwhelmed with all the crowds and noise," I say, leading her to a bar full of crayons and TGG-themed coloring pages. "This is a quiet space where they can recharge. Want to color?"

"Um, *yes.*" She snags a twenty-four-count box of crayons and a line drawing of Gwen Lestrade in her epic trench coat and heads straight for the nearest high-top table. I grab a John Watson sheet then hesitate when my eye catches the Andante Teas logo across the room.

It's a loose-leaf tea bar. My biggest non-fandom, non-writing obsession. This place could not be more perfect.

My feet carry me straight over to the table before I have a chance to think too hard about it. Does Teagan like tea? Should I make her a cup, or is that presumptuous? What if she doesn't drink caffeine? It's late, after all. After a moment's hesitation, I hit the button on the electric kettle and set about preparing two cups of decaf tea. I'm being brave and putting myself out there, right? That means sharing something I love, even if it might not go over how I want.

The sound of the kettle heating and the scent of dried tea leaves puts me instantly into a calmer place. I'm a total Andante Tea addict, and I make my own fandom tea blends on their website all the time. The chance to do it in person where I can see and smell all the different teas and mix-ins is *awesome*. I use the baby spoons in each dish to create a decadently sweet-smelling blend for Teagan. Cream tea, hazelnut tea, vanilla tea, and a tiny pinch of cinnamon, something easy to drink and impossible to hate—one of my most popular blends. For myself, I make something a little weirder and more complex, taking the chance to fiddle with the ratios of one of my other character blends. When the kettle clicks, I pour boiling water over my creations, drain the leaves after the exact right length of steeping time, and bring the mugs back to the table where Teagan sits, still totally focused on her coloring.

Her Gwen Lestrade picture is *gorgeous*. Not only has she stayed inside the lines like any good kindergartner, but she's done some seriously complex shading and added background details with a pack of colored pencils she scrounged up from somewhere.

"That's incredible," I say, and she jerks as if startled then blinks owlishly.

"I am so sorry, I get kind of zoned in when I do art stuff. You weren't . . . standing there long, were you?"

I smile and set her tea down in front of her. "No, not at all. Do you do a lot of art?"

"Yeah, kind of," she says, and pulls out her phone. "I mostly do custom, hand-painted clothing."

She leans her head against mine and holds the phone between us, scrolling through an Etsy shop full of shirts, skirts, dresses, and accessories. They're *unbelievable*, gorgeous, and complex, and mostly geeky or rainbow themed.

"Oh my *God*," I breathe, snatching the phone from her and zooming in on a few of my favorites. "Teagan, these are amazing! They're so detailed. They must take forever."

"Some take a while if they're really intricate," she says, her voice wavering between pride and modesty, "but I've been doing these since I was fourteen, so they're pretty second nature now. I do fan art sometimes, too."

She flips her coloring page over, grabs a black pencil, and starts to sketch. As I watch, what initially seems like a few random lines transforms into an adorable miniature Sherlock Holmes in his signature hat. She spells her name in neat block letters at his feet and hands it over to me with a little smile.

"You're so talented," I say, running a finger over tiny Sherlock's face. "Where did you learn?"

"Ah . . ." She hesitates for a moment then shrugs. "I went to an art therapy group for a while after my mom died, and now I volunteer with them every weekend. Lots of time to practice. My dad travels for work a lot, so it keeps me busy. And it's fun."

My heart pangs in sympathy. "My dad's gone, too. Though I guess he's still alive, probably. Just an asshole."

I don't know why I'm telling her this. I never talk about it, not even with Ami and Cakes. I try to hand the drawing back to Teagan, but she waves it away.

"Keep it," she says, then seems to notice her cup of tea for the first time and pulls it close. "What's this?"

"You don't have to drink it if you don't want." I pull my own cup close and bury my nose in it, letting the warmth and soothing scents of the different components drain away my tension. "I make tea blends designed after different characters from the show, and one of my friends out there—the white girl, Cakesforall is her Scroll username—she makes these fandom-themed cupcakes to go along with them. That one is my most popular one, the one non-tea drinkers usually like the best. Can you tell what character it is?"

She sniffs the warm, amber liquid then takes a careful sip, and her eyebrows shoot up. "It tastes like cookies!" She takes another sip, and her eyes crinkle at the corners. "Mrs. Hudson?"

I grin. "She's always bringing John and Sherlock biscuits. Cakes does a delicious cinnamon-spice cupcake filled with hazelnut ganache for that one. Here, try this one."

I pass her my cup, and she puts her mouth right where mine had been, her lips cupping the rim. Her brows furrow as she holds the tea on her tongue then drinks again.

"It's kind of smoky but sweet at the same time. Smooth." Her mouth twists in a wry smile. "I sound like a tea snob, but I really have no idea what I'm talking about."

"No, you're exactly right! That's what I was going for," I say, pulling up the blend on the Andante Teas website and spinning my phone around for her to see. "It's the same cream tea as the base, to give it the sweet and homey feel, but then it's blended with aged Pu-erh to make it dark and grounded and just a pinch of lapsang souchong to give it that little hint of smoky danger."

"Johnlock in a cup." She glances at me over the rim of the cup, meeting my gaze dead on, and takes another long, slow sip. When she passes the cup back to me, our fingers brush, and I feel the color rushing to my cheeks. I suddenly feel every spot on my body where we were pressed together earlier so intensely, and my brain recoils from the overwhelmingness of everything.

"So, uh," I stammer, floundering for a new topic and landing on my earlier question that never got an answer. "How has your first con been so far?"

She hesitates, and that wary look is back, but I can see the moment her brain says *screw it*. She leans in close and lowers her voice, her eyes fixed on her tea. "It's been . . . kind of weird."

I tense, but she quickly continues, "Not like *bad* weird. Like . . . this is going to sound mushy as hell, but I feel like I can be more myself here, you know? Most of the time, I have to hide so much. My sexuality, my fan art, you know? All of it."

I bite my lip and look away. "No, I completely get it. Seriously, I was just having similar thoughts today. I met some of my longtime Scroll friends for the first time earlier tonight, and it was like . . . puzzle pieces, as cliché as that is. I just *fit* here, with them. Not only do I not have to hide my fic from these people, but they actually want to read it! And . . ."

I hesitate, but now, *now* is the time. If I let it go too much longer, it'll get awkward bringing it up out of the blue later. And if it's going to be a deal breaker, better to know now.

"And," I continue, steeling myself. "I feel like I can ask people to use they/them pronouns for me here without being looked at like a freak. People here at least mostly know about pronouns and . . . everything."

My stomach clenches in anticipation of rejection, my heart racing, but Teagan's eyes soften, encouraging me to continue. I hesitate, waiting for the hammer to fall. But it never comes. Teagan just looks understanding, expectant. Listening. My mouth takes this as a cue to keep going.

"It's . . . it's just wild. I keep thinking I should feel ashamed or something. I have a little mini panic attack every time I mention my fic out loud. Even just now, like I've lost my mind and mentioned it at school or something. In some places that might not be so bad, but in my part of North Carolina, writing gay fanfic and being maybe nonbinary or something won't exactly win me any favors. Pitchforks, maybe."

Her face lights up with a brilliant smile, a tiny dimple on the left side, and something passes between us—an understanding, a feeling of . . . of *yes, you get it*. It's so *easy* here. It's like a safe little bubble, a whole different world.

"You're the first person I've told, actually," my mouth word-vomits without my permission. "Or, asked, I guess. To use those pronouns. I just . . . wanted to try it while I was here."

Teagan bumps her knee against mine under the table. "I'm glad you told me, though, and I'm sorry if I used any wrong terms for you earlier. I should know better than to assume."

I shrug. "Honestly, it's just how brains work. We put people into categories without thinking. I still do it, too, and I'm the one questioning my gender on a daily basis. It takes a lot of work to unlearn that reflex."

"I know," she says. "I still have a lot of that work to do. I'm glad I'm not the only one who feels that way, though, about the con. Like this is almost a space outside of the real world. Another dimension, where it's safe. Where anything can happen."

She shifts a bit closer, her grin sliding into something shy, and—

"Hey, Kay!"

I jerk, startled like I've been caught cheating on a test. Cakes, Lady, and Ami let the door to the break room fall shut behind them and approach our table, eying up my new friend with curiosity.

"We're heading back to the room. You coming with?" Ami asks.

Lady rubs her hands together like a Looney Tunes villain. "Time for our first angsty watch-along of the weekend. Watch-Along 1: A New Pain. Because it's not bad enough online—we have to die together in person, too."

I hesitate. I've been looking forward to this exact thing for months, but . . . I sneak a look at Teagan, and she's completely blank, all her spark gone. Cakes must catch the direction of my gaze, because she immediately jumps in, ever the peacemaker.

"Hey, want to join us?" she says, addressing Teagan directly for the first time. "We're watching the last episode of season two tonight, because apparently we like to suffer."

"Yeah, join us! We have plenty of room," Lady adds. Ami nods, too, looking like a proud mama bird watching her baby fly.

"I really shouldn't," Teagan says, but trails off in that way that means she just needs a bit of convincing. I'm happy to oblige. I'm not ready for this to be over.

"Come on," I say, nudging my shoulder against hers. "Join us for a bit. We can shield you from your evil chaperones on the way back to the room."

I reach out and tug the hood of her purple sweater over her head, tucking as much of her hair underneath as I can. It feels like silk under my fingers, and there's so *much* of it, but I manage to get most of it hidden away. One more tug to get the hood down low over her eyes, and she should disappear just fine.

"What do you think?" I ask, as she studies me from under her lashes, the hood casting her face into shadow.

She bites her lip, then a smile breaks free. "Yeah. Okay, yes, I'll come, if you're sure you don't mind."

"Not at all!" Cakes says, shooting me a not-so-discreet wink.

I roll my eyes, but I can't keep my answering grin from breaking through.

I'm glad this isn't "good night."

Not yet.

Chapter Seven

TEAGAN

Jess: WHERE ARE YOU

Jess: It's already an hour after curfew

Teagan: I'm sorryyyyyy, I'm still out. I'm okay though. Has anyone noticed?

Jess: Not YET

Jess: Come back while that's still true

Jess: You need sleep for tomorrow. It's almost 11. You'll look tired.

Teagan: just a bit longer. We're coming up to watch an episode of TGG. I'll be right next door. I hope you had a fun science nerd hangout!

Jess: . . .

Jess: Be careful

Jess: This better be worth it

Teagan: it is. I promise.

Teagan: thanks for checking on me

Teagan: I miss yooooou, we'll hang out tomorrow

Teagan: promise

Jess: I will kick your ass in the morning if I have to

Teagan: love you too 🐱

[unread] Jess: EMERGENCY

[unread] Jess: Get back here RIGHT NOW

[unread] Jess: NC was just here

[unread] Jess: I tried to get rid of her but she's like butt glue I swear

[unread] Jess: I told her I had no idea where you were and that you weren't there when I got back

[unread] Jess: So you better make up something GOOD

[unread] **Miss NC:** Still out, huh?

[unread] **Miss NC:** I guess I have to get a chaperone.

[unread] **Miss NC:** Because I'm so worried and all.😒

Chapter Eight

KAYLEE

O ut in the main room of the annex, the party has somehow both thinned out and gotten wilder at the same time. Teagan pauses by the outside door then snatches a con program off a nearby table and holds it open in front of her face. I wince in sympathy.

"Come on," I say, guiding Teagan in front of me with a hand at the small of her back. "Let's go before someone sings another Adele song and we all start sobbing. Y'all, surround Tea as best you can once we're outside, okay? The dragons that keep her locked in her heteronormative tower will be on the prowl."

Tea gives an indelicate snort from behind the program. "You certainly have a way with words."

"They didn't rack up a quarter-million hits on their fics in one year for nothing!" Cakes adds, and I have to bite the inside of my cheek to keep from grinning like a loon. The number sounds more impressive than it is, considering those hits are spread across twenty-five different fics, but it's still pretty damn good, and the pride in Cakes's voice makes my chest feel full and light at the same time.

"I meant to ask about that, actually," Teagan murmurs once we're back inside the main hotel, her eyes darting down to my con badge. "Your username sounds really familiar, so I assume I've read some of your stuff before, but I'm not really good at keeping track of specific authors. What's something you've written that I might have read?"

I open my mouth, but no sound comes out. *Hi, yes, hello, I have written many popular and well-loved fics, including one or two recent ones that include my first attempts at writing sexy stuff. Oh, you've read them? NOT WEIRD OR EMBARRASS-ING AT ALL, NOPE.*

Fortunately/unfortunately, I have my number one cheer-leader and fangirl, Cakesforall, right here to advocate for me.

"Oh, you *must* have read 'Say Something,'" she says. "I feel like the entire fandom has read that one and bawled over it. Well, except non-Johnlockers, I guess, but to each their own. 'The Start of Tomorrow' and 'Every Small Thing' also get recommended a lot."

When Teagan gasps in recognition at the titles, I'm torn be-tween pride and wishing wild raptors would appear out of no-where and eat me alive.

"Those are some of my favorite fics!" she gushes. "I have all of those bookmarked on the Archive on my 'cheer me up' re-reads list. I normally stick to femslash pairings, but your John-lock is so good! You're fantastic!"

Nooo, she's read them?

"Um," I squeak. "Thanks? I guess? Oh God."

She whirls around, and we stop right in the middle of the lobby as she takes me by the shoulders. "Don't you dare get all embarrassed! You have something you're really good at, and you should be proud of it. I know the rest of the world makes us feel like we should be ashamed of what we do, but you have real talent and no reason to hide it here. We have to do enough of that everywhere else."

Her cheeks are flushed, her eyes intense and bright. I flash back to our earlier conversation, our shared feeling of belonging, and . . . I guess I'm kind of taking that away right now, by being ashamed of my work. If ever there were a place to celebrate my accomplishments, this is it.

I bite my lip then nod. "Yeah, you're right. I'm sorry. I didn't mean to be a jerk, I just have a hard time talking about my writing online, and it's even harder face-to-face."

"Kay writes original stuff, too, but they won't let us read any of it," Ami interjects, sticking her tongue out at me.

"I will!" I protest. "You know. Eventually."

Ami makes a face.

"No, really!" I say, turning to Teagan. "Do you know about the short story contest they're doing this weekend?"

She nods.

"Okay, so, if I win that contest, my story will get published. And I'll let whoever wants to beta read the book I've been working on."

Ami makes a face even harder, and Teagan joins in.

"If you don't win, that doesn't mean your original stuff isn't worth sharing," she says. "You're such a good writer. Are you really going to just give up if this one thing doesn't work out?"

I sigh. "Not give up, I just— Oh shit, hide me!"

I throw myself at Teagan and bury my face in her neck, my lips moving against her skin as I frantically whisper, "The girl in the white robe. Ami and I know her from school. She's horrible to me, and if she sees me here the whole school will have read my fic by the time I start senior year!"

Teagan scans the lobby then stiffens and snaps her head back to me. She must have seen her—Madison is the only one in the lobby who doesn't work here. She stands up at the check-in desk, giving the attendant an earful about the air conditioner or something. She's dressed in pajamas with a ridiculously expensive silky white robe clutched around her, gesturing wildly with one hand as she complains. The others draw closer to block us.

"Come on," Lady whispers. "Let's go while she's distracted. We've got you surrounded. Just keep your head down, and she'll never notice you."

I give a shaky little nod, and Teagan and I hunch over in the middle of our group. She's taller than all but Cakes, but she manages to blend in, and we make it to the elevator long before Madison finishes her complaining. The ride up to the fourteenth floor takes ages, as always, and when we finally step off the elevator, it's into an empty hallway.

If anything, Teagan seems even *more* frightened, walking with comically bent knees. I reach forward and rest the tips of my fingers at the curve of her waist, where they lingered while we danced earlier. She stiffens at first then relaxes and snakes her hand back to cover mine for a brief moment. Comforted, I hope.

The rooms with glittery crowns and state cutouts are graveyard silent, no light creeping out from under the doors. Don't they get to have *any* fun while they're here? On the other hand, noise spills from every room with a Scroll or Archive handle on the door—laughter and the occasional shriek, a blurry mess of overlapping voices. Every time a door opens in the hallway, Teagan practically climbs out of her skin, but every single time it's someone on Team Fandom, running to get ice or snacks or join a different party.

When Ami finally unlocks our door, Teagan all but tackles her to get inside as quickly as possible.

"Sorry," she gasps once we're all in. "Just . . . you don't know how bad it'll be for me if I get caught by the people I'm with. Thanks for hiding me."

"And me," I add. "If Madison manages to figure out my username, I'm dead. Actually . . ."

I stick my head back out into the hallway and rip my name off our door.

"Can't take any chances. What if she's staying on this floor and sees me walk out? Not too hard to make the leap from Kaylee to KayfortheWinnet."

"Smart," Ami says, then ducks out the door one more time to take her name down, too. "ConsultingMi is a bit more of a stretch, but it's worth being careful."

Lady and Cakes make cooing noises of sympathy for us both as they get Netflix cued up and pull drinks and snacks from the fridge. We all take turns slipping into the bathroom to change into pajamas and take care of various nightly routines: hair wrapping (Lady), detailed skin care routine (Ami), and deep curl conditioning (Cakes). I have a mini crisis in front of the mirror when it's my turn, my gender comfort falling away as I peel off the layers I carefully designed for tonight's look. My sleep shirt is too low-cut. The sleep shorts emphasize my hips and are too short, revealing too much leg. My hair still works, at least. Focus on that. With a breath, I fix my eyes on my face, not allowing them to wander down my body, then throw open the door and flee the mirror before I can second-guess myself any further.

Once we're all together again, we pose for the obligatory group selfies in front of the show logo on the screen, which Teagan makes us *swear* to keep off social media. Lady and Cakes tuck themselves into their bed with the remote and a bag of popcorn, and Ami flops back on the bed she and I are sharing.

Teagan hovers awkwardly for a moment before sliding to the floor at the foot of our bed, her back propped up against it. I hesitate and glance over at Ami, but she waves me away silently with a grin. No hard feelings, then. I shoot her a grateful smile then sink down next to Teagan as the theme music for *The Great Game* pounds through the hotel TV's tinny speakers.

"You want anything to munch on or drink?" I ask. "We have all kinds of snacks, and I have some of my tea blends here. Not as good when made with water from the little hotel coffee maker, but still drinkable."

She throws a lingering glance at Lady's buttery popcorn but shakes her head. "I'd love some tea if you have decaf. I'm fine on food, though. I have weird dreams if I eat too close to bed."

The episode begins in the background, but I already know most of the words by heart, so I focus on Teagan instead. Bracing one hand on the floor between us, I turn slightly toward her and quirk an eyebrow. "Really? What kind of weird dreams?"

The corner of her mouth turns up just a bit. "Just. Weird. You know how some dreams are just a jumbled mess of things from real life in an order that makes no sense? Usually like that. And for whatever reason, I'm almost always a preschooler in them."

I sputter a laugh. "The hell? Why preschool?"

"How should I know? All I remember about preschool is one really embarrassing incident involving poop, and there's no way you're getting that out of me."

Oho. She hasn't known me very long, so she doesn't realize what she's just done.

I will have that story.

The night rolls on, with alternating soundtracks of pained

moans over the *angstiest TGG episodes of all time* and stifled giggles as I worm more and more embarrassing stories out of Teagan over steaming cups of tea. The more we talk and quote the episode back and forth to each other, the more of her weight she leans into my shoulder, and the deeper the flush in her cheeks becomes. Her smile is infectious, that dimple doing more to draw laughter from me than the crackiest fic ever did, our fingers a hairsbreadth apart on the stiff hotel carpet between us.

When the ending credits music comes on, her pinky nudges over mine, just a bit, and I look up, catching her steady gaze and hesitant smile. She leans in closer. My breath slows, but a smile starts to grow on my face without my consent, and I—

"Um, y'all?" Ami says, shattering the moment. She stands with her eye pressed to the peephole, peering out into the hallway. "There's something going on out here. The pageant moms are going door to door and inspecting things with a magnifying glass like weird Sherlock impersonators."

"Shit!" Teagan jumps, scrabbling in her back pocket for her phone. As soon as she lays eyes on the screen, she sucks in a breath.

"Oh no, shit, shit, *shit!*"

"What? What is it?" I ask, following as she leaps to her feet.

"They're checking for people breaking curfew. They're looking for *me*. My room is right next door. My friend tried to warn me, but I didn't see her texts, and . . ."

She trails off, looking around the room with wild eyes as she finally notices us all staring.

"So, you're . . . ," Lady begins, but trails off.

Teagan winces, drawing in on herself. She glances up at me just long enough to meet my eyes for the briefest second then shoves her hands in her hoodie pockets and looks away.

"Yeah. I'm Miss Virginia."

Chapter Nine

*

TEAGAN

The shift in the room is instant, just like I knew it would be. This was a terrible idea to begin with. There's nowhere on earth where these two parts of me are equally welcome, the pageant queen and the fangirl, and I was naive to think otherwise. I never should have gone out. I should have just stayed in my room and studied for tomorrow's interview like everyone else, should have been there to hang out with Jess once she got back and soaked up the rare time with her. I never should have let myself get sucked in by this amazing, beautiful person who, if I'm honest, *I don't even really know.* Now the whole point of me being here this weekend is about to be snatched away.

With a deep breath, I summon my practiced poise, lift my chin, and straighten my spine. "I have to go. This probably ruins any chance I have of winning the scholarship this weekend, but it'll only be worse if I put it off. Thanks for inviting me. I'm glad I got to see at least a little bit of the con."

I turn without meeting anyone's eyes and take two steps toward the door before a hand on my shoulder stops me in my tracks. I turn . . . and it's Lady, one of Kay's roommates. She gives me a little half smile and lets her hand fall away.

"Hold up a sec," she says, glancing over at Kay. "We could help, right?"

I allow myself the briefest glance at Kay then tear my gaze away. They seem . . . lost. Or confused, or something. Still processing the revelation that the girl who had her hands all over them all night is a pageant queen, I guess. Does not compute. Cakes speaks right up, though.

"Yeah, we could create a distraction! You said your room is right next door, right?"

"Yeah," I say, hesitant. "But I don't want you getting in trouble for me or anything."

"Psh," Ami says, finally bursting into the conversation with full enthusiasm and total fearlessness. "Those pageant chaperones have no authority over us. We got this. Right, Kay?"

Kay seems to shake themself awake, mustering up some semblance of the energy they'd had up until moments ago. "Yeah, we can do this. Just give us about thirty seconds and watch out the peephole. We'll cover you. Shall we start the Discourse on the way out?" they say, turning back to their friends.

I wince. I'm not sure how rehashing every fandom-wide argument that's ever taken over Scroll will help in this situation, but I have to trust them. I don't really have another choice.

"Okay," I say, and they all leap into action a second later, murmuring to each other on the way over to the door.

"Thirty seconds," Kay says, turning to look at me one last time. Our eyes meet, and the moment pulls taut. Their lips part like they're about to say something, some parting words that will make everything okay.

Then the door closes, and Kay is gone. Just like that.

I allow myself exactly five seconds to mourn the evening: the touches, the laughing and stories, and most of all, the intense lingering Gay Eye Contact™. The feeling of safety, of belonging.

Then I shove it all away, right along with the con program I picked up this evening, which goes up under my hoodie and into the waistband of my jeans. I press my face to the door, eye struggling to focus through the peephole. Kay and their friends manage to take up the whole hallway with both bodies and personality, waving their hands around in fannish enthusiasm. I can't hear their exact words, but it's loud enough for me to pick up their muffled voices through the heavy hotel door, probably annoying everyone in the hallway—group moms included. Then, to my astonishment, they actually stop and talk to them, seeming to drag the moms into their Discourse . . . and like magic, turn their backs to the door.

That's my cue.

As quickly and quietly as I can, I open the door a crack, look left and right lightning quick, then yank my key card from my pocket and make a break for it. The door behind me closes with barely a click, but the beep when I press my card to the reader on my door seems horrifically loud. I don't stop long enough to see whether I'm noticed, just get my body through the door with every bit of speed I can muster while crouch-running at half height.

As soon as I'm through the door, I replace my jeans and sneakers with yoga pants and bare feet then rip off my hoodie and snag my con program from where it fell on the floor. Jess . . . she must have been up the whole time I was gone, because she's there in an instant, wide-awake. She doesn't even bat an eye, just takes my hoodie and program and hides it under her pillow.

In a quiet, stern voice I've never heard used on anyone but her younger sisters, she orders me to summon some tears and shoves a wad of tissues in my hand.

I don't know what I'm meant to be fake crying over, but the tears come easily, and once they start, I can't make them stop. I'm not normally a crier—not a strength, just a fact that's been true since my mom died—but right now I feel utterly exhausted right down to my core. In the background, I hear Jess at the door to the room, whispering to the moms over my sobs. She says something about the pressure of the weekend, my parents, my dad being gone all the time, and doing yoga on the roof. It paints a lonely picture, I can't deny.

I had the best time tonight, hanging out with Kay and their friends. It felt so *good* to be with them, the complete opposite of lonely. *Seen*, and welcomed. And I ruined it all by lying to them all night. Now I'll never see them again, and it feels like my chest is being crushed under the weight of everything I've been hiding.

I wish I could hate the pageants. That would make it all much easier, if I could just scorn everything pageant related and identify wholly with fandom alone. Then I could at least be all righteously angry as I go through the motions, knowing with certainty who I am and where I truly belong, drawing fan art with one hand and self-righteously accepting their scholarship money with the other.

But I legitimately love the pageants, despite all their obnoxious trappings. I love the confidence they give me and the places I get to see. I've made so many friends, people I know I'll stay in touch with for life, like Jess. And I love the clothes, too. I love to feel amazing in a great dress, to walk across that stage and feel comfortable in my own skin. And I love that it's given me a chance at college and a chance to do good in my town and throughout the country with my charity. Girls come up to me after pageants all the time to ask me questions, tell me about their art, and ask advice so they can get into the pageant world, too, and those moments mean more than all the rest.

I love it.

I really do.

But right now, alone in this room, in the dark of night with no eyes to judge me?

I'd skip it all for another hour with Kay.

Chapter
Ten

KAYLEE

*a*s soon as the door shuts, a solid barrier between us and the bewildered pageant moms, I flop back on my bed and blink.

I think I have brain whiplash.

What . . . just . . . happened? Did I really just spend all evening lusting after a pageant girl like Miss North Carolina?

"Well, that was fun," Lady says from her bed, wiggling under the covers to get comfortable again after the sudden interruption. "I do so love to annoy uptight white women. Huge bummer ending to your night, though, Kay."

Ever the optimist, Cakes gives me an encouraging smile. "Yeah, she seemed really cool and really into you. Maybe we'll see her again tomorrow."

"Yeah," I murmur. My stomach twists itself into a knot at those words: *into you.* "Maybe."

But after the close call she just had? I don't know. I seriously doubt it. And do I even want that, now that I know who she is?

"Maybe it's for the best," I say, staring blankly into the middle distance. "I mean, she does pageants. She probably only cares about hair and makeup and dresses and stuff like that. Pageants are so shallow. Those girls just walk across a stage trying to look pretty for judges, and somehow that makes them worthy of scholarship money that real people could use?"

"Yikes," Ami says, chiming in with her characteristic succinct opinion. "Check yourself, Kay."

"Yeah, I like makeup," Lady says, gesturing to the bulging makeup pouch sitting on top of her suitcase.

"And I like doing things with my hair," Cakes adds, tucking a blue curl behind her ear, still sleek and shiny somehow despite a day of travel and dancing.

"And I wear dresses," Ami concludes with a significant look at the day's Sherlockian dress, thrown haphazardly over the back of the room's only chair. "Are we shallow?"

If I could trip over myself while lying down, I definitely would with how hard I'm backpedaling right now. "No, no, that's not what I meant at all! Y'all are awesome and I love you, you know that. And you're into fandom, and fanfic, and you're so . . . *you*. You know?"

Lady tips her head to the side then shakes her head. "No, I don't think I do know. Teagan was into fandom, too, and she's even read your fic."

"What is it about pageants that makes you think so badly of her?" Cakes says, turning fully toward me under the scratchy hotel comforter. "It's like you did an instant one-eighty as soon as you found out and became this Judgy McJudgepants. You liked her, right? *And* you were attracted to her," she adds with an eyebrow waggle.

Ami plops down cross-legged on the end of our bed, looking me straight in the eye. "Is this about Teagan? Or is it about Madison?"

I open my mouth to protest, but she tilts her head and raises her eyebrows in that "nuh-uh, think before you speak" look she's perfected over years of being friends with me. My jaw clicks shut.

I mean, how can it *not* be about Madison, at least a little? She makes my life a living hell at school, and she's queen of our town all because of her pageant career. She's practically famous, and everyone treats her like it. And she uses that attention not to do good in the community or model how to be a decent, empathetic human or anything but to write garbage on my locker, spread rumors, harass me in class, and set her minions after me. Why should I believe she's the exception, not the rule?

"Okay, I can see that you're struggling, so here's the obvious solution: Let's google her," Lady says, pulling out her phone and joining the pile on our bed.

"And the pageant," Cakes says, grabbing her own phone from the nightstand. "If it's the competition aspect that bugs you, then maybe if we know more about it, it won't seem so shallow."

Ami nods and lies down, happy to take a step back now that things are moving in a better direction. She reaches out a toe and pokes my knee, tilting her head again—but this time, it's her "are you okay?" face. I manage a weak smile then look away.

"Okay, look, here," Lady says, flipping her phone around for me to look. The headline reads MISS VIRGINIA MENTORS KIDS THROUGH ART THERAPY. I skim the article, noting the quotes from Teagan and the kids, but my eyes get stuck on a photo of her beaming at a kid who couldn't be more than seven holding up a painting for her approval. Her eyes are bright and kind, and her smile looks sincere enough, not forced or bored or anything.

"And here's a recent article from a feminist blog about pageants in general, but it talks about Miss Cosmic Teen USA specifically. 'Although the stage competition itself remains regrettably focused on physical appearance and retains many of the misogynistic trappings of its predecessors, it is unfair to judge the pageant on that aspect alone. The majority of a contestant's score is based on a portfolio and interview, which both emphasize charity work and career or educational aspirations. Miss Cosmic Teen supports those aspirations with scholarship money for the top three contestants. Though the travel, garments, makeup, and other requirements of the pageant still largely limit participation to a certain class, there are other avenues. Miss Virginia, one of the favorites to make the top five this year, is almost entirely sponsored by local businesses and pageant-wear companies.' Well, there you go," Cakes adds. "Even a specific shout-out for Teagan. And she's apparently really good if she's Top Five out of fifty-one contestants!"

Lady's hand slaps down on the bedspread in an excited interruption. "WHAT. Okay, look at this. I think this is her Etsy shop? Have you seen this?"

She holds the phone out for the rest of us to see and scrolls through the same shop Teagan showed me earlier with all her hand-painted creations. "Your girl is hella talented, Kay. You better jump on that."

"Literally," Cakes *has* to add, of course, which makes my cheeks go scarlet. I hate that I'm such a blusher.

"OKAY, okay, I get it. I'm being judgy, Teagan is not Madison, pageants are not all bad, and I'm a jerk."

"And?" Ami asks, poking my knee with her foot again.

"And," I add with a sigh, "I appreciate y'all calling me out on my bullshit. I will do better. And I love you."

"Aaaaaand?" Cakes draws out with a wicked grin. "Tomorrow you will find that girl and kiss the hell out of her?"

"Oh my God, *stop*," I say, grabbing the nearest pillow and

crushing it to my face. My voice comes out muffled through the layers of stuffing and fabric. "Your point is made, can we please move on?"

"Move on to bed, definitely," Lady says, whirling around to her own bed and settling back down with a happy sigh. Cakes is already snuggled up with her pillow, feet moving under the clean hotel sheets like a happy cricket. Ami gives me a silent hug then crawls under the covers where she'll inevitably play her Nintendo 3DS until she passes out with it on her face.

And me?

The red numbers of the beside alarm clock burn 1:56 A.M., and I'm barely even tired. My panel is first thing in the morning, but my brain is buzzing with *something*, and I can already tell it's going to be a while before I can get it to shut up. Maybe some words will help.

I grab my laptop, climb into bed next to Ami, and open my fic in progress. Lips . . . too many lips. I was having trouble writing kissing earlier today.

Not anymore. The words flow with heat and vivid detail as I craft their love onto the page, spinning sentences into paragraphs long after the others have dropped off to sleep. I don't know what happened, but the tap has been opened, and the result might be some of my best writing yet.

I reread the new chapter one last time, click POST, and smile.

Part II

SATURDAY

Chapter
Eleven

*

TEAGAN

S hit!

I sit straight up in bed, glancing blearily at the glowing numbers of the hotel alarm clock. 5:27 A.M. The alarm would have woken me up in three minutes anyway, but a horrible thought did it first: *I forgot to get Kay's number.* Or their email. Or their damn Snapchat or *anything*. Their Scroll username was Kay-something, but my foggy brain can't remember the rest.

They probably don't want to talk to me anymore anyway, considering I lied to them all night, and they didn't seem thrilled with my revelation at the end. But I poured my soul into them for hours last night, nearly got caught by the group moms, then was saved by Kay and their friends, and for what?

To *never talk to them again*, apparently, because I'm hopeless.

I roll myself out of my scratchy hotel blanket cocoon with a quiet groan, doing my best to avoid waking Jess. If she gets up now, she'll want in the bathroom, and the only reason I'm dragging myself out of bed at this unholy hour is for as many uninterrupted minutes in there as possible. Jess, for all her amazing qualities, is not much of a morning person. Normally I don't have a problem waking up early. I'm one of those sick people who roll straight out of bed and into an overly ambitious schedule: exercise, shower, skin care, smoothie, and fanfic, then school.

Today? My face feels stiff and crusty from dried tears, and my eyes have that saggy, groggy feeling I earned staying up *way* too late. It was a terrible decision, I know that, but even with a three-cup-of-coffee sleep hangover, I can't bring myself to regret it. I sneak back out into the room, grab the Red Bull I always bring to get me through late rehearsals and interview studying, then close the bathroom door behind me. A crack, a hiss, and the sharp taste on my tongue—the flavor always starts to wake me up long before the caffeine can actually take effect. My body and I, we're used to this routine by now.

I lean over the sink to inspect myself, and the puffiness under my eyes spells out my bad choices for all to see. I could try the forbidden Preparation H under the eyes trick, but it never works for long, and I'd rather not risk going blind. My head feels puffy, too, though there's no magic pageant trick for that. I'm normally hyperfocused on the first day of competition, but my mind is a clanging, discordant mess of typical pageant nerves, worry about my friendship with Jess (I'm such a jerk, I owe her big), and long, lingering thoughts about the curve of Kay's neck and the feel of their fingers under mine.

The shower pulls the tension from my shoulders and clears some of the fuzz from my brain. First item on the agenda is the interview with the judges. The interview portion is worth a full 40 percent of my final score, the largest part, and fortunately the one I'm the best at. It's all about brains, confidence, charm, knowledge of current events, and the ability to utterly rock a sleek business outfit. I've got it on lock. If I can keep my head in the game, that is. One of the first lessons I ever learned about pageants: Interview. Is. Everything.

The makeup for the interview is more toned down than the stage makeup I'll need later today. Soft, natural, polished, and professional. I'm halfway through my meticulous eyeliner routine when I jerk in realization, nearly stabbing myself in the eye.

Kay's fic.

I have their fic bookmarked on the Archive. With that, I should be able to track them down on social media and contact them. It's a bit stalkery, but totally worth it, right?

I drop my eyeliner in the sink and scramble for my phone. As soon as it unlocks, the big group selfie from last night fills the screen. It was the last thing I looked at before falling asleep. My gut tugs at the sight of Kay: short, feathery hair, bright eyes, that *damn* lip ring . . . I want to see them again so badly, and I only just met them a few hours ago.

I swipe the photo away and pull up my Archive bookmarks, waiting while the awful hotel Wi-Fi takes its dear, sweet time, then smile. *Yes.* KayfortheWinnet's fics are right on the first page of bookmarks, and their Archive profile has Scroll and Posted accounts linked—plenty of ways to contact them. I open Posted first, log in, pop open a direct message . . . then hesitate.

My Posted account is completely pageant sanitized, full of excitement over the upcoming competition, information about my community service platform, and lightly Photoshopped pictures of me at pageants and around town. If Kay gets curious and scrolls my feed or looks at my bio, they'll probably think, *Who is this person?*

I bite my lip then close Posted and bring up their Scroll

instead. I have an ancient Scroll account of my own, one that's strictly fandom stuff and gay feelings, completely secret, anonymous, and separate from my pageant identity. I stopped using it six months ago because I couldn't shake the paranoia that someone would find it and link me to all the angry lesbian feminist posts and queer fan art, but this persona will be much more familiar to Kay. A reminder of everything we have in common.

I log in, click the MESSAGE link on Kay's Scroll, and stare at the blank text box for a moment. How can I make this sound as minimally creepy as possible?

Dear Kay, I had a great time meeting you last

Delete. Too formal.

Hi, I hope this isn't creepy but

Delete. Pointing out the creep factor only emphasizes it. I think for a moment then start again.

Hi, Kay. It's Teagan. The girl from last night who for some reason overshared embarrassing preschool memories with you. Sorry again for the poop story. We just clicked, and . . . yeah, that's no excuse. Anyway, I woke up this morning and realized that I never got your phone number last night. I know we probably live on complete opposite sides of the country and will never see each other after this weekend, but I had a great time hanging out with you and I don't make friends that easily, so I hate to just give up.

Hope to hear from you before the weekend is over. It would be great to see you again, but if I don't, I just wanted to say good luck with the writing contest. I really hope you win. If you don't, though, please don't stop writing. The world needs your words.

-Teagan

I read it over one last time, hold my breath, and hit the SEND button before I lose my nerve. My heart flutters like I'm about to walk onstage. They're going to think I'm a total creepy stalker, but there was no way I'd be able to let it go all weekend. At least now I've done all I can do. I doubt I'll really be able to sneak away to see them again before the pageant is over, but I have to at least put it out there.

Now, time to focus on what I actually came here to do: win this pageant.

I fish my eyeliner out of the sink, lean forward, and bring the tip to my eyelid.

BAM BAM BAM!

I nearly stab myself again, though this time I'm tempted to let it happen.

"Good morning, Miss Virginia!" a voice trills, and not the one I'm expecting. North Carolina? Where's Jess?

"Oregon is having a bad hair morning," she continues, syrupy sweet. "And my hair is going to take at *least* an hour! Can I borrow your bathroom until she's out? Jess said it was okay."

Oh, *did* she now? My jaw tenses, but I force myself to relax. Why, oh *why*, despite all the awesome North Carolina girls I've met at other pageants, did Madison have to be the one here this weekend? This girl almost caught me last night, called the moms on me, and she apparently knows Kay from school. I have to be more careful, and that starts with—ugh—being nice to her.

"Sure, Mads, it's all yours. I'll be right out."

Mads? Where the hell did that come from? Gross.

I huff a sigh, gather up my bags, and set up shop in front of the mirror out in the room. Jess shrugs helplessly, mouthing *sorry* to me in the reflection. I throw my hands up in a universal "what can you do?" gesture. She couldn't have said no without getting on Madison's bad side, and our dear North Carolina is one of the few vicious, conniving girls to slip past the judges and make it this far. She's dangerous, and it's better if we play it safe. We'll have plenty of time to do full hair and makeup and get dressed in the dressing room on-site, but the judges will definitely be down at breakfast and watching us make the short walk next door to the theater where the interviews will be held. That calls for at least basic makeup right now. I'm not taking any chances. This is one of the few areas where pageant officials enforce some form of equality, so the rich girls can't just hire a team of hair and makeup artists. We all have to do our own hair and makeup, though some blow hundreds or thousands at Sephora while the rest of us realize that grocery store products can be just as good. They can spend all the money they want, but it won't do anything for them that trial and error, years of practice, and a *lot* of YouTube videos have done for me.

I pick up the eyeliner, finish the last sweep with a flourish, and inspect the result.

Totally killing it. I've got this.

Miss NC will be in the bathroom for the next eternity, which gives me a perfect opportunity to more carefully plan out my next chance to drop in on the con. I lift up the blank hotel stationery to pull out the program I stashed under it last night, after drawing giant dorky circles around Kay's panel and tonight's Cosplay Pageant.

THE ONE TRUE ME AND YOU

But it's not there.

Panic sends my heart fluttering, and I look under everything else on the desk one at a time, biting my lip to keep from swearing where Miss NC can hear me.

I know I brought it back from Kay's room last night. Jess took it from me and hid it and my hoodie under her pillow while she got rid of the chaperones, then she gave it right back afterward . . . right? Though, I was deliriously tired from crying at the time. Maybe I dreamed that? I spot the purple hoodie in my suitcase and dig around under it, but no luck. It's nowhere to be found.

"What are you looking for?" Jess whispers, barely making a sound.

My eyes cut to the bathroom door out of sheer paranoia, where Miss NC is humming cheerfully to herself. "Where's the con program? I swear I put it over here last night."

"You did," Jess confirms, dread growing in her face. "Madison was standing over there earlier. Could she have . . ."

I shake my head, unwilling to even consider it.

Okay. Not a big deal. This is fine. Let's not embrace that paranoid life. Realistically, someone would probably look at the program and be like "Huh, maybe Jess or Teagan really likes that TV show" and then forget all about it. There's no reason to go from zero to *all my secrets are now un-secret and I am DOOMED* in three seconds flat.

But that's exactly where I'm at, because this is Madison. If she saw that program, if she took it and spotted the circled events I was interested in, then . . . what? I don't know what she could possibly do with that noninformation, but I wouldn't trust her with a dull safety pin, much less any private information.

Nothing to do about it now, though. Can't let the paranoia

distract me from this morning's missions: crush the interview and figure out how to see more of the con.

I flop down on the bed, bring the con schedule up on my phone instead, and turn on some upbeat music.

The melody does little to soothe the prickling sense of danger in my stomach.

Chapter Twelve

KAYLEE

*Y*ou could always wrap an Ace bandage around your boobs," Ami shouts through the bathroom door, her voice muffled and exasperated. I roll my eyes at my reflection and throw the door open, letting a billowing cloud of steam escape into the room.

"Friends don't let friends practice unsafe binding," I say, my unsuccessfully buttoned shirt flapping open at my sides. "I don't *love* my boobs right now, but I'd rather not have them wither away because I choked them to death."

My feelings about them change by the day, honestly. Sometimes I want to embrace them as an essential and beautiful part of my body. Other days I wish they were gone. Either way, I can't afford a real binder right now, and I don't have anywhere to wear one back home anyway. Another thing to add to the college column.

"Well, I don't know what to tell you," Ami shoots back from behind her Nintendo 3DS. "But that shirt is definitely not going to button."

I groan and flop back on the bed. I'm supposed to be on a panel in forty-five minutes, I haven't eaten, and my Army John Watson cosplay outfit for today doesn't fit because I always gain weight in my chest before anywhere else. Might sound fun to people who like breasts, but it mostly means all my screen-printed T-shirts are going to get boob-stretch cracks and the rest won't fit at all. Forget about button-down shirts altogether. It's so frustrating. I saved the tiny amount of money I make stocking groceries for months to buy these cosplay pieces, and now they don't fit.

My phone chimes, and I scoop it up from the bedside table. Probably Cakes and Lady wondering why we aren't at breakfast yet when we swore we'd be down in "just a few minutes." The screen is still lit with a new Scroll notification: Hi, Kay. It's Teagan. The girl from last night who . . .

I suck in a sharp breath through my nose and swipe three times trying to get the damn phone unlocked to see the rest of the message. She found me on Scroll. Does that mean she saw that NSFW art I reposted? Did she see that explicit-rated fic I recommended yesterday? Did she read my late-night vagueblogging about orientation and gender and all that mess?

Hope to hear from you before the weekend is over. It would be great to see you again . . .

Oh God, this nervous fluttery thing does NOT work on an empty stomach. I'm gonna puke. I bite my lip and glance over my shoulder then back at the screen.

She wants to see me again.

I tap on her Scroll URL (paintmeinviolet) and read her bio:

17, she/her, very lesbian. Ride or Die: Virene (TGG),
Korrasami (LoK), Clexa (100). Quickly becoming
Supercorp trash. Occasional fan artist. [On Hiatus]

Scroll, scroll, scroll. Lots of pictures of girls kissing. Fan art of girls from her fandoms cuddling or being badass, some of it hers. Reposted rants about gender and sexuality, occasionally with witty or insightful commentary tacked on. A cat picture. (It had to come eventually.)

The roiling in my stomach kicks into high gear as I remember the feel of her hips against mine, her body molded to me, her breasts pressing into my back. She's obviously really certain about being *very lesbian*, as stated, but I'm . . . I don't know, something? I mean, if she's gay, does that include only cis and trans girls? Or are nonbinary people included? Definitions can be flexible, but did she only like me last night because I came across as femme enough? Or maybe I misread the entire thing. I wouldn't put it past myself to have imagined . . . everything. All the tension. Girls dance together like that all the time, and if that's how she viewed me . . . how am I supposed to know when it's just two friends having fun together and when it's potentially more?

I drop the phone on my bare stomach and close my eyes, reining in the utter panic thrumming through my veins. It's pointless to even think about it. My only goal this weekend was to *kiss* a girl, not find someone to have some kind of long-term thing with. It doesn't need to go any further than that. It *can't*. Besides, I've only ever dated guys. I have no experience in this arena. I wouldn't even know what to do with a girl if I had the option for more.

My heart gives a tug in time with a lurch of my stomach.

Okay, maybe I have a *few* ideas to consider.

At length.

In private.

A soft bit of cloth hits me in the face, half covering my eyes. I pick it up and hold the sand-colored T-shirt out in front of me.

"Just wear this as an undershirt with the camo jacket open over it," Ami says, "instead of lying there and making yourself sick thinking about that girl from last night."

"I wasn't . . ."

My cheeks burn, and I trail off with an awkward cough.

"Okay, yes, I was."

I chew the inside of my cheek for a moment, pick up my phone, turn it over in my hand once, then close the Scroll app. I *should* be focusing on Cakes, Lady, and Ami this weekend. This is *our* time, and we've been waiting for this weekend for months. It's selfish of me to have made this weekend all about me and my ridiculous checklist. *And then I don't have to deal with any of this,* my brain exults. It's such a lazy asshole.

"Ami."

She turns, shrugging on her Gwen Lestrade trench coat and slipping her 3DS in a pocket.

I close my eyes and sigh. "I'm sorry for ditching y'all last night. It was shitty of me. We never get to see Cakes and Lady, and hanging out with you should be my first priority this weekend."

Her stern lips twitch into a tiny smile, and she waggles her phone at me, open to our group chat. "Come on, there are apparently waffles at the breakfast buffet. You know how I feel about waffles."

I gag a little. "Yeah, I know you put eggs, butter, bacon, and whipped cream on them all at the same time, you disgusting human. No one needs to witness that."

"One day you will understand my genius."

I pull on the undershirt she gave me, whose plunging neckline is definitely not military appropriate, then toss the button-down desert jacket over it. Authentic British army dog tags complete my preparations: KayfortheWinnet, reporting for duty as army-era John Watson, complete with authentic military-issue boots, desert camo pants, and the (irritating) jacket. It was a lot of work to get it all together, but it's worth it to get to cosplay my favorite version of my favorite bisexual disaster.

And if I ended up with certain assets a bit more on display than usual, well, better than forcing the jacket to button and being uncomfortable all day. I'm having a hard enough time breathing through the anxiety of this morning's fic author panel without a too-tight jacket strangling me, anyway.

Now all I have to do is get my brain together enough for the discussion. No more thoughts of gorgeous girls with their hands all over me. Definitely not. Clear head, ready mind.

Time to channel my inner John Watson and be a BAMF.

No one will come to a 9:00 A.M. panel, they said.

It'll be fine, they said.

As the fortieth person walks through the door (not that I'm counting), I shoot Cakes and Lady a mental middle finger and struggle to get a real lungful of air. Ami flexes a fake bicep at me, her signal for "be brave, you got this." Yeah, okay.

This. Is. Terrifying.

People continue to trickle in even after our panel moderator taps the microphone to silence the chatter. My friends give me thumbs-ups of support as the mod welcomes everyone and thanks them for dragging themselves out of bed for the first session of the day. Throughout the room, there's hardly a single person without a cup of coffee in their hands, though a few who are in particularly elaborate cosplay outfits lean away from their coffee-bearing neighbors. The moderator, utterly adorable in a punk Mrs. Hudson costume, gestures broadly to the four of us seated at the head table.

"The title of our discussion this morning is New Authors for the Win! Getting Your Start in Fan Fiction. We have four authors with a variety of backgrounds and levels of experience here to discuss how they got into this whole fic writing deal and how you can get ready to dive in yourself. Without further ado, I'll hand it over to our panelists so they can give us their names and pronouns, tell us a bit about their works, and share how they got started in fandom."

The girl on the end launches into her introduction, and I wipe my sweaty palms over my thighs. I'm still shocked that I was invited to be on this panel. I'm definitely the newest and youngest author here, though I guess they must have heard of my work if they asked me to speak. I have decent numbers of hits and comments on my fics, but it's hard to know how that actually matches up with real popularity. The other people at the table with me are much heavier hitters. SpaceGlee221b has been writing fic since *he* was seventeen, back in the early '90s. Cait started back when season one of TGG aired four years ago, and even Darslie has been around longer than me, though she only started writing two years ago.

And pronouns. God. It's standard to introduce yourself with pronouns at a con like this, but I feel like I could choke on the words. I've never been so public about it before. There are a *lot* of people here.

Introductions move down the line until it's my turn, and the room falls silent.

Breathe. Speak.

I lean in and accidentally bump the base of the mic. The light tap reverberates through the room. The moment stretches for an awkward eternity, a blanket of heavy silence over the room. I shove my hands in my lap to hold them still and lean in close (but not too close) to the mic again.

"Hi, I'm KayfortheWinnet on Scroll and Archive, and—" *say it say it say it* "—my pronouns are they/them. I'm—"

The door in the back of the room swings open, admitting a group of three people in their thirties and forties. My tongue stumbles over my words, and my thoughts come to a screeching halt.

Two of them I recognize immediately from the GreatCon website: Les Vanetti, the editor who's judging the publishing contest, and Mariana Heimish, a big-shot literary agent who happens to be his wife. My stomach lurches in protest.

And the last of the trio? Irishtea23. My all-time favorite fic author. The author who inspired me to start writing fic is at *my panel*. Listening to me talk.

Or *not* talk, because I'm sitting here with my mouth hanging open, no words coming out of it, painfully awkward. *Say something, damn it.*

I force a weak, self-deprecating laugh to cover in case anyone noticed my lapse. "I'm definitely the youngest and newest writer on this panel. I'm seventeen, and though I've been reading fic since I was about thirteen, I was always too nervous to try writing my own—forget about actually posting it somewhere where other eyeballs might touch it."

I shudder. "The thought still gives me that fluttery, panicky feeling in my chest sometimes, even though I finally posted my first work over a year ago, and two dozen more since then. It's all . . ." I wiggle my fingers over my breastbone in an approximation of butterflies and shrug.

A few scattered warm laughs ease a bit of the tension in my gut, and I manage a wan smile.

"It took me a long time to get my courage up to write something of my own. I kept reading all these beautiful fics that would completely turn my mood around when things at school were rough. They'd make me cry, make my heart ache, or make me grin to the point that my mom asked once what evil I was plotting."

That wins a bigger laugh from my fellow panelists, and the coiled spring in my chest relaxes a fraction more. "So, one day, after reading a really emotional fic by one of my favorite authors—who's in this room today, I'm totally dying—I finally decided I wanted to try to share some of the feelings that her fics evoked in me. I felt like I was overflowing with it, and pouring some of it onto a page really helped me process it."

I feel like I've been talking *forever*, but several heads around the room are nodding in approval, so I guess it's going okay. The moderator takes over again and poses some questions to our panel for discussion. We ramble on for a few moments each about our weird writing rituals, techniques, and beta reader relationships. Turns out all of us have at least one beta reader in the room (Lady, in my case), so we have the chance to applaud them all for their hard work. I'm glad—beta readers definitely don't get enough attention in the fandom. SpaceGlee gets a great discussion going about how so much of fandom centers on romance between cis men but prioritizes cis women's gaze over actual real-life queer men like him and brings up the objectification queer men in fandom deal with. That morphs into tips for new writers dealing with the darker side of fandom: shipping wars, drama, problematic content, and so on. I'm glad we get a chance to talk about it—as much as I adore fandom, it is definitely not all sunshine and roses.

Everything is going surprisingly well, and by the time the moderator finally opens it up to questions from attendees, most of the tightness has left my shoulders and lungs. Cait fields a question about the world-building in her novel-length sailor AU fic, and I manage to intelligently answer a vague question about balancing schoolwork with writing fic. (Answer: Get homework done the second it's assigned to avoid panic stress! Avoiding it only makes it drag out longer and leaves less brain space for Johnlock. I'd rather be done and not think about it.)

Near the end, though, with about five minutes to go, someone asks: "Could you each name a few fic authors you've found particularly inspiring or influential to your own writing?"

My blush is instantaneous, and I must have made a noise because the moderator turns to me first. "Kay, you want to start us off?"

A nervous laugh burbles up from my chest. "Hah, uh, it's a bit awkward because they're almost all in this room right now. Um, everyone at this table, for one," I say, gesturing down at the others. "They were all already writing in this fandom when I joined up, so I've been seeing their works come across my dash from the start. It's a huge honor to be on this panel with them today."

The others all make polite protestations, but I wave it off.

"No, it's true! But I have to say my biggest influence is the person who wrote the fics I talked about earlier, with the spilling feelings and all that." I swallow, take a breath, and look over at my friends so I don't have to see the reaction. "Irishtea23 has been a huge inspiration to me from my first day in this fandom, both with her writing and her kindness toward everyone in the community, and I wouldn't be writing at all if not for her amazing fics. So, thanks, I guess!"

I look up to address the last part to her . . . but she's gone. Something must show on my face, because the moderator immediately sweeps in.

"And speaking of Irishtea: All the writers in this room, from experienced vets to complete noobs have the opportunity to learn from her this morning! There's been a bit of a scheduling issue, so her flash fiction workshop has been moved to . . ." She checks her watch. "Ten minutes from now. We'll end this panel a few minutes early so you all have a chance to get over to Conference Room D, and I hate to cut that last question short, but I have one last thing for our panelists to wrap up: What do you appreciate most about being in fandom? What does it mean to you?"

I mutter something short and quick about meeting amazing new friends, which earns a whoop from Cakes and Lady, and the others chime in with quick words about feeling part of a community. Darslie, who has been lost in thought since the question was asked, finally speaks up, her voice slow and thoughtful.

"What I appreciate most about fanfic and fandom in general is the way it's opened me up to different sexualities and gender identities that I had no idea were, like . . . actual things," she says, nodding as if she's thinking out loud. My heartbeat speeds, and the rest of the room falls away as she speaks. "I've learned so much about asexuality and about nonbinary genders, but most of all I've learned a lot about *myself.*"

She grins. "I finally was able to accept that I'm bisexual, that it wasn't just a phase or intense friendship or something. I came out to my family and got my first girlfriend this year because fandom gave me a safe place to figure things out and the context I needed to understand what I was feeling. I wrote that one story, 'Another Option'—"

Someone in the audience squeals, provoking a smattering of laughter. Darslie grins. "Ha, thanks, I think? Yeah, I wrote that story, my first femslash pairing, and that was a big turning point for me. I'm grateful to fandom for helping me get there."

Everyone applauds, the moderator says something, and people begin to funnel out of the room with the scooting of chairs and shuffling of feet. But it's all a dull background roar to me.

She's right. She's *so* right, God, I've learned a ton over the past year of being in fandom, and yet I've obviously learned *nothing* if I'm still feeling like I can't possibly be nonbinary, can't possibly be bi or pan for real because there's nothing unusual about acknowledging that girls are beautiful.

Except when it makes my skin feel warm, my heartbeat go wild, my fingers *itch to touch*.

I'm so oblivious sometimes.

It all seemed so abstract and logical when talking about fictional characters or people on the internet, who sometimes feel like fictional characters themselves. But it's real, and it might apply to me.

I want to know. I want to find out.

I scramble under the table to pull my phone out of my pocket, bring Scroll back up, and tap out a quick message:

I want to see you again too. I had a great time. When?

Chapter Thirteen

TEAGAN

I'm five minutes from lining up for my interview session and the thought that's running on repeat through my head?

My outfit matches Kay's hair.

I'm wearing a sleek pencil dress in a rich, bright burgundy, almost the exact shade of Kay's dyed hair, donated by one of my local sponsors. Little cap sleeves and a stitched-in, jacket-like flare at the waist both keep the outfit professional and emphasize my curves, one of the things I love most about my body. I'm still not sure the color is right for this, though. It's so bold, and most of the other girls are wearing much *younger* colors like pink, white, or bright blue.

I have a pale-purple version of this dress with me, and I'm sorely tempted to change. It wouldn't take me more than a minute to slip into the other one. I study myself in the mirror, tuning out all the other girls bustling around me—until my ringing phone startles me out of focus. I glance at the screen and groan.

My pageant coach, doing her psychic thing again.

Normally I almost miss her stern guidance and unwavering

confidence at these things, but this weekend, I'm happy to have one less person breathing down my neck when I sneak out. Physically here or not, though, she is never a woman to be ignored. I paste on my best smile and hit the ACCEPT CALL button. She always tells me she can *hear* when I'm not smiling.

"Good morning, Rhonda!"

"Nice smile, good girl," Rhonda says from four states away. "Interview in just a few minutes, right? I'm calling to make sure you don't panic and sabotage yourself by wearing that awful lavender dress instead of the burgundy. You're wearing the burgundy, aren't you?"

I sigh internally but externally keep my smile fixed. Trust Rhonda to hear my doubts from hundreds of miles away and come sweeping in at the last second. I'm honestly not even surprised. I swear she can *sense* when I'm about to screw something up. I'm more shocked she didn't sense the gay radiating from me last night and call in the middle of my dance with Kay with a lecture on pageant propriety. "Yeah, I'm—"

"*Yeah?*"

I roll my eyes. "*Yes*, I'm wearing it, but everyone else is wearing pastels or navy and I really don't think—"

Rhonda cuts me off. "No, stop right there. I am right and you are wrong, as always. Listen to me. You are a *powerful* speaker. You have presence and dedication, and your enormous brain comes through in your interview. If you walk in there in pastels and give the kind of intense, focused interview you always do, the judges will be jarred by the contrast between your appearance and your attitude."

She sighs the dramatic sigh of the vastly superior in the presence of lesser mortals. "You need to dress for your *personality* more than your body, and your personality is strong and bold. Burgundy is the right choice, and I bet you're the only one wearing it.

You better believe those judges will remember you. Just walk in there with your chin up and those fierce eyes like you always do, and they'll be completely swept away. Tell me I'm right."

I study myself in the mirror, trying to see the burgundy suit as the judges will. It's a more cool-toned shade of burgundy that works well with the undertones of my skin, and the white band around the middle provides a bright pop that draws the eye to the dip of my waist. The big, dark waves of my near-black hair combine with the deep color of the suit to create an aura of power and professionalism. I look like someone an employer would want to listen to. Someone with opinions worth hearing.

I smile for real this time. As much as she frustrates me, Rhonda really is great at what she does.

"Yes, okay, you're right. Thanks for talking me off the ledge. Again."

"Good girl. You'll be amazing. Call me after prelims! Mwah."

She hangs up without giving me a chance to say goodbye, like usual, and I turn the phone over in my hands a few times like I can somehow absorb some of Rhonda's confidence through it. The pageant coordinator calls the one-minute warning, her voice shrill and thin over the tittering of fifty-one girls going through last-minute sprays and plucks and tugs. It's boiling hot in here, with too many bodies, too much nervous energy, and energy-sucking, low-efficiency light bulbs burning bright above each dressing station. It's suffocating, and I turn away to get some air just as Jess pushes her way through the crowd of pastel skirt suits. Her eyes widen when her gaze lands on me.

"Wow, Tea. You're going to kill it. You look like some kind of super CEO warrior woman."

Her praise fills me with even more confidence than Rhonda's, and I instantly breathe easier. Jess is the greatest pageant bestie I could ever ask for. I smile and pick a piece of lint off her shoulder, smoothing the short sleeves of her dress.

"You look incredible, too. Did you read the newspaper this morning?"

She grimaces. "Yeah, I'm all caught up on current events. It would be just like them to pull an interview question from to-day's headlines."

"*I* hope they ask you about climate change so they can see you literally light fires with your eyes," I say, grinning. She puffs up as if to launch into a tirade then takes a serene breath in and blows it out slowly.

"I see what you did there," she says, shaking a finger at me as she backs away to take her place in line. I blow her a kiss for luck then unlock my phone again. I barely had time to skim the headlines myself this morning, so I stick at my station to scroll through *The New York Times* on my phone until the pageant co-ordinator claps her hands to catch everyone's attention.

"Ladies, it's time! Please line up in alphabetical order by state outside the interview room and have a seat."

I groan internally. That means I'll be close to the end. I was hoping for reverse alphabetical or by last name. At least Miller is in the middle. Virginia leaves me fifth from the end. More time to brainstorm smart answers, but more time to psych myself out, too. Also, the judges are tired and bored by the end—I'll have to work twice as hard to get them to no-tice and remember me. Hopefully I can pull it off and be one of the last people on their minds. Unless they already have their favorites by the time they get to me. Rhonda has told me how this works a thousand times, though, and I repeat it to myself again: The judges have an agenda. The producers have told them what kind of girl they want as a winner, what kind of person they want representing the Miss Cosmic organization for the next year. I have no way of knowing whether this year is a cute-and-sweet year, or a brainy year, or a fierce political year. It's infuriating and frustrating, working so hard with college money on the line and having no idea what standard I'm actually being judged against. I've heard that the judges can go rogue occasionally, though, if someone is really, really good. All I can do is play to my strengths and hope they match the judges and producers' checklist.

Unfortunately, even this waiting game is a judged test. We're supposed to sit quietly and make small talk with our peers like polite society types. Vermont and Washington State are both nice enough. I've never met either of them before this weekend, and they both have outdoorsy interests that drive the conversation. But before long, Miss North Carolina's voice raises above the din, her drawling words loud enough for all to hear.

"I just don't think it's right, all this TV convention stuff. Like, why don't these people do something *useful* with their time like we do?" Her voice drips in fake concern and syrupy sweetness. "We volunteer in our communities, while they just sit around in their bedrooms all weekend with the curtains closed."

Tittering laughter follows.

"No, honestly!" she starts again. "One of the fan freaks from my school is here this weekend, and she's so useless. She has like one friend. Might be her girlfriend, actually, I think she's a *lesbian*."

She says *lesbian* in a stage whisper, like it's a swear word and she's in a public place. I close my eyes and start counting, though all I want to do is chant *they, they, they* for every misgendered *she* on Kay's behalf. If I let myself get tense now, I'll blow the interview, but panic sinks its nails into my heart and starts to squeeze anyway. If she saw Kay, does that mean she saw me *with* her?

As she stands to take her turn in the interview room, Miss NC delivers her parting shot: "I hope they give me a current events question about the transgender whatevers going on in my state, because let me tell *you*, I've got some opinions!"

And no one gives a shit about your bigoted, closed-minded opinions, you utterly vicious harpy.

I start counting back at zero.

All the A state girls got their full five minutes in the room with the judges, but the pace has definitely picked up. North Carolina got maybe four at most. By the time Jess stands from her seat to approach the interview room, turning briefly to receive my encouraging smile, it seems like everyone's in and out in only three minutes.

Not good. This is my strongest portion, and I want every second I can get with that panel. Maybe if I can be compelling enough, they'll keep me in there for the full five minutes.

Then Miss Vermont walks out after only two and a half minutes, and I know for a fact she's a straight-up math genius with an incredible education platform.

Really not good.

The coordinator pops her head out and waves me forward. My turn.

The next ten seconds are critical. If I can capture them now, it could be my ticket to the top fifteen. I stand up straight, lift my chin just a bit, arrange my hair into big waves over my shoulders, take a deep breath . . . and nod.

The coordinator holds the door open and stands back.

I make my entrance.

One of the tricks Rhonda taught me was to imagine your own soundtrack as you're walking to exude the right "presence." I'm sure she meant some kind of peppy pop song, but for me, for this powerful image I need to portray, I let raging, distorted guitars and throbbing bass fill my mind. My dad's obsessed with this '90s band called the Prodigy, and for as long as I can remember, he's called me his *little firestarter*. I let the relentless beat and thrashing melody drive my steps and smile in a way that's just a shade too bold. In this bland, beige room, I'm a pop of audacious red.

I'm a firestarter, a wicked firestarter.

The judge on the end, an aging man in a pin-striped suit that probably costs more than I make on Etsy in a year, raises his eyebrows at my entrance. The others, a somewhat younger man and a middle-aged woman, look like they're biting back smiles. The woman immediately scribbles something on her judging sheet. Hopefully something positive. I reach the single chair placed before the table of judges, smooth my dress, and sit primly on the edge of the seat without bending to give them a view down the front of my dress. Legs crossed tightly, perfect posture, smile in place—I'm ready. I can do this.

I make eye contact with each judge in turn, smile, and speak loud and clear.

"Good morning! My name is Teagan Miller, I'm seventeen years old, and I'm representing the Commonwealth of Virginia in this year's Miss Cosmic Teen USA scholarship competition. It's a pleasure to meet y'all today." I let just the barest hint of Virginia drawl creep into my voice. Not enough to take the polish off my enunciation, but enough to add a bit of southern charm.

It works. The older man cracks the tiniest smile before he can stop it, notes something on his sheet, then introduces himself. They go down the line, listing their names and affiliations, and I nod politely at each one and rattle off an automatic thank-you for each. Come *on*, let's get to the questions, we're wasting time! Finally, the oldest man on the far left begins.

"Miss Virginia, if you were to win this competition and move on to the Miss Cosmic Teen World pageant, how would you describe your home state to your roommate from another country?"

Ugh, a fluff question right off the bat. I can salvage this one, though—this was in my sheet of practice questions, and I can turn this around into something intelligent and thoughtful.

"It starts with listening first. How I would describe Virginia depends on where my roommate is from and how they talk about it, because I would want to do my best to start by drawing similarities between my home and theirs. It's so important to connect on a personal, human level and emphasize how fundamentally similar we all are, no matter what languages we speak or where we live. With a great state like Virginia, it's easy to draw comparisons to many places. We have beautiful beaches, abundant farmland, big cities with great cultural arts, and the stunning Blue Ridge Mountains. The state and its diverse people truly have something to offer everyone."

Thoughtful nods, smiles, good. I made that one work. The second male judge lingers on my outfit for a moment before meeting my eyes to ask his question. I fight back a shudder at his attention and listen carefully.

"Miss Virginia, do you think a college education is necessary to succeed in today's society?"

Ooh. My opinions on this topic might not be the right ones to win favor, but I'm the most obvious liar in the world, so I have to go with the truth. They aren't *supposed* to judge us on our opinions, anyway, only on our poise and how well-spoken we are. (Yeah, right.) But one of the missions of the Miss Cosmic organization is to give young women a platform, so I mentally step up onto my soapbox and dive right in.

"No, I don't think a traditional four-year college education is necessary for *everyone* to succeed in today's society. My goal of going into art therapy requires a degree, and I fully intend to pursue one. However, there are many respectable, well-paying careers essential to the functioning of our society that a person can pursue with limited post-secondary education, such as electricians and other skilled trades. We also need retail workers, waiters, fast food workers, and so many others who don't get anywhere near the respect or compensation they deserve. Should we look down on those people because the work they do doesn't require a high level of expensive education?"

I lift my chin, let my smile harden just a bit with my resolve. If I go down, it won't be for lack of poise or commitment.

"In my opinion: absolutely not. Those people, including my own family members, work *so* hard, and they provide for the people in their lives. There are many measures of success and happiness in life, and post-secondary education and a degree-requiring career do not automatically ensure either of those. Even if a college education were free for everyone, which I believe it should be, college is not the right path for every person, and it wouldn't lessen our society's need for people in those non-degreed positions. That said, I *do* think that education of some form is important to being a well-rounded person. It's important to get outside your own experiences and learn about your fellow human beings to develop empathy and create a more peaceful society."

The judges blink in stunned silence, and it takes everything in me to hold back a crowing laugh of triumph at their expressions. Bet they didn't expect such a meaty answer to that one. I've already been in here nearly three minutes, so I've at least managed to hang in there longer than Miss Vermont. But there should still be one question left, and if I can nail it, I'll walk out of here like a rock star.

The woman on the end recovers first and pulls her question list to her then discards it in favor of a sheet with my bio on it. *Noooo*, I think at her, willing her to go back to the sheet of prepared questions. *Ask me about my platform, ask me about my charity work, ask me about my ideal date and I'll play the pronoun dodging game, anything, just—*

"Miss Virginia, how has the loss of your mother affected your pageant career?"

Only the fact that I've been asked this question at least three times before keeps me from completely losing my composure. I've practiced this question with Rhonda dozens of times since it lost me the title the first time it happened. I let sadness soften my eyes and smile but refuse to look away. It feels like a punch in the stomach, every single time.

But I've learned to deal, and I won't let my mom down by blowing it now.

"I actually got my start in pageants *because* of my mother's death. I adore my dad, and I have some amazingly strong women on his side of the family, but they all live in California or New Mexico, and I rarely get to see them. My dad thought I needed some adult women mentors in my everyday life. So, when I was eleven, he started letting me spend the night at our neighbor's house every Friday and Saturday. She and her daughter did lots of local pageants, so I got to help with all the prep work and attend with them. People kept telling me I should join in, too, so I decided to give it a shot. And I won the title at my first pageant."

And winning is addicting, I add silently. I take a deep breath and push on. This is my last question, so I have to cram as much in as possible.

"My mother's death also influenced my choice of platform. She died by suicide after a years-long struggle with physical and mental health, so I've dedicated a lot of my free time to working with Art Buddies. They're a nationwide art therapy volunteer network for children and teens living with depression, anxiety, grief, and other struggles. I really believe in the ability of art therapy to help people understand and process their thoughts and feelings, and the creative outlet can provide strong support to other forms of more traditional mental health treatment."

Here we go, stick the landing, almost there.

"If I'm selected as this year's Miss Cosmic Teen USA, the best part of the whole winner's package will be getting to travel to all fifty states, because I'll be able to meet up with fifty local Art Buddies chapters to lead workshops and meet local kids and teens. I would use my voice to advocate for mental health awareness and fight the stigma so people like my mother will have a better chance of surviving their struggle."

I end with a winning smile, still tinged with very real, achingly heavy sadness. I was in therapy with Art Buddies for years, and volunteering with them has been one of the best things in my life. Not just because of my mom, but because they work with a lot of LGBTQ+ kids who are fighting bigoted families or trying to figure themselves out. I love the work, and the chance to travel and do it for a year would be fantastic.

A tiny voice in my head whispers that being out of the closet as a public figure might be more helpful to those kids than teaching them to draw their feelings, but I shove it away. The timing isn't right. Scholarships to college first, *then* I can be out. Besides, no one is ever obligated to be out.

Either way, my sincerity seems to have melted the judges' hearts. They thank me for my time, I stand and shake their hands, and they look on me with indulgent smiles. Time to make my exit.

I hold my head high and stride out of the room, exuding all the same power and authority as when I arrived. And when I get outside, I check the time.

Six minutes.

Top *that*, North Carolina.

Chapter
Fourteen

KAYLEE

*B*y the time I escape the people lingering after the panel to meet me (unbelievable, and utterly embarrassing), it's already 9:58. Cakes, Lady, and Ami all hover around me, being supportive and telling me how professional I sounded, but my impatience must show through because Lady grabs my arm and pulls.

"We're going to miss Irishtea's fic workshop if we don't go now," she says, loud enough for the others to hear.

"Yeah, we're meeting up with y'all for lunch before Lady's panel, right?" I add to smooth things over.

We exchange quick hugs with Cakes and Ami, make our exit as quickly as we can without offending anyone, then race down the hallway to Conference Room D. Every hall is decorated with the exact same subtle, off-white textured wallpaper and gray, patterned carpet, the plaques marking the rooms tiny and discreet. I hope we're going the right way. If we can get there before the panel starts, maybe I can talk to Irishtea for a minute or at least get a seat in the front so I can talk to her right after.

My laptop bag bites into my shoulder as I round the corner into Conference Room D . . . only to find the panel already in progress. Irishtea looks up and smiles at me as I walk in, but I'm forced to take a seat in the back, far from her and her co-presenter, Bryn. Sighing, I plop down at an empty round table with Lady beside me and take out my laptop while Irishtea explains the morning's writing exercise.

"Everyone will randomly draw two index cards with characters from the show," she says, "and trust me when I say the options aren't limited to ones typically written about. The whole point here is to get you thinking about the building blocks of romance and attraction, rather than the specific characters themselves. You'll have to look for ways to get these characters together, reasons they might be attracted to each other, situations where they might interact. You might have to invent backstory for them that doesn't exist in the show or take liberties with what we know about them. Let it be weird, let it be so out there, you think no one will ever want to read it. Let go of your judgment and be open to possibilities."

Her co-presenter cuts in, his voice gravelly and pleasant. "You'll also be drawing a random object and a random bit of dialog to use as inspiration. Finally, you'll draw a number one through five. That will be your group number for share time online after the panel is over. Since this is not an age-restricted event and we have folks under eighteen in the room, please keep your stories rated Teen for now. You can always continue working on them and increase the rating at a later date."

I snort softly, and Lady and I exchange an eye roll. It's not like lots of us don't read the occasional explicit fic *anyway*, though we're technically not supposed to. It's like our generation's version of stealing mom's romance novels. I understand that they need to cover their own asses, though.

I'm nervous about sharing this bit of writing I'm about to do, though. I've made something of a name for myself writing Johnlock fic. It's the only pairing I've ever written, and I'm not sure I'm capable of writing anything else. What if I'm not creative enough to get two completely random characters together? What if I share something terrible and everyone thinks *all* my writing is like that or that I'm a total fake?

What if I draw Violet and Sherlock? I will walk right out of this room before I'll write Violock. They have *no* chemistry; I seriously don't understand how some people ship them so hard. Then again, any time a cis man and a cis woman are on-screen together in any show, people are automatically like *Ooooh, will they get together?*

I gag a bit and join the line forming to draw cards. Better to get it over with than worry myself to death wondering what could happen. If it really turns out badly, I can always pretend I lost my group's contact info.

But then I see Irishtea taking cards to join in the exercise. What if I end up in her sharing group?

Ugh. I'll just hope for the best.

When it's my turn, I draw my five cards quickly, like ripping off a Band-Aid, then scurry back to the table to see my fate in private. I flip over the two character cards first. My heart leaps into my throat when the first one reveals Violet's name in bubbly writing staring back at me.

No, no, no, I can't write this, I can't—

I flip over the second card, and my breath leaves me in a huge *whoosh.*

Gwen. Not Sherlock.

Two women.

I've never written femslash before. Haven't read much of it, either, though there isn't much out there to begin with. It's a big sticking point for this fandom. The femslash writers are total unsung heroes. They get way less attention: fewer reads, fewer comments and kudos, fewer subscribes, all of it. It must be hard. It's probably misogynistic of me to ignore femslash, but in a show with two male leads and mostly male supporting characters, it's kind of hard to make it happen. I know people *do*, but how do I even start? I don't think these two characters have even shared screen time in the show, much less interacted in any way. I could text Cakes for ideas—I know *she's* a big fan of this pairing—but that feels like cheating. The whole point of the exercise is to think creatively. Maybe the other cards will inspire me somehow.

I flip over the object and dialog cards: a beverage glass, and "I've never done this before." Okay. That's . . . something. Maybe the drink glass can give me the setting somehow. They can be out to dinner? But how would they have met to be out at dinner together, since they've never interacted before? I take a long, slow breath to calm the anxiety curling in my chest and lean back in my chair to think.

Okay. What do Violet and Gwen have in common in the show? They're both single for most of the time. They both have demonstrated bad taste in guys. So, for this fic to happen, they have to both be bisexual or pansexual. That's a start. They're also both professional women, a detective inspector and a professor, so they're both strong, smart, and competent. Presumably they both live alone, so they probably live in a cheaper area of London. Maybe they live in the same neighborhood? Maybe they frequent the same restaurants or pubs?

My phone vibrates in my pocket, and I slide it from my pocket with clumsy, distracted fingers.

New Scroll message. Teagan. I suck in a sharp breath.

paintmeinviolet:
I just finished with my morning stuff, and I have a bit of
free time before I have to be somewhere this afternoon.
I can only sneak about 15 minutes, but it's something.

My stomach churns with nerves. I sneak a glance at Lady,
but she's completely absorbed in her new ficlet, oblivious to
the blush staining my cheeks. I'm really doing this. I reread the
message three times then begin to tap a reply, but another message
pops up.

paintmeinviolet:
We'll have to meet somewhere the chaperones won't
be able to find us. Any chance we could meet in your
room?

A flare of panic bursts in my chest. That's kind of . . . private,
with everyone else down at the con. But there's only so much
we can get up to in fifteen minutes, and I can always say no to
anything I don't want. This could be my chance to . . . check
something off the list. Maybe. If she's up for that.

KayfortheWinnet:
I can ask my roommates, but it should be fine.

I hesitate, glance at the cards in front of me. Maybe it wouldn't
hurt to manage expectations a bit. I bite my lip then copy the bit
of dialog from my index card into the message.

KayfortheWinnet:
I've never done this before.

And now that I've sent the message, it seems like the most ridiculous thing I could have possibly said. What if she wasn't thinking that at all? What if she just wanted to talk? There's no instantaneous reply, so I lay my phone down and pull up a blank document on my laptop, typing my prompts at the top just to get my fingers moving and conquer the blank page, to distract myself. Okay. Violet. Gwen. A beverage glass. Never done this before. They live in the same area of London, they meet up somewhere with a beverage glass and are attracted to each other . . .

A sense memory of the night before hijacks my brain for a moment, filling me with swaying hips, sweat, pounding music, and mysterious smiles.

A dance club. They meet at a club in their neighborhood, share a drink, share a dance. Maybe they've met briefly, in passing. Maybe Gwen's consulted Violet as a subject expert for a case, just enough times that they do a bit of a double take, recognize each other, and the different atmosphere is enough for their walls to come down a bit.

My phone vibrates against the table with a buzz. I scramble to unlock it.

paintmeinviolet:
I'm not sure what you're expecting, but I promise I'm not expecting anything. I just want to see you. And . . . if it's okay with you . . . maybe continue where we left off last night?

Last night, when we were pressed together on the floor of the hotel room, her pinky over mine, leaning in closer . . .

A pause, then another message:

paintmeinviolet:
Never done what before? Kissed someone?

My cheeks burn, and I glance around the room like someone might be looking over my shoulder. Everyone's typing away on their short stories, paying me no attention whatsoever, of course. Lady is smirking, but her gaze is firmly fixed on her computer screen, so I tap out a quick reply.

KayfortheWinnet:
Never been with a girl. In any way.

I drop my phone to the tabletop the second I hit SEND, the clatter overly loud in the room filled only with clicking keys and quiet snickers. I can't believe we're actually talking about this. I can't bear the thought of her somewhere in this same building, reading my message and thinking . . . whatever she's thinking. I pull my laptop closer, lay my hands across the keys, and start typing what I already know to get more words moving through my fingers.

Violet and Gwen live in the same neighborhood.
They both work hard, have fought for their positions.
They both need to unwind after work.

Thoughts of Teagan, of her long body against mine, push their way into my brain, demanding attention. The memory of sweat, the cool slide of condensation against my wrist after—
Oh.
I know how they can get together. The condensation on the beverage glass is key. My fingers fly over the keyboard.

Violet Hunter wasn't too good with people. She spent her days hunched over her lab equipment at the university and her nights at home cuddled with a book and a cat, the world closed away behind her floral-print curtains. Dance clubs weren't her native environment, but she needed a place where everyone didn't know about her unfortunate habit of falling for the wrong men, and the internet (all-knowing as it is) hadn't been able to come through. The anonymous mass of writhing bodies before her wasn't ideal, but—

My phone vibrates. Oh God.

paintmeinviolet:
I don't mind. If you don't mind, that is. Am I hitting on someone who is totally uninterested in girls again? If so, please tell me to shut up and go away.

I snort. That's the big question, isn't it? But either way, I don't mind it. I really don't. At least I know now that she's definitely hitting on me. Definitely *interested*.

KayfortheWinnet:
Please don't go away. I don't really know what I am, though. I'm still figuring things out. Does that bother you?

I hold my breath until her reply appears.

paintmeinviolet:
It's fine. Experience isn't everything. It's about how you feel. It doesn't bother me at all if you're inexperienced. Have you ever kissed anyone?

I wince. This is where I'll lose her, but I can't just fake it. If I'm going to figure all this out, I want to be honest with both her and myself.

KayfortheWinnet:
That's the thing, though. I'm not inexperienced. I'm actually not even a virgin.

I don't completely spell it out for her, but that should be plenty for her to figure it out. She's smart and a quick thinker. She'll get it. I fiddle with another sentence of my fic, but the anxiety building in my chest makes focus impossible. At the front of the room, Irishtea announces that we have five minutes left to finish up our stories. Beside me, Lady types even faster, determined to finish her ficlet in time.

I freeze up entirely.

Between waiting for Teagan's reply to my awkward revelation and the fact that I'll finally be meeting Irishtea in just a few minutes, I'm on the verge of bolting from this room. But if I leave now, I'll miss out on getting to talk to Irishtea *again*, and this is the last program she's hosting this weekend. There's always the chance that I'll run into her at another panel or event, but no guarantees. This is my last sure chance to be in the same room with her for the weekend. She's my biggest inspiration, my influence, the one who got me writing.

Then my phone buzzes, and my heart leaps into my throat.

But it's not Teagan. It's Ami, saving me from myself once again.

Ami: So excited for you to finally meet Irishtea!

Ami: Don't be nervous. You are a fandom powerhouse.

She's amazing, but you are In Her League and it's not weird at all for you to introduce yourself.

Ami: So don't chicken out. 🫠

Caught. She knows me so well. I send back a quick flex emoji and look up as Bryn calls time and thanks everyone for coming. The panic threatens to well up again, but I reread Ami's words then stand to find my share group, number three. Irishtea isn't in my group, but there are several other familiar names, and we all exchange Scroll usernames and email addresses so we can share our fics later. As the conversation winds down, I start to choke up again. How do I approach Irishtea? What do I say? Do I just . . . walk up to her?

Then a hand lands on my shoulder, and I nearly jump out of my skin. I whirl around . . . and there's Irishtea, smiling brightly at me.

"Kay! It's so great to finally meet you!"

Uh . . . what?

I clear my throat and try to summon up a smile. After all, I've been waiting to meet Irishtea all day (all year, let's be real), and now I'm face-to-face with her with a completely blank brain and *nothing to say*. What do you say to a celebrity?

"You," Irishtea says, shaking a fist at me and breaking the awkward silence. "I stayed up last night getting caught up on your latest fic, and it completely wrecked me. The way you write John is so on point, it makes my heart ache!"

I stare at her for an awkwardly long time, blinking. "You . . . read my fic?"

She laughs. "Of course I do! Who in this fandom doesn't? You're one of the new greats carrying this poor fandom through the season four hiatus. Not to mention, your work is fantastic."

I shake my head, my lips parted in surprise.

"But . . . but you're the whole reason I'm writing in the first place! Your fics made me *feel* so much that I had to do something with all of it, so I started writing, and it just sort of got out of control. How can *you* read *my* stuff?"

Not to mention she's been in fandom so long and has so many followers and hits on her fics that the rest of us must seem tiny in comparison.

"I know what you mean about the writing getting out of control. I sat down to write one little missing scene fic, and eighty thousand words later, I had 'Nature Knows' and a thousand subscribers. Things get away from you really quickly in fandom." She smiles and shakes her head ruefully. "But now it's *your* writing that's making other people drown in their feelings. Things come full circle!"

"Yeah, I guess they do," I say, dazed. What is even happening right now?

"Anyway, I gotta pack up and run, but I'm looking forward to the next chapter!" she says with a wave as she walks backward toward the head table. "I can't wait to be put out of my misery."

"Wow, uh, thanks! Thank you. Bye?"

What. Just. Happened.

I walk back to my table in a daze, where my laptop sits still open to my partially finished femslash fic. I shake my head at Lady, who's doing a little happy dance for me.

"You met her! She knows you! You're *famous*," she says as she slides her laptop back into her bag. "Also, your phone was about to vibrate off the table with like, a hundred messages. Is it Teagan?"

Ahh!

I snatch it off the table and swipe the first notification I see.

Scroll pops open to the direct message screen, showing a whole string of messages.

> **paintmeinviolet:**
> So maybe you're bi, or pan. Which is fine, by the way.
> Obviously. I hope you aren't ashamed of not being a
> "virgin" or something.

> **paintmeinviolet:**
> virginity is fake and you're awesome.

> **paintmeinviolet:**
> When I think about you, all I see is the burgundy color
> of your hair, your gorgeous eyes, and the way you felt
> pressed up against me last night.

> **paintmeinviolet:**
> I've been thinking about it nonstop since we went back
> to our rooms.

> **paintmeinviolet:**
> I woke up thinking about the way we danced, the way
> your hands felt on me . . .

> **paintmeinviolet:**
> I'm sorry, this is too much too fast, isn't it?

> **paintmeinviolet:**
> I hope this is okay.

> **paintmeinviolet:**
> Are you still there?

paintmeinviolet:
I'm sorry

My breath comes in shallow pants, and I can feel it all, *see* it all. Last night, we were molded together, her hips rolling against mine in a way that made me feel impatient and desperate. Her hands slipped over my waist, up and down my sides, wrapped around my stomach to pull me back against her, until her chest was pressed into my back. I imagine that hand on my stomach, pinning me in place, her mouth next to my ear, the hand drifting lower . . .

My eyes drift to the fic up on my screen. Violet and Gwen, a chance encounter, standing on the edge of something new.

I can be brave, too.

KayfortheWinnet:
More than okay

KayfortheWinnet:
So very okay

KayfortheWinnet:
When can you meet?

Barely thirty seconds pass until she replies.

paintmeinviolet:
Now. Can you come now?

Without Ami to push me, I would normally back out in a heartbeat. I'd hesitate until it was too late. It's who I am.

The burning low in my belly makes the decision for me.

KayfortheWinnet:
I'll be there in 5 mins.

I shove my laptop in my bag and look up to find Lady smirking at me. I can't even be embarrassed.

"I'm gonna meet up with Teagan really quick. I'll only be about twenty minutes. I promise I'll be at your panel. Okay?"

"Stop talking to me and go!" she says, shooing me away with a wicked grin.

I shoot her a grateful smile and race out the door without a backward glance.

The elevator can't get here fast enough.

Chapter Fifteen

TEAGAN

I never thought I'd actually *hope* for Miss North Carolina to take forever sucking up to the judges after the interviews ended, but I'm sending every ounce of mental energy I have at the elevator door, willing it to *stay closed* as I peer out at the hallway through the peephole.

I managed to change into my "business casual" luncheon clothes in record time. My makeup and hair are still done from the interview, as they should be for the lunch event, but hopefully they won't look too out of place to Kay. I removed most of the lipstick to tone it down a bit, but—oh God, will my lipstick come off all over them? Does my breath stink? I wish I could get some mouthwash from the bathroom, but Jess is in there right now, singing her way through her pre-pageant routine, and I've messed with her weekend enough already. Do I have a breath mint?

I pause and take a long, deep breath. I have not suddenly developed severe halitosis between the interview and the room. This is ridiculous. I've kissed people before. I don't need to freak out about this. At most, this is a weekend hookup. And probably not even that, honestly. Low pressure, low stakes, no consequences if it doesn't work between us. Just spending some time getting to know someone I can't get out of my head. Where's all my hard-earned stage confidence now?

Of course, if this is terrible, I could put them off girls forever. *Breathe.*

I should probably have a cover story in place, just in case Miss NC sees me sneaking around and starts something with one of the chaperones. I whip out my phone and text Jess really quick.

> **Teagan:** Need to take care of something. Going to be off the grid for about 15 mins. If NC or a chaperone comes looking for me, could you tell them I ran to get something at the cafe? Then text me if you can? I'll be right next door to you.

I press my eye back to the peephole and hit SEND without looking. Jess's text alert sounds from inside the bathroom over the sound of her pageant prep playlist. The phone vibrates in my hand barely ten seconds later.

> **Jess:** So basically you need to go "take care of" this con person you met and you need me to cover for you.

I wince. Not like I didn't know it would be obvious to Jess, but she makes it sound so callous. Granted, last time we were in this situation, it *was* kind of callous, just a random rebound hookup resulting from the creation of my "don't date pageant girls" rule. I can't blame her.

My phone vibrates again.

Jess: They better be really hot, T.

I grin.

Teagan: They're totally worth it, I promise.

Jess: Don't be late for lunch. I won't be able to cover that.

Teagan: I won't. I'll walk down with you. I want to hear more about how your interview went! ♥

Then a Scroll notification pops up and blocks the top of my messages.

KayfortheWinnet:
I'm in the elevator, on my way up.

A flurry of nerves explodes in my stomach. This is ridiculous. I can't just pounce on them as soon as I get into the room. Actually, if it's their first time with a girl, maybe they need to make the first move. I have to wait. I can wait. We can talk more, like we did last night. That was . . . good. Really good. I told them things I could never talk about with my pageant friends, even Jess. It was easy. Comfortable. And now that they really know all of me, even the pageant side, and they seem to be accepting it . . .

I take a deep breath to calm my racing blood. We're just going to talk. No pressure. Probably nothing else will even happen.

A faint *ding* filters through the door as the elevator down the hall reaches the fourteenth floor, and there they are, walking down the hall to their room with quick, eager steps. Their burgundy hair is recognizable even through the blurry view of the peephole.

They disappear from my field of view, and a few seconds later I hear the door next to us slam shut. *Now!*

I open the door, do a quick check for group moms, then dart to the next door down. Three knocks in quick succession, and the second the door opens, I push my way inside and shut it.

"Sorry, sorry," I say, and turn to look at them. And my eyes go wide.

They're cosplaying Army John today and wearing it damn well. Their fatigues look authentic, like something purchased from a British army surplus store. The trousers are tucked into the top of desert combat boots and slung low on their hips, held up by a functional uniform belt. A matching uniform jacket hangs open over a tight, tan shirt cut low enough to give me an amazing view. Some folks try to adjust their appearance to match the gender of the character they're portraying for maximum accuracy, and some play a completely gender swapped version of the character—and then there's Kay, who has managed to strike a balance somewhere in between.

The result is unbelievably hot.

Then I realize it's been silent for several long, awkward seconds, and my eyes are still locked on their chest. *Eyes up, eyes up!*

"Um," I manage, wrenching my gaze back to their face. "Amazing cosplay. Looks . . . really great."

They give me a faint smile and smooth over the wrinkles of their shirt.

"I know it's not totally accurate, but I couldn't get the jacket to button, and this was the closest thing to a British army undershirt we had between us. I know some hard-core cosplayers won't agree with it, but I think it works."

"It definitely works," I say, then snap my eyes back up to theirs. Again. "So, uh . . . how's the con going?"

They sit down on the floor at the foot of the bed and look up at me, their expression serious and drawn. "It's been kind of . . . heavy this morning. I've only been to two panels. It's not even noon yet, but I've already spent the whole morning analyzing and questioning myself, trying to process everything."

My heart gives an aching pang in my chest for them, for what they're going through. It's so hard, and I feel so lucky that I got my crisis out of the way pretty early. I drop down next to them and prop my back against the bed, tipping my head to face them. "It's confusing, and it's so hard to sort through everything the world has been telling you your whole life."

They laugh at that, a harsh note to the sound. "See, it's kind of funny. Fandom is such a queer-positive place to be most of the time, and it's so open, and discussions of queer issues are so common that you'd think I'd *know*. You'd think it'd be easy to figure myself out and to come out about it, especially at a con where probably a good fifty percent of the people here are queer in one way or another. I really shouldn't have *any* baggage about my sexuality or gender. Why is this so hard?"

Tears prick at the corners of my eyes at the desperation in their voice, and I purse my lips for a moment to keep them at bay. I hate that this is so messy for people like us.

"It's difficult because no matter how open fandom is, the rest of the world isn't like that. Some places less so than others. What we learn about ourselves in fandom has implications for who we are to the rest of the world, too. Our entire selves, not just our internet selves. And I think, no matter what the particular issue is, it's always hard to accept big things about yourself."

Kay's mouth twists into a smile I know well—one part amused, one part self-deprecating. I see it in the mirror all the time. They wipe a tear from the corner of their eye before it has a chance to fall, then meet my gaze head-on.

"How did you know?"

I feel my lips twitch into a faint smile. Past me was *so oblivious.*

"I went through a really hilarious phase when I was maybe twelve or thirteen where I was really judgy to all my friends for being so obsessed with boys. I was all self-righteous like 'I don't need a boy, my friends are my top priority!' And some people legitimately are like that, which, you know, high five, ladies," I say with a wave of my hand. My cheeks darken with remembered embarrassment.

"But I was just completely physically uninterested in guys and *very* excited to go swimming with my female friends. I just want to go back in time and pat Past Teagan on the head and tell her it's okay to be queer and to stop being such a jerk to everyone."

Kay gets a good laugh out of that, their shoulder shaking where it's pressed against mine. "But that sounds like you still didn't know. When did you *know*?"

Blood rushes to my cheeks at the memory. I haven't told *anyone* about this before except Jess, and that was over text message, not face-to-face. It's so embarrassing. I tip my head back against the bed and fix my eyes on the ceiling.

"One of those friends I was so devoted to finally called me out, right in front of our whole group. Told me to stop being a bitch about their boyfriends and to stop staring at her boobs because she wasn't an 'effing dyke.'"

Kay sucks in a sharp breath and leans closer for support. "Middle school is the *worst.*"

"God, it really is," I agree. "But it wasn't all bad, because one of the other girls in our group came to my house the next day and said she didn't mind me staring at *her* boobs, then gave me my first kiss. So that was me at thirteen, a total hashtag confirmed lesbian and definitely less judgy after that, because I was as obsessed with her as my friends had ever been with their grabby boyfriends."

"So what happened?" Kay asks.

I shrug. "What happens to any middle school relationship? She started liking someone else, and I had started doing pa—" I catch myself then remember: I can say this. Kay already knows. "—started doing pageants and was spending a lot of time on them. Also, I never wanted to 'come out' in a big way at school, and I think she started to hate me for the secrecy. But I have a lot of reasons for not being out, and I'll come out when I'm ready. My dad and my best friend know, and that's all I care about."

"That's fair," Kay says, turning their face toward mine. I glance down at them, and our noses brush.

"So, you just knew instantly, as soon as she kissed you?" they murmur into the scant inches between us.

I wet my lips. "Pretty much, though I'd been very deliberately avoiding plenty of other evidence up until that point."

Their cheeks darken, and their shallow breaths speed up.

"I want to know for sure," Kay says.

Oh God, please *let me help you find out.* Are they asking? But there's still one thing that needs to be said.

"You know you don't have to *prove* your sexuality or anything, right?" I whisper. "If you're attracted, then there's your answer. You don't have to have done anything."

"I know," they say, their gaze dipping to fix on my mouth. "But I want to."

Every inch of my skin is electrified, every hair standing on end where we almost touch. We're pressed together at our knees and shoulders, and with the tiniest effort, I nudge my fingers over Kay's on the floor between us. They respond immediately, curling their pinky finger around mine, just like we were last night. My gaze flickers from their lips to their eyes, needing permission.

Needing *Kay.*

"Can I kiss you?" I breathe.

The corner of their mouth turns up in a small smile, and they whisper:

"*Yes.*"

The first contact is barely a brush of full lower lip against lip, a faint exchange of breath and texture. We separate just a fraction, the air taut and alive between us, until I lean in to press my mouth more fully against Kay's, then again, and again, until they surge against me, the tension breaking over us in a heavy wave of snapping electricity. They trap my lower lip between theirs, trace their tongue along it and—*oh God.* When our tongues touch, I feel it like a thousand volts straight to my gut, and we both gasp aloud into each other's mouths, pressing deeper. Kay swings a knee over my legs and settles into my lap, their arms wrapped around my neck, my hands running up their sides, up under the back of their shirt to touch hot skin, and—

My phone alarm goes off, chiming over and over and over, and UGH.

I break away with a sharp exhalation and jam a finger down on the screen to shut the damn alarm off. It's time to go. It's already been fifteen minutes, and I need to sneak back to my room to get fully ready for the luncheon and preliminary stage competition.

But how can I leave with Kay sitting in my lap, cheeks flushed and eyes bright, their chest rising and falling with the speed of their breathing? They sway back into me, and I press up into them one last time, pulling them flush against my front until I have to break off the kiss before I get carried away.

"I have to go. There's a horrible boring lunch thing I have to go to," I say, every word dripping with reluctance. God, I hate this. "I'm sorry for leaving. You know I don't want to, right?"

Kay smiles when I pull them tighter against me again, our stomachs and chests sliding in a completely delicious way. Their fingers sink into my hair as they pull me in for one last lingering kiss, then they climb off my lap to collapse against the foot of the bed beside me.

"Well. That answers that," Kay says, a bit dazed but with an uncontrollable grin on their face.

I stand and brush a messy length of burgundy hair back from their face, my fingers lingering on the soft strands. "I really want to see you again tonight. It'll have to be late, but can we—"

"*Yes,*" Kay says, and we break into giggles at our own eagerness. I give them a hand up, dive in for one last quick peck, one last taste . . . then back away before my hands get out of control.

"Message me. I don't care what the event is, or if it's just hanging out back here again. Just. Let me know, okay?" I say, walking backward toward the door.

"I will. I promise," Kay says.

It takes all my willpower to turn around and look out the peephole then crack the door open to see if the coast is clear. The hallway is empty, so I dart out and close the door behind me, reaching out with my key card to unlock my own room.

The door next to ours opens before I get there, and panic floods my system with adrenaline. With shaking hands, I do the first thing that pops into my head—I fling open the door to our room, nearly smacking Jess in the face when it turns out she's just on the other side. Miss North Carolina pokes her head out of her room and fixes me with a suspicious stare. "Teagan, there you—"

Jess stands in the open doorway before me, dressed and

polished for the luncheon in front of the room's full-length mirror, holding an iced latte in her reusable tumbler with a puzzled look. I babble the first thing I can think of.

"Hi, yeah, I know, I've only been gone like ten seconds, but did I leave my coffee in here?"

Never let it be said I don't think quickly on my feet. I silently plead with her to catch on, to back me up here, and my utter panic must show through because she purses her lips in frustration, frowns down at her mostly full drink, and thrusts it into my hand. I'm going to owe her so many coffees after this.

"Yeah, I was just about to bring it to you. Don't drink the whole thing! You don't want to be jittery for the stage competition," she grinds out, only sounding slightly bitter. I wince. I've been a terrible, *terrible* friend to her this weekend.

"Thanks so much," I say, pushing as much honest gratitude into my voice and gaze as I can without giving myself away to NC. "You're the best, Jess. I mean it."

Her expression softens into something fonder, and she shakes her head ruefully, but she still closes the door in my face. As I deserve. From the next door over, NC eyes my new coffee drink and shakes her head.

"All that sugar, Teagan, honestly! On the weekend of a pageant? And you know milk messes with your vocal cords. What are you thinking?"

Joke's on her—knowing Jess, this is an unsweetened organic almond milk latte. I take a halfhearted sip, and the sharp flavor bursts on my tongue. Pretty good, actually. The quick hit of caffeine brings me back from the haze of Kay's kisses and into the real world—the world where I have a luncheon in fifteen minutes and I'm not wearing my sash.

"Shoot, my sash!" I say, playing it up. "I'm having such a forgetful day. I'll see you at the luncheon, Madison!"

I pull my room key from my pocket and let myself back in before North Carolina can scold me any further, awash with relief the second the door closes behind me. Jess is still in front of the mirror, picking at the ruching of her top until it lays perfectly. I offer her the latte back, which she takes with a raised eyebrow.

"I'm sorry, Jess," I say, holding her gaze. "Really, really sorry. It won't happen again."

"I thought you were already heading down," she says, giving her hair one last touch then slipping on her sash. I do the same, giving myself a quick once-over to make sure I'm not rumpled and flushed from my time with Kay. I still feel like I'm about to combust, and I've gotta get it together before I can be in public.

"Hey, I said I would walk down with you and I meant it," I remind Jess. "I want to hear about your interview. Did you get to rage at them?"

She turns to me with a big, pageant-winning smile and sharp eyes then puts on her interview voice. "In five years, I see myself finishing up my last summer with the Pittsburgh hub of the Sunrise Movement and preparing to graduate college with a degree in environmental science. *As you know*, climate change is the biggest threat our society has ever faced, and we are all complicit. I've made it my *personal mission* . . . and so on. They never expect to get their faces melted on that question, and it definitely woke them up."

I grin as we walk down the hall to the elevator together, reveling in Jess's fire and determination. "Did you get to tell them your ideas for making pageants greener?"

She purses her lips and raises her eyebrows at me. "Mm, I wouldn't say I *got to* as much as I shoved it into the conversation at the slightest opportunity. 'Why, yes, my favorite color is green! And speaking of green, here is my fifteen-step plan for lowering the carbon impact of pageants and fostering good environmental stewardship within United States pageant systems.' I don't know what it is about me that makes them throw those softball questions, but I smash it right back in their faces every time."

"Damn right you do," I say. "I'm surprised they still let us do these things. We never play nice."

She flaps a hand at me dismissively. "What's the point of that? If they ever need a climate warrior queen, I'm a shoe-in. If not, well, at least I had fun, tore it up in a great dress, and made my mom happy. I may as well try to inspire a few Karens to believe in climate change along the way."

I mean, I could really use the scholarship money, too, so there's definitely a point. But I get what she means. The odds of winning are so small that it helps to feel like we're accomplishing *something* positive on a larger scale. I love the chance to promote my platform just as much as Jess does, and if they won't give me an opportunity, then I'll create one.

We walk through a huge crowd of fandom people on our way to the ballroom they have set up for the luncheon, and a brief ache for the safety of the con makes my steps slow. I'm looking forward to the luncheon, though. Free food is always a plus in my book, and it's one meal I don't have to pull from my very tight budget. I like getting a chance to sit and meet some of the other girls without having to juggle choreography, hair and makeup, or stage nerves. Sure, the judges are watching our table manners, but who doesn't like being treated to lunch?

My stomach is still fluttery from the memory of Kay's eager kisses, though. Their mouth was hot and demanding, skilled and confident, their hands wandering and teasing. I think Kay is well on their way to sorting things out, and I couldn't be gladder to be the one helping them with it.

I glance over at Jess, and she hands me her iced coffee without a word. I take a sip to cool the burning in my cheeks and clear the fog from my head. Hopefully I can get myself back under control before I have to be social and use real words.

But if not?

Worth it. God, *so* worth it.

I run a thumb over my newly kissed lips and smile.

Chapter Sixteen

✴

KAYLEE

For several long minutes, I stand in the exact spot where Teagan left me. Lips burning, heart hammering, insides hot and unsettled.

I just made out with a girl.

I, for the first time ever, had a girl's tongue in my mouth and her legs between mine.

God, it was *fantastic*.

I catch a glimpse of myself in the framed mirror over the hotel room desk and see the giddy grin on my face stretched ear to ear then immediately blush a deep red and look away. I can't go out in public like this. People will think I'm out of my mind.

I step into the bathroom and splash some cool water on my face, shocking myself back down to earth. It's fine. It's all fine. I just made out with a girl, a gorgeous, amazing girl who kisses like a firecracker, and everything is fine. Better than fine, *amazing*, because making out with a cis boy has never done anything like that for me. This was *new*, and hot, and much more like what people—like *I*—am always writing about in fanfic. Connection, and a needy push and pull of mouths and hands and—

I splash another handful of water on my face in an attempt to cool off then press the soft white hotel towel to my burning cheeks.

Maybe this means life will be different now. Maybe I can have girlfriends. Maybe when I get home, I can find—

Home.

No, I can't. I can't do any of that.

Because this place, this situation . . . none of it is real.

My stomach heaves, and I drop to my knees in front of the toilet in case my innards decide to become out-ards.

I can't have a girlfriend in *Plainsborough.* My mom will find out. My teachers will find out. Miss freaking North Carolina will find out *immediately* and make my life even worse than she already does.

I made out with a girl, and it was *fantastic*, and I can never do it again outside of this con.

At least, not until college. An entire year away.

My phone's text alert echoes off the bath tiles, surrounding me with its tinny rendition of *Dear Evan Hansen* lyrics. The distraction settles my stomach slightly, and I lean back against the bathtub to read it.

Cakes: So how did it go?? Are you coming to Lady's panel? It starts in 5 mins

Kaylee: It was amazing. More than I ever thought it could be.

Kaylee: But no, I don't think I can come to the panel.

Cakes: Why not??? Are you ok?

Kaylee: Fine. But. Panicking a bit.

Kaylee: a lot actually

Cakes: So am I coming up there, or are you coming here? Because you shouldn't be alone while you panic.

I lay the phone down next to me on the tile and rest my forehead on my knees. I want to just hide up here all day. Maybe work on some fic. The distance of online interaction sounds comforting right now, actually. This is all just . . . way too much. Way more immediate than I'm used to.

I pick my phone back up and start scrolling through all the notification emails from the Archive I've gotten since posting my latest chapter last night. I've already gotten a ton of comments, and reading them slows my heart rate and calms my racing mind. This is what I can do. This is who I am, how I'm known. I don't have to show my face here for that. I can be this person just as well from inside this hotel room. Why do I even care about the writing contest? I don't need to share my original stuff. I can just enjoy these readers, write only fanfic, and major in something boring to keep my mom off my back. She can't take these readers away from me. This is who I am. I smile a bit at one particularly effusive comment and click the link to respond on the website, but then a new text alert drops down from the top of the screen:

Cakes: that's it, I'm coming up there

No! I shoot back immediately.

Then I hesitate.

Why am I so against being . . . seen right now? I'm not embarrassed, exactly, but I feel . . . different. Scandalous or something. Why? I would never judge anyone else for doing what I've done. And having what I've always suspected—what I've always *known*, if I'm honest—confirmed in a very real way doesn't change who I am. Why am I feeling so shy? Or vulnerable or something. What's *wrong*?

I'm not a different person. I'm just queer. Like my friends have always known me to be. Like most of my friends in this fandom are. I don't judge them, and I know they won't judge me. They'll be happy for me.

And until I'm out of Plainsborough and at college, where I can be out, they'll be my safe space. Like they always have been.

Damn it, Cakes has been right all along, with all her teasing and knowing looks. Suddenly, she's exactly who I need to see. And I need to see her out in public, surrounded by the loving, accepting fandom I adore. Need to shake this feeling. What better place in the world to finally embrace who I am?

Kaylee: Stay put. I'm coming to you. Room #?

Cakes: W304. I'm right in the back with an empty seat next to me.

I pick myself off the floor and study my appearance in the bathroom mirror one last time. I don't look any different. I feel completely new in my own skin, though. Before I can lose my nerve, I grab my key and race out into the hall.

And nearly run straight into Miss North Carolina and a pack of pageant girls.

Madison whirls around, and I think faster than I've ever

thought in my life. I flip over my con badge so my username is hidden and charge right past them, into the stairwell, their laughter echoing after me. If it's a choice between taking the eternal elevator fourteen agonizing floors down with eight pageant princesses or walking down fourteen flights of stairs . . . seriously, stairs every time. No contest.

My heart hammers from more than the exertion of the stairs. She saw me. She definitely, *definitely* recognized me. But without my username, she can't do anything she doesn't already do. I've tried googling every combination of my name and *The Great Game,* and nothing comes up. I'm still safe.

For now.

In the lobby, it takes me two tries to find the right hallway, but I finally figure out that the W stands for West and locate room W304. The door stands open to welcome latecomers, fortunately, so I don't need to feel too awkward about sneaking in after the panel has started. The topic is Thrift Store Cosplay, and we're here to cheer for Lady, who is one of the speakers on the panel. I feel like a complete ass for stalling. She catches my eye as I walk in, and I give her a little wave in apology, sliding smoothly into the seat beside Cakes at the back.

Cakes vibrates with excitement next to me, dying to pry out every last detail. We'd never think of being so rude, though, especially at our friend's panel. We're here to support.

So she blows up my phone instead.

Cakes: so what happened?

Cakes: you're smiling like you got laid or something

Cakes: DID YOU GET LAID OH MY GOD

Cakes: tell me everything

Cakes: what happenedddddddddd

I snort so loud, a guy in the row in front of me turns around to look, but I manage to school my features into . . . well, something? I press my lips together and concentrate on the panelists for a minute until the urge to laugh uncontrollably subsides then flip my phone over and type.

Kaylee: Of course I didn't get laid, I've known her for like twelve hours

Kaylee: I'm not going to go from zero to vag in four seconds

Cakes's shoulder shakes against mine with her muffled laughter, and her fingers fly over her phone screen.

Cakes: but SOMETHING happened and I know it did so just stop

Cakes: WHY ARE YOU TORTURING ME

I hesitate, scrolling through the emojis on my phone to kill time while I think. I'm *not* embarrassed. But. How exactly does one just come out and say, by the way, definitely confirmed queer, definitely just made out with a gorgeous girl and sat in her lap and probably would have done more if she didn't have to freaking leave so soon. My cheeks heat at the memory, and I blow out a slow, calming breath.

Well. I guess I could just say exactly that.

Kaylee: well, I'm definitely queer

Kaylee: so take your victory lap or whatever because I know you called that

Kaylee: and we talked for a bit

Kaylee: then we made out

Kaylee: with me on her lap

Kaylee: OH MY GOD CAKES IT WAS 🔥🔥🔥

Kaylee: I am DEAD

Kaylee: 100% DECEASED

Next to me, Cakes makes a tiny, almost entirely suppressed, high-pitched screeching sound, and just like that, I'm grinning from ear to ear again. I bite the insides of my cheeks to try to keep my face looking somewhat normal, but it may be hopeless at this point. I'm in full-blown giddy crush mode like I haven't been since . . . maybe ever, and it feels amazing.

I look around the room and the more I look, the more I see little signs here and there: rainbow bracelets, tiny bi pride flag pins, two girls holding hands a few rows up. I'm surrounded by people like me, and now that I'm out of the hotel room, the feeling of being a stranger in my own body is fading. The fact that Cakes is obviously ecstatic helps, too.

Cakes: *victory dance*

Cakes: You're right, I totally called it. There's platonic admiration of Gwen Lestrade's legs, and then there's you.

Cakes: but I'm not here to gloat. I'm here to be happy that you got to make out with a girl who is totally hot

Cakes: which I hope you don't mind me saying, because damn

Kaylee: nah, not at all. It's completely true. No wonder she does pageants. She's utterly gorgeous.

Then another notification drops down, and my heart leaps into my throat, thinking it'll be Teagan. But it's Ami, who's sitting on the other side of Cakes, actually trying to pay attention to the panel and ask thoughtful questions like a good friend.

Ami: what are you two giggling about?

Ami: 💪 ?

Ha. Yeah. I guess I need to tell Ami, too. Come out to her officially. It's weird to think of it in those terms, but I guess that's what it is. I tap her message to reply, then . . . freeze up completely. This should not be weird. We've been friends since middle school and know everything about each other. She's been there for my failed relationships and lukewarm feelings about my cis dude exes. But we'll have to see each other every day at school, in Plainsborough, and she'll *know*.

But she's my best Real-Life Friend. She's the only reason I had the courage to go through with everything. She's always pushing me to be braver.

Well, here I go.

Kaylee: Everything is fine. More than fine actually.

Kaylee: Check another thing off the list, thanks to superhot make-out times with Teagan.

Kaylee: 💪 💪 💪

I hold my breath while I wait for her reply. She's leaning back in her chair, so I can't see her expression when she reads the messages. But the second she does, her legs bounce in a silent excited dance, and she leans over to give me a huge grin.

Buzzzzz.

Ami: Congrats kay. I'm happy for you, seriously. I know figuring this stuff out has really been weighing on you.

Ami: I'm so proud of you for being brave enough to follow your heart

Ami: or your tingly vag feelings, whatever

I blow out a slow breath and smile down at my phone. It's fine. Ami knows. And most important, Ami actually used the words *tingly vag feelings*, and that is getting screenshotted *yesterday*.

Kaylee: Thanks. ☺

Kaylee: I don't know about "following my heart," it's not serious or anything. I'll only get to see her one or two more times this weekend before it's over.

Kaylee: But it's been a good thing for me, for sure. I'm glad it happened.

Happened. Past tense.

Just like that, my giddy joy evaporates. Only one or two more times seeing Teagan, and I'll have to go back to good old homophobic Plainsborough. It's only for one more year, senior year, and then I can get out of there and head to a university town with an LGBTQ+ students group far, far away. But it's a year that I have to keep this hidden and pretend that this beautiful girl who is so easy to talk to didn't turn my world upside down in a matter of hours. One press of her lips, and I was gone.

I smile wryly. Looking back, a lot of things make more sense now. That picture of Rika from *Last Fantasy X* in her bathing suit I had as my desktop background for months because "the colors were pretty" (even though Rika was my least favorite character). My inexplicable hatred of Grace Younger's boyfriend in seventh grade (who took all her attention away from me). My obsession with that retro dress website, despite the fact I never wear dresses (but they looked so good on the models). I guess the brain will do a lot to make sure you believe what you want to believe.

Well, I want to believe something different now.

I want to believe I can find a community like this in my everyday life.

One day.

Just not now.

Chapter Seventeen

TEAGAN

*I*t's two minutes to curtain, and they're passing the Vaseline down the line. God, how has this not died out completely yet? Barely anyone actually uses it anymore—it's more of a strange holdover from years ago, and only the legacy girls with super strict moms or coaches still slather it on. It's supposed to keep your lips from sticking to your teeth when they dry out from smiling for too long, with the bonus effect that the more you let your smile droop, the more you taste it. I tried it once when I was a pageant newbie, just to see why it was even a thing, and there are times where the mere thought of the taste makes me throw up in my mouth a little. Never. Again.

All around me, girls perform their mini pre-pageant rituals, trying their best to focus through the rank cloud of nervous sweat and hair products. Some are mentally rehearsing choreography, counting under their breath with tiny movements. Others quietly say prayers either alone or holding hands with others, or take a quiet moment to meditate and center. This group has everything: the hard-core scholarship seekers, the future news anchors and lawyers, the social media influencers and future models, and the girls who straight up have hearts of gold and hands made for volunteering. Some of them want this title more than anything, and others are here only to please family members, bring attention to their charity, or enjoy the sisterhood and confidence-building. We spend much of the weekend getting to know each other and bonding in the way that only intense, short-term events can create, but right now, right before the competition begins, we're all understandably self-focused.

It's a cliché, but it's true: This competition isn't really girl versus girl. It's a mental competition against yourself. And for many of us, we're our own worst enemies.

The preliminary stage show is the first public portion of the competition, which sets plenty of girls on a razor's edge of panic. The judges no doubt have already cut their list of potential Top Fifteen candidates in half. No less than twenty-five of the girls standing in this room have already screwed their chances somehow. Usually by bombing on the interview, but occasionally by displaying bad character at the luncheon or making bad life choices during off time that the undercover judges caught.

Hopefully I'm not one of them. *Hopefully* the judges have no idea what I've been up to in my spare time.

My cheeks flush as I think of my morning activities today. It went pretty much as well as I could possibly have wanted. Kay figured things out, they were eager, they were confident once they got their head sorted out, and *God*, they were an amazing kisser. And that cosplay, damn. My blood sings hot under my skin at the thought of Kay's mouth on mine, their body pressed against mine as they sat in my lap, drinking in my kisses like water in the desert.

At least the thought keeps my smile firmly in place.

When the opening music for the preliminary competition begins, I practically float onstage behind Miss Vermont, my body following the choreography on autopilot. Our last rehearsal after the luncheon had been short but effective, solidifying the steps in my head, so I manage to at least nail the key poses while I'm in the front of the group. The thunderous applause that follows is exaggerated; these opening dance numbers are never exactly spectacular, but everyone's happy to be here cheering on their loved ones, reliving their glory days, or ogling all the girls onstage.

The next bit always makes me nervous. It's not difficult or anything, but we each have a chance to do a carefully choreographed walk up to the microphone to say our name and state. Sounds straightforward, but one year my voice cracked, and I sounded like a boy going through puberty. It didn't end up costing me the title, but Rhonda reamed me out afterward—never a fun time. The problem is that I'm always near the end, so my voice goes a bit stale from disuse. I figured out a trick last year, though—to hum a bit as the group advances up the stage right before my turn. It warms my vocal chords up just enough that when it's my turn, I can lean into the mic and say with total confidence and pep:

"Teagan Miller, Virginia!"

I walk my route to the back of the group, giving up the mic to Miss Washington State, and resist the urge to breathe a silent sigh of relief. While onstage, it's easy to get overwhelmed by the crowd, the lights, the pressure, by the way my cheeks and lips twitch from the effort of holding my smile, and no matter how much I try to *not think about it*, I have to give my brain something to focus on, or else I'll choke. So, I choose to focus on something completely different. Not four hours ago, I had my tongue in Kay's amazing mouth, and now I'm prancing onstage among all these (presumably) straight girls.

I, an avowed gay, am up here working this stage so damn well. Witness me, bitches.

Once the last of the introductions are done, we all file off-stage while the second-string hosts engage in painfully bad banter to a practically empty room. They manage to sell a few tickets for the preliminary competition, usually, but the very small audience is mostly composed of parents and siblings. For some people that makes it easier, but I personally find the emptiness a whole lot more awkward. You're supposed to be rocking the stage, and the room is practically silent except for the thin, cheesy synth music they pick for you and your own heels clicking. Makes the whole stage presence and energy thing a bit difficult. It totally threw me off during my first preliminary competition, but by now I can compensate like a pro. The finals will be completely different, with a packed house.

We only have a few minutes to change into our casual fashion outfits. To keep it fair, they give everyone the same amount of time, no matter where you fit in the order. No time to tweak makeup or hair except to swap out lipstick colors. Less than five minutes to yank off the horrid skirt and crop top from the opening number, slip into my next outfit, check for wrinkles and showing bra straps, and adjust to walking in the new pair of shoes. I use the last ten seconds to smooth some anti-frizz serum over my hair and wipe my shaking hands, then race to the end of the line, taking my place behind Miss Vermont again. So far, so good.

The waiting is the worst. I want nothing more than to fidget with my clothes and run my hands over my hair, but without a mirror, I could be making it worse instead of better. Instead, I take a long, slow breath to calm the adrenaline pumping through my veins, close my eyes, and focus on the image I'm trying to portray.

The casual fashion wear segment has two purposes: to allow each contestant to show off her personality through style, and to gauge our potential for future modeling gigs. I know I get no points for the latter, because I'm just not typical runway material.

Personality I can do, and in a competition that rewards con-
formity in so many ways, I appreciate the chance to put a little
of myself into the mix. They funnel us out onto the stage in
groups of ten until, finally, it's my group's turn.

One by one, the girls in front of me take the stage as the host
reads out their cheesy taglines. Miss Vermont almost wipes out
over a taped-down cable on the floor but manages to salvage
the walk with an adorable, self-deprecating shrug. Then it's my
turn. I carefully note the location of the cable, step over it, and:

"Miss Virginiaaaaa! Teagan is a lifelong artist and loves to
paint gifts for her friends and family. She spends many of her
weekends volunteering with Art Buddies, an art therapy organization that works with teens and young adults."

I hold my head up and soften my usual pageant smile into
something a little more relatable, a smile I'd use with the kids at
Art Buddies. The walk happens automatically, one foot directly
in front of the other the way Rhonda taught me so my hips sway
with each step. I genuinely love this outfit: a long, slouchy, yellow patterned flannel shirt belted at the dip of my waist over a
short, white lacy dress that hits me at mid-thigh. Deep-blue jeg-
gings emphasize the line of my legs, strong and sculpted from
soccer, and their dark color combined with my heeled mid-calf
boots make my legs look superlong and graceful. Not only do I
feel beautiful in this, but I feel *comfortable*. The flannel is soft
and drapey, and it feels like something I'd wear to the studio or
to one of my Art Buddies sessions.

Not to mention it absolutely thrills me to wear something
considered stereotypically lesbian. I'm a flannel kind of girl,
wink, nudge.

While in my interview I did my best to exert an image of
power and competence, here I go for something a bit more free-
flowing and creative. My smiles slide into place slower, my hip

pops are more natural, and I turn with a more fluid grace that lets the big waves in my hair whirl in a soft, bouncy dance. I can't see the judges with the stage lights in my eyes, but the energy in the room feels right, and when I turn to make my exit, the polite applause seems just a bit louder. Win.

I rejoin the line backstage, and our group does a quick review walk for the judges, then we all race backstage to change into our evening gowns. I want so badly to run over to Jess's dressing table and see how she thinks she did, but all I have time for is a quick wink in her direction. I'm sure she was fabulous. There's a minor scuffle as Miss Montana launches into a straight-up panic—she left the lipstick she brought to match her evening gown back at the hotel, it sounds like. I don't have a shade that'll work, but all the girls immediately around her launch into a search, and someone quickly comes up with the perfect color. Crisis averted, the pageant fam comes through again.

I blot my underarms to keep any sweat or deodorant from getting on my dress then shuck my whole outfit and slip into the sleek, shimmery gown. Rhonda found a sponsor willing to donate something so long as I could pay for the alterations, and it was worth every penny of the alteration fee. It's gorgeous— almost the same deep burgundy as my interview suit but with more of a shine and a sheer, black overlay that makes the dress move over my body like liquid. The overlay flows down and away from the dip of my waist as I walk, and the neck and waist-lines are emphasized with delicate, subtle beadwork that draws the eye. It's a good complement to my other outfits. A good choice.

This is the last category of the competition. One more walk across the stage and I'm done until dinner.

And after this? I'm spending as much of the evening with Jess and Kay as I can.

I rein in my thoughts before they have a chance to wander too far in Kay's direction and study the other girls' gown choices as I wait my turn to walk. My inner judge provides a running commentary in a voice that sounds eerily like Rhonda's:

1. Deep-blue velvet: too heavy, especially for a teen. In Orlando. In summer. We're supposed to wear the same gown both days when possible, but I hope you brought a backup.

2. That leg slit is *way* too high for a teen pageant, even though it looks *amazing*. You can get away with that in the Miss pageant. The judges won't have that here.

3. Miss North Carolina's glowing white dress is so tight, it looks painted on . . . and unfortunately, it's really working for her. Ugh.

I manage to distract myself with the gown analysis enough that the wait doesn't seem so horrifically long. Finally, it's my group's turn again, and I close my eyes. Time to remind the judges of the girl they interviewed this morning. The wicked firestarter. Fierce eyes, intense energy, a confident walk to raging drums. Miss Vermont makes her final turn at the end of the stage, and they call me out.

"Miss Virginia! Teagan hopes to earn dual degrees in art and psychology before attending Drexel University for their highly rated art therapy graduate program. A young entrepreneur, Teagan often sells hand-painted clothing and accessories at her local co-op stores and online."

It takes everything in me to keep my focus and not roll my eyes. Sometimes the "fun facts" Rhonda chooses to submit for me are ridiculous, and sometimes they border on excessively ef-fusive. A *young entrepreneur*, seriously?

I strut to the edge of the stage, place my hands on my hips *under* the gown's overlay like I was commanded, then sweep my hands under the sheer material to give it a whirl as I turn. I can feel the crackle of my stage presence taking hold, even with the awkward near silence of the tiny crowd, even though I'm not allowed to say a word. My heels click as I move to the other side of the stage, twirl again, and here it is—my last chance to make a solo impression.

With a toss of my hair, I fix the area of the crowd where I know the judges are placed with an intense look and let my smile edge just a bit toward the wicked. *See me? Yeah? Under-estimate me—I dare you.* Then I'm gone, whirling around to give up the stage to Miss Washington State. I actually feel a little bad—in her pastel-pink gown with the cutesy young-and-fresh look going on, there's no way she'll be able to follow me.

I reach the back of the line just in time for the group to take the final review walk. Five more minutes. Five more minutes and I'm *out of here*. They invite all fifty-one contestants onstage for a final look, most of whom make it to their correct spots, then make us stand there as they go through the obnoxiously long list of thank-yous and invite everyone back tomorrow evening for the final competition where the top fifteen will be revealed.

And you know what? I think I'm in. I think I'm easily Top Fifteen material. I know when I've done well and when I haven't, and tonight? I completely and utterly rocked it.

We all pile onto the catwalk to make our way backstage, and I'm already thinking ahead to tonight. Hopefully I have a message from Kay waiting for me, telling me where to meet them for whatever the con has in store for us later. What will it be? I didn't have a chance to look at the con schedule again, but I really hope it's something that involves dancing. Now that we've kissed—and oh *God,* that *kiss!*—I'm dying to get my hands on Kay again, to dance up against them with my hands on their waist, feeling the lines of their body, breathing in their—

Riiiiiiiiip!

A shocked gasp, then: "Oh no, Teagan, I am *so* sorry!"

The group erupts in murmurs as I turn to face the drawling voice. Miss North Carolina, standing with one high-heeled shoe on what used to be the back of my gown. The jagged, frayed edges of the cloth peek out from under her heel spike, and I feel a draft on my calves. For a moment, I'm completely detached, staring at the torn fabric with a blank expression. Then I look up at Miss North Carolina, and though her face is doing all the right things to spell contrition, her eyes gleam with victory in the backstage darkness.

She did this on purpose.

"It's fine," I hear myself say as if from a distance. Play it cool. Don't let anyone see you rattled. Jess rushes to my side and stoops to pick the scrap of gown off the floor with a burning glare at Miss North Carolina, who stands radiant in her false horror and sparkling, pure-white gown.

I don't know what I'm going to do. This gown was the perfect finishing move. The best possible way to end my portion of the competition. It tied into my interview suit, it made me look powerful.

(It matched Kay's hair . . .)

I take the scrap of fabric from Jess and force a cold smile.

"It's fine," I say again, balling the cloth up in my hand. There's no saving the gown, so no point to keeping it unwrinkled. "I'll think of something before tomorrow. Accidents happen, right, Madison?"

Miss North Carolina stiffens. I can see her turning it over in her mind. Is it a threat?

I'm not sure. It might be. I haven't decided yet.

Either way, I have less than twenty-four hours to come up with a gown solution that will win me this competition. I brought a spare, of course. Everyone does. But I never thought I'd need it, so all I brought was an old dress that got me low scores in a previous pageant. It was all I had—most of my best gowns have been loans from designers who made me give them back after whatever pageant they wanted it to be seen at. The fit of my backup gown is perfect, and there's nothing *wrong* with it, but it's plain, solid white with no decoration whatsoever, way too similar to Madison's. Rhonda thought it would work like a blank canvas, "allowing my natural beauty to shine through."

It didn't work. That was the only pageant I bombed. If I have to wear that gown tomorrow, it won't matter if I scored Top Fifteen today. I'll never make Top Five, never have a chance at an onstage question to get the win.

Never have a chance at the scholarship money I need so badly.

And, when I sit down at my dressing table and turn my phone back on, I have two new messages:

KayfortheWinnet:
Pizza and watch-along in our room, whenever you're free

KayfortheWinnet:
then the cosplay pageant at 9:00pm! You in?

I purse my lips, look between the messages and the scrap of gown.

Is there any point to either?

With a blank expression, I lay the phone gently down on the dressing table and drop the torn fabric over it like a shroud.

It's all pointless now anyway.

Chapter
Eighteen

KAYLEE

I 'm starting to worry that I'm never going to hear from Teagan
again.

I messaged her hours ago, but it's almost five thirty and
still nothing. Maybe she changed her mind about everything.
Maybe the kiss wasn't any good for her. She *seemed* into it. Really into it, actually, so I don't know what happened. I guess she
could just be really busy with . . . whatever it is pageant girls
do all day. My phone lights up again, and I scramble to unlock
it . . . but it's just another text from my mom. Her fifteenth one
today. It's like the longer the weekend goes, the more paranoid
she gets. Asking what I'm wearing, what I'm doing, am I eat-
ing well and watching my portions, reminding me what "good
girls" don't do. Ugh.

I settle back into my pillow and shove another slice of veggie
supreme pizza in my face, because obviously the solution to my
big gay drama is *more pizza*. Or big enby drama, I guess. Queer
drama? Labels are confusing. The words still sound weird, but
I've been thinking about it all day, and the more I do, the more I

feel this sense of . . . fullness in my chest. Happiness. Completeness? Is that cheesy?

I don't know, but if my very first girl kiss ends up ditching me completely, it's gonna tarnish this feeling a bit.

I'm just about to pick up another slice when my message alert *finally* goes off.

paintmeinviolet:
I don't know if I can come tonight

paintmeinviolet:
something bad happened and it's kind of consuming my day

My heart sinks. I should have known it was too good to be true. This sounds like an excuse, a convenient way to get out of this. Next to me, Cakes, Lady, and Ami shake the other bed with bouncing and shrieks of laughter as they argue over which episode to watch tonight. Their antics nearly upend the pizza box, and I drop my phone to the scratchy hotel blanket just in time to snatch the lid before it goes over and push it back between them. Good save.

Maybe I should let Teagan off the hook so she doesn't feel like she has to keep messaging me all weekend. I could focus on my friends, my cosplay, the writing contest—all the things I actually came here to do. The smudgy phone screen glows under my fingers, awaiting my input.

KayfortheWinnet:
Look, I'm sorry if I made you uncomfortable or something. You don't have to explain or anything. Sorry for bugging you.

The reply is nearly instantaneous.

paintmeinviolet:
No!

paintmeinviolet:
That's not what I mean. I'm serious. I want to come over.

paintmeinviolet:
This morning was amazing

paintmeinviolet:
Really, REALLY amazing

paintmeinviolet:
I want to see you again

KayfortheWinnet:
Then DO. Let me take your mind off the bad thing.

paintmeinviolet:
It's complicated

What does that even mean? I assume it's pageant related. If so, the chances of us being able to help are nil, but I feel like I should offer at least. That's the good thing to do, right?

KayfortheWinnet:
Why don't you come over for five minutes and talk it out with us? I doubt we can do anything, but we're here to be angry on your behalf about whatever it is, at least.

Three dots appear as she starts typing a reply, then disappear, and reappear. Finally, another message pops up.

paintmeinviolet:
I'm in the room right now, actually. Be over in a sec?

KayfortheWinnet:
Yes!

Which . . . I should probably tell the others.

"Hey, y'all, Teagan finally got back to me," I say, hesitant.

"Oh, is she finally coming over?" Lady asks. "There's plenty of pizza."

I nod and smile faintly as Ami gets up and cracks the outer door open so Teagan can come right in when she's ready. My friends are so much better than me. So instantly welcoming in a situation where I'd probably be irritated or jealous of someone else taking up my friend's time.

"Yeah, she's coming over for a few minutes," I say. "But she said something bad happened, so—"

Teagan comes flying in before I can finish my heads-up, shutting the door behind her and letting out a long breath. As soon as she looks up and meets my eyes, I can tell something is really wrong.

"Hey," I manage, scooting over to make room for her next to me on the bed.

"Want some pizza?" Lady says, hoisting her own slice in greeting.

"Or a pastry?" Cakes adds, pointing to a box of deliciousness from a famous local bakery she idolizes.

Teagan studies the pizza for one longing, desperate moment before she shakes her head.

"No, but thanks. I have a dinner thing I have to go to in—"

She glances down at her phone. "Like twenty minutes? So I can't stay, I just . . ."

She trails off and looks so lost and sad that I shove aside my cowardice and stand, wrapping her in a hug.

"Tell us what happened?" I ask, drawing her back to sit down. She sits heavily on the edge of the bed and stares at her hands.

"This is going to sound like nothing to you all, I'm sure, but . . ." Her face goes hard with anger for a moment then smooths out into neutral nothingness. "Miss North Carolina—you know, Madison?"

A bolt of terror strikes deep in my heart. Oh God. Does this have anything to do with me? I look up, and my friends are all staring back, holding their breath. Teagan continues.

"God, you're gonna think this is so shallow, but . . . she stepped on the back of my dress after the preliminary competition today. On purpose. It ripped, and it's totally unsalvageable." Her words tumble faster and faster as she tries to explain. "I *know* how ridiculous that sounds, but the gown was donated by a sponsor who wanted to do a photo shoot when I got home, and I'm probably going to have to pay to replace it, and it was so expensive, and my shoes were dyed to match it, and I've been *killing* it this weekend and had a real shot to win. First prize is a twenty-five-thousand-dollar scholarship, and I really need it, so much more than a lot of the other girls who are competing. That gown was perfect for me . . ."

She trails off for a minute, her eyes locking on to my hair, of all things—is it because I was always wearing it up when she saw me before?

"But now," she says, her eyes growing shiny. "Now I have to wear my backup gown, which is . . . it's just awful. It lost me the state pageant last year when I rocked every other part. *That's* how bad. And I know, it's just a dress, it's just a pageant, but . . ."

"It's not *just* anything," Cakes cuts in, wiping her pizza-greasy fingers off with a napkin. "A musician would be wrecked if their instrument had an issue right before a big performance. A hockey player would be just as upset if their skates . . . broke or something. That much scholarship money is a big deal. Not to mention, like . . . winning a pageant must be a big check on a college application, right?"

Teagan tips her head back and blinks rapidly, chasing away the tears. "Yeah. And there are so many doors that open for you. Internships, chances to do charity work, media appearances to support your platform . . . just, a lot of stuff. All gone."

Lady frowns. "Well, hey, hold up. The pageant isn't over yet, right? The main competition is still tomorrow? Let's see this dress you think is so horrible."

Teagan sighs and pulls out her phone, scrolling through her photos. "I know it's not going to seem that bad to you, but trust me when I say that the judges at last year's pageant did *not* agree . . ."

She flips the phone around to show us a photo of her on a stage in a stunning white gown with subtle shimmer that seems to glow under the stage lights. It's a sleek, slim silhouette that hugs her body all the way from the fitted V-neck bodice to the floor, but there are also these . . . I don't even know what to call them. Side panels? Wings? It's like an extra layer of fabric that starts at her hips and flows outward, all the way to the ground, when she holds them open. Her hair falls over her bare shoulders in big, shiny waves, and her makeup is perfectly applied, as far as I can tell. She looks utterly gorgeous.

Of course, I might be biased.

"Hmm, I see what you mean," Lady says thoughtfully. I look up at her like she's lost her mind, but the others nod in agreement, and she continues, "It's a beautiful shape for you, and you wear it perfectly, it's just a little . . . bland."

Teagan nods. "That's exactly what the judges said. Too plain, didn't match my personality, didn't add anything to my appearance. There were these two incredible girls in the state pageant last year, and everyone knew it was all but a guarantee that one of them would win, so my pageant coach decided to take a risk and see if it would be a good strategy for my future pageants. She called it 'a blank canvas allowing my natural beauty to shine through.' Totally backfired. I didn't even make Top Five. It's the only time she's led me wrong."

Cakes blinks. "Wait, pageant coaches are a thing?"

"Oh yeah," Teagan says. "Most people who are really competitive have a coach who teaches you poise and elocution, advises you on outfits and strategy, drills you on interview questions, and tons more. I wouldn't have gotten this far without mine."

"Okay, but the dress," Ami interrupts, shooing away the excess information like flies. "If this is your only option tomorrow, then there's got to be a way to salvage the situation. Lady is amazing with cosplay . . . any ideas?"

Lady takes the phone from Teagan and zooms in, squinting at something. "When you aren't holding the overskirt open, does it lay pretty flat against your sides?"

Teagan nods. "Yeah, it looks like a standard A-line silhouette when I let it hang naturally."

"The angled pleats on the bodice add really nice texture," Ami says, pointing at the top of the dress. Does she mean the folds?

"Yeah," Cakes agrees. "And the belt at the waist is the perfect accent for your shape."

It's like they're speaking another language that I only know how to say "hello" and "where is the bathroom" in. I know what dresses are. I know long and short. I know strapless and . . . not strapless. But this conversation is light-years beyond me.

"What size shoe do you wear?" Lady asks, her eyes lighting up. Does she have a real idea that can help? I'm glad someone here can be useful, because it sure isn't me.

"Seven," Teagan says, and Lady hands the phone back to her and launches herself at her cosplay suitcase. She comes back with a pair of strappy, *very* high heels in a beautiful shade of rich purple. "Okay," Lady says with firm confidence. "Here's my idea. If you want to do it, message Kay the supplies you'll need, and we'll make sure you get them. If you don't think it'll fly, that's totally fine, *but* I think this is just the thing to bring this dress to life."

Lady outlines her plan, gesturing at different areas of the photo and pulling up other references on her phone as examples. Teagan listens politely at first then leans forward, asking more and more questions and talking faster with every word. I gather all my courage and reach out, laying one hand on her knee to give a supportive squeeze. She drops her hand to mine instantly and squeezes back, turning to me with a grin.

"This could actually work," she says, eyes bright and alive for the first time since she walked in the room. "Thank you so much, everyone. It's a big risk, but it's my only shot, right? I may as well take it."

We all look at each other, waiting for one of us to make the inevitable *Hamilton* reference, but it never comes, and we all burst into laughter instead. Teagan glances down at her phone and swears, launching to her feet.

"I'm so sorry, I have to go, or I'll be late for the dinner, but . . . Cosplay Pageant tonight, you said?"

I nod, looking up at her. "Yeah, 9:00 P.M. Do you think you can make it?"

"I'll make sure of it," Teagan says, stepping between my legs and tipping my chin back so she can place the lightest of kisses on my mouth. It straight up lights me on *fire*. Cakes squeaks from somewhere, but the kiss is otherwise met without commentary. Teagan steps back toward the door but pauses, looking over the group.

"Thank you again, everyone. I really mean it. I'm basically a stranger, but you've been so cool about me barging in on your weekend, and you've given me hope when I thought I was doomed. You didn't have to do any of that, and I just wanted you to know how much I appreciate it."

Her eyes slide over to meet mine, and she gives a small smile.

"See you tonight."

She practically floats out of the room, so different from how she came in, and as soon as the door clicks shut, I flop back on the bed with my hands over my burning cheeks.

"Y'all," I say. And that's *all* I say. Because. Damn.

"Oh my God, you have it *so bad* for her!" Lady cackles, clapping her hands together.

Cakes launches herself onto the bed next to me and shakes my shoulder. "I mean, can you *blame* them? I gotta get me a pageant girl, too!"

My phone chimes its email alert, interrupting my fantasy of what might happen *after* the cosplay pageant tonight before it can even really get started. Probably another Archive notification for a fic comment or—

My heart leaps into my throat.

FROM: contest@greatcon.org
SUBJECT: Pastiche Publication Contest

I suck in a sharp breath and jab the screen two or three times before I manage to open the email. I skim it once, then again, then again, my grin widening with each pass.

Dear Kaylee,

Thank you for your submission to the GreatCon-sponsored Pastiche Publication Contest. We are pleased to inform you that your entry has been selected as one of the final two to be considered by the editor from 221b Press for inclusion in their next Sherlock Holmes anthology. We hope you will be able to attend a late luncheon with the editor on Sunday afternoon, June 19 at 4:00 P.M. for the announcement of the winner, presentation of the contract, and details about 221b Press and the world of small-press publishing. Congratulations on your selection! There were many fine entries, and the choice was incredibly difficult. No matter what the result, you are to be commended for your contributions to the Sherlock Holmes community. We hope to see you tomorrow afternoon!

Best wishes,

Aiden (ImprobableEgg)

Contest Coordinator

The sound starts as a thin, high-pitched whine in the back of my throat and turns into a full-blown screech when it really sinks in.

I'm a finalist.

I'm a finalist!

The others crowd around my phone and read for themselves when I prove incapable of making anything resembling words, and before long, all four of us are squished together on the one bed, a giant, screaming mess. Someone has the forethought to remove my laptop from the vicinity (probably Ami) before we all end up sprawled half on top of each other across the length of the bed, arms wrapped around whoever happens to be closest. The screams eventually subside into giggles then into contented, surprised silence.

"I can't believe it, you guys. Is this real? You read it, too, right?" I ask into someone's ribs. The ribs vibrate with laughter then speech.

"Of course it's real," Lady says. "You're an awesome writer. Did you think everyone was lying to you this whole time?"

"No, but," I sputter. "I mean, you're my friends. I thought you were just being nice and supportive."

"Nice and supportive friends also do you the favor of telling you when you suck so you don't embarrass yourself," Ami adds, her hand squeezing mine. "We would do that for you, if it were true. But it's not."

"The mark of true friendship," Cakes murmurs into my neck. "Honesty. We got your back."

"Does this mean you'll finally let us read the story you submitted?" Ami asks with a poke.

The familiar automatic panic reaction flares, but for once I don't let it sweep me away. Instead, I think of Teagan's words from earlier: *You've given me hope when I thought I was doomed.*

I have hope.

And I have some truly amazing friends.

"You know what? Yes. After the con is over, I'll send it to all of you."

"And a few chapters of that book you've been writing, too?" Cakes asks with raised eyebrows.

"Whoa now, baby steps. Let's not go totally wild."

We lie there for another minute or two, during which I message Teagan the good news, then someone makes a crack about the episode still playing in the background, and we all turn our attention back to the show that brought us together, still glowing with contentment and closeness. My mom always complains that I don't have enough "real" friends because Ami is the only person I hang out with back home.

But these people in this room? All four of us *are* real, true friends. We were before this con, honestly, but being here all together has only solidified it. Lady and Cakes, whom I never met in real life before this weekend, both feel closer to me now than any of the people I share classes with or even sit with occasionally at lunch. We all understand each other on a different level. I don't know if it's the fandom connection or the similar mindsets or what, but I feel a completely different kind of friendship here. It's beautiful.

And on top of it all, these are the only people in the world who know about my . . . recent discoveries. About myself. Well, the only people who weren't actively involved in the discovery, that is. And that means I can go to them for just about anything.

"Hey, y'all, can I ask you something?" I say, propping myself up on one elbow. "I started writing this fic earlier at the flash fiction workshop, and it's Violet/Gwen, which I've never written before. Can you give me some quick feedback on the beginning?"

I swallow down my nervousness at sharing something so different from anything I've written before and at what I'm about to say next.

"I think I want to gift it to Teagan on the Archive, if I can finish it before she comes over for the cosplay pageant. What do you think?"

And what do my friends do? What they do best, of course: They squeal and gush and gently suggest improvements and new ideas, and just generally make me feel so loved and supported that the idea of leaving on Monday morning seems a million miles away.

This place, right here, is perfect.

The fic grows out of control, of course. Typical. But by the time I'm done, my cheeks are flushed with exhilaration and something else entirely, the words honest and revealing and simmering with heat. It's obvious to me in hindsight: It wasn't the femslash pairings I was avoiding all this time. It was myself, and the feelings they stirred up in me.

When I click POST, it's with the confidence that it's some of my best writing, and I'm proud to put it out in the world.

Title:

And the Night Belongs to You

Author:

KayfortheWinnet

Rating:

T

Archive Warning:

No Archive Warnings Apply

Category:

F/F

Fandoms:

The Great Game (TV)

Relationships:

Violet Hunter/Gwen Lestrade

Additional Tags: Femslash, Coming Out, Sweet lady kisses, Flirting, Dancing, Clubs, Bisexual Violet, Bisexual Gwen, Violen?, What is the name for this ship?, I don't know but it's one of my new faves

Summary:

When Gwen and Violet run into each other at a club, they're both way out of their element—and yet surprisingly fine with it.

Notes:

Written for paintmeinviolet

Chapter Nineteen

✴

TEAGAN

I must be out of my mind, choosing to sneak out for the con after what happened today.

"You must be out of your *mind!*" Jess says, waving her arms in my face. "After what happened today, you're going to go out with this girl after curfew?"

Is there an echo in here?

"Person. Not girl. Look, there's nothing else I can do about my situation right now," I say. "The first changes need to set before I can keep working on the dress. I honestly think at this point it would be *worse* for me to sit around all night and be pissed off. I need to blow off some steam so I don't try to take revenge."

"Meaning you need to stick your tongue down someone's throat. Teagan, you are *so close*. You and me, we are *killing it* this weekend, and I really feel like one of us could win. You, especially. Don't get me wrong, I crushed my interview and my dress this year is—" She does a chef's kiss. "But we both know how this works."

I want to protest. I've seen that dress, and I know how she interviews. She's *amazing*. So smart and driven and funny, and she's so passionate about climate change, she'll probably be the one who saves us all with her science in the end. But I also know what she means. She's very dark-skinned and wears her hair natural, and I'd be an idiot to deny the role that plays in a pageant world where participants in the early days used to have to trace their lineage to prove they were white.

All you have to do is look at past pageant statistics to see how the racism and colorism play out. Even though 2019 was an amazing year, where all the winners of all the major pageants were Black women, pageants are full of girls of color just as beautiful and talented as Jess every year, and one year of big wins doesn't lift all those girls up. The standard of beauty is slowly changing, but we still have a *long* way to go, and it affects Jess in a way that it will never touch me. If everything else is equal, the odds are always going to be in my favor. If I win this pageant over Jess, it'll be partly or mostly because I'm white.

Jess sighs, seeing my protests flare up and die, then leans in close to take my hands. "I love you, girl. But if you get caught out tonight? They'll knock you out of the top fifteen in a heartbeat. We've dreamed of being in the top five together since we were thirteen. Do not blow this for baby Teagan and Jess."

I bite my lip and look up at the ceiling. I know. I know, I know, I really, *seriously* am aware of how bad an idea this is.

This should be a clear-cut decision. A hookup with some random person I'll probably never see again and a few hours at a con should be *nothing* compared to the thought of standing up there with Jess and maybe even winning this pageant, the culmination of my pageant career. I could keep competing in this circuit until I'm nineteen then compete in the Miss pageants after I turn twenty, but I was really hoping I wouldn't have to.

I want to focus on school. I want to be out and free. I want to fall in love and not have to hide it. I need that twenty-five-thousand-dollar scholarship *now*, not later. I need the opportunities the crown will bring. This could make or break the next several years of my life. But . . .

What is it about Kay, about GreatCon, that has me so out of my right mind?

Part of it is undoubtedly that fic they wrote me. God, *that fic.* When I first got the notification email that a work had been gifted to me on the Archive, I was confused. No one really knows me well enough in fandom to gift me anything. Then I saw the username, the pairing, the description . . . and promptly melted. It was three thousand words of pure sexual tension between two amazing women who don't get nearly enough love in the show or the fandom, and I devoured every word of it, starting in the elevator on the way back from dinner, with a reread immediately after.

And knowing those words were written for me? That fic lit a fire low in my belly that hasn't gone out ever since. It was so well written, dripping with the heat of two beautiful people discovering their attraction. It was honest and relatable, and Kay's talent shone with every line.

I have to see them again.

"There's just something about Kay," I say as shorthand for all the complicated feels. "Like . . . I will admit I was terrible at Miss East Coast Teen. It was a huge risk for something that meant literally nothing to me except as a way to get back at Priya, and you probably should have been ten times *madder* than you already were and just friend-dumped me altogether. I would have deserved it. But Kay is . . ."

I shake my head and smile. "The con is such a different world. Safer for most queer people, for people like me. Anywhere else,

Kay and I may have never looked twice at each other, but here, we just clicked instantly, you know? Mentally and, uh . . . physically. That first night, I didn't come back for so long because I spent almost four hours just *talking* to them. I haven't been in sync with someone like that since you and I first met four years ago! Not that I ever felt like this about you—I mean, no offense."

She huffs a breath and rolls her eyes. "Obviously."

I pause, take a deep breath, and finally allow myself to think it. "You know . . . Plainsborough, North Carolina, isn't that far away from Charlottesville. Only about three hours. Maybe we'll be able to see each other again."

Jess's expression softens at that, and she shakes her head. "You really do have it bad, don't you? You didn't visit Priya once, and you were supposedly madly in love with her."

I sit down hard on the edge of the bed and put my head in my hands. "I don't know what it is. It's not just the fandom connection, it's like . . . I just feel the potential, you know? We've only known each other for a day, so it's not like I'm trying to say I'm in love with them or anything. That really *would* be ridiculous. But it feels . . . possible, you know? Eventually."

The bathroom door opens, and Oregon comes out in comfy-looking PJs, makeup free and with her earbuds in. Miss North Carolina apparently had a bunch of her groupies over and she couldn't deal, so she's hanging in our room until curfew. She shoots me a little smile as she flops down on Jess's bed and pulls a book off the nightstand, instantly absorbed in what looks like a doorstop of a fantasy novel with an orange cover. Trying to give us privacy, probably. Sweet of her.

Jess sits back, resigned. "Just be careful, okay? I mean it when I say I think you have a real shot at winning this. I'd hate to see you lose out on a scholarship to your dream school because of this."

I stand and shove my hands in the pockets of my hoodie. "I know. This is a terrible decision, honestly, but it still feels like the right one. I spend so much of my time hiding, and at this con, it's just . . ."

How can I even explain what the atmosphere at a fan con is like? I shake my head, at a loss for words.

"Anyway, are you okay with me leaving my dress hung up in the bathroom for now? It's not in your way?" I ask, dropping the subject and hoping Jess will take the cue.

"Of course, love. We've got your back. Go, have fun. Don't stay out too late this time. But *do* think about how much fun we'll be having without you, because Oregon and I are doing face masks and a bad movie marathon, and you are completely missing out."

"I definitely am," I say, as I hug her and turn to leave.

"Wait!" Jess whispers, then shoves a bundle of flowers tied up with a ribbon into my hand. One of the centerpieces from tonight's formal dinner. The colors, ironically, are a perfect match for the GreatCon logo.

"I thought you wanted to take this home to your little sister," I say, trying to pass them back to her, but she holds up her hands and steps away.

"Eh, she probably would have ripped them apart and made her dolls go all Godzilla on them. Look, if you think this thing might be real, then get out there and woo this person," she says with a wink. "Lesbians still do flowers, right?"

I roll my eyes, laugh, and shoot her a middle finger on my way to the door, flowers in hand. A quick check through the peephole, then I let myself out into the hallway, my hood pulled low over my face. Ami must hear me coming, because she lets me right in before I even knock. "Kay's just putting their cosplay back on. They'll be right out."

The bathroom door opens as if on cue, and out steps Kay in that same Army John Watson outfit from earlier, looking just as gorgeous and badass. They can rock some combat boots, seriously. The corner of their mouth turns up in a shy smile, but their eyes burn as they drag over every inch of me—until they catch on the flowers.

"What are those?" they ask, eyes wide.

"Um, for you," I say, thrusting the flowers toward them like a sword. Ugh, why am I like this? I step closer and hand them over a little more gently. "To congratulate you on being a finalist in the story contest. They were decorations at our dinner tonight, but I thought you . . . might like them, I don't know. Do you even like flowers? I guess I don't know you well enough yet."

"I . . . think I do?" Kay says, taking the bouquet from me and bringing it to their nose. "No one's ever given me flowers before. Thank you."

Their cheeks turn a faint shade of dusky pink, and they suck on their lip ring in that way that drives me wild every time. Lines from that fic they wrote me drift through my head, words like *mesmerized* and *needy* and *lips*. I need a distraction before I instigate a repeat of this morning's activities, so I cast around for a discussion topic.

"Are you competing in the cosplay pageant?" I ask, the words tumbling out in a babble.

"Ha, not really," Kay replies, finally looking up from the flowers and running their free hand over their hair. "I signed up to walk the stage, but I didn't enter myself to actually win. I just want to see all the costumes and enjoy the show."

I turn to look over the rest of the group to see what they're wearing . . . and feel strangely out of place in my plain, non-fandom-ish clothes. Ami is wearing another custom TGG-themed dress, tea-length and patterned with the iconic wallpaper that hangs in 221B Baker Street in the show. Cakes wears a T-shirt from one of my favorite fan artists and carries a bag covered in pins, buttons, and patches relating to TGG and other Sherlockian fandoms.

Lady is on a whole other level. She *is* Violet Hunter, computer whiz extraordinaire, friend, and occasional co-consultant to Sherlock and John on the show. The details of her cosplay are incredible; if I looked at a side-by-side comparison of Lady versus a photo of Violet from the show, I don't think I'd be able to spot a single difference in their outfits or accessories, right down to the slouchy hat and tablet covered in stickers. I knew she was really into cosplay and liked to sew, but I didn't realize she was pro-level good at it. Now I'm extra grateful she took the time to help me with my dress.

"We're going to be late if we don't go now," Ami warns, shooing us all toward the door. Kay hesitates for a second, turning the bouquet over in their hand before placing it reverently down next to the TV.

"I'm just gonna leave this here," they say. "I don't want to accidentally leave them somewhere. Is that okay? I don't really know flower-getting etiquette."

And I don't want anyone to see you carrying flowers from a pageant event and wondering what's going on, I think. Can't believe that didn't occur to me.

"Totally fine," I say. "Let's go see some amazing cosplay."

I tug my hood down again and tuck myself up between Kay and Cakes out in the hallway. My skin tingles, being so close to Kay without touching them, but I hesitate before reaching out. It's one thing when it's behind a closed door where no pageant chaperone or undercover judge will ever see me. And what about Kay's friends? Are we allowed to be together-ish around them? Will anyone mind? I guess I did kiss Kay in front of them all earlier, but I really should have asked first. I was just so over-whelmed by actually having hope for tomorrow's competition again. I want to feel their mouth on mine again, want to wrap an arm around their waist, or—

Kay's hand snakes down to take mine, squeezing to get my attention. I glance up, catch their gaze, and their eyes are warm and shy.

"Thank you for the flowers. It was sweet," they say, looking at my mouth again, and I can't think straight with our earlier kisses replaying in my head. I lean in and press our mouths together right there in front of the elevator. Down the hall, a door opens and closes, and our elevator dings its arrival, but I can't bring myself to care. No one will recognize me with my face hidden behind Kay's, under a purple hood, surrounded by obvious con goers. I kiss them again, and again, gently, with my heart in my throat. *Please tell me I can keep having this after tomorrow. Please, please . . .*

Cakes finally drags us into the elevator, one hand stuck out to keep the doors from closing. We laugh and apologize, our fingers still tangled together, and join in the group's discussion of a cosplay panel that Lady was apparently on earlier. The conversation flows, enveloping me easily as if I've been part of their group all along, and by the time the eternal elevator ride dumps us into the lobby, the dress disaster is all but forgotten. Lady's solution will work. I've still got a good shot.

For now, I have other priorities.

Chapter Twenty

*

TEAGAN

*B*allroom B glows with hundreds of rainbow twinkle lights, completely transformed for the cosplay pageant. The normally bland, blank-slate room now hosts a small stage with overhead spotlights, a sound system, and hundreds of full chairs. The audience for this pageant is nearly twice as large and ten times as enthusiastic as our families-only audience for the preliminaries today. The pageant hasn't even started, and the crowd is alive, cheering for friends waiting in the wings and chattering excitedly.

Kay and I lean together on the end of a row, our hands entwined and our shoulders pressed together. My insides feel calmer than they have all day, with my hand in theirs. This is starting to feel too real. They lean close, their warm breath ghosting over my ear and raising the hairs on the back of my neck as they ask, "Have you ever done cosplay before?"

I turn my head just a fraction toward Kay. "No, never had a chance to try it. I've done commission work for other people's cosplays, though. Sometimes it's easier to have someone paint a design for you than sewing on all that detail. I'll have to paint something for one of yours sometime."

Their smile dims just a fraction, and they glance down at our joined hands with flushed cheeks. "Um, yeah, maybe."

It takes a moment for me to realize what I've said, and when I do, I have to bite my lip to keep from groaning out loud. It's the first time either of us has definitively mentioned anything about after the con. Maybe they think I'm just in this for the weekend? Does this reaction mean they'd be open to staying in touch? Maybe even dating?

"I actually have some family in Chapel Hill," I say, trying for casual. "It's not a very long drive from Charlottesville to there."

Their smile falls even further, and they angle their body more toward the stage and away from me. "Yeah, Chapel Hill isn't that far. We go there sometimes on the weekend."

Okay, so this isn't going over well. Maybe Kay is the one who doesn't want anything after this weekend. I really don't know what to do with that possibility, after the strength of everything I've been feeling this weekend and that fic dedication.

I've just about gathered the courage to ask what's wrong when a blast of music sends a jolt of adrenaline through my veins, and I jerk back away from Kay, who bolts to their feet.

"Shoot, I gotta get in line, I'm in the first group! Be back soon," they say, dashing off around the back of the ballroom to join the row of costumed people at stage left. *The Great Game*'s theme song crescendos to a peak, and the crowd roars its approval as a guy with electric-green hair skips onto the stage with a microphone. Ami and Cakes shout loud whoops of support from the other side of Kay and Lady's empty chairs.

"Good evening, GreatCon!" the host shouts, to another wave of thunderous applause. "We're here tonight to witness the amazing talent and beauty of our fandom's fantastic cosplayers!

Some costumes are bought, some are handmade, some are hilarious, and some, I hear, were even cobbled together ten minutes ago in someone's bathroom, so thanks to that person."

He pauses for uproarious laughter that's much more about the charged atmosphere than the joke, then he continues, "We're going to be giving away a few great prizes tonight for best overall costume, most accurate costume, most creative costume, and best crack costume, which will be determined by your laughter, so don't be shy! We have so many fantastic cosplayers here tonight, though, and they *all* deserve your love, so let's kick this off with a big round of applause!"

The crowd obeys with gusto as the guy leaps off the stage with the microphone and sets himself up on a podium at the foot of the stage. A tiny light illuminates his face as he shuffles through his cue cards then leans into the mic to announce each contestant.

"First up is Scroll user JohnlocksInferno with their rendition of Bird!lock. Mark this one down for the creativity category, judges, because look at those feathers!"

Kay's friends explode with cheers as Bird!lock flies across the stage, doing a quick twirl in the middle to show off the back of their costume. Sherlock Holmes's signature hat and coat, but with enormous wings and a beak. Hey, why not?

"They're a friend of ours from Scroll," Ami says, narrating so I don't feel left out. "They really love birds *a lot*, so their costume is particularly fitting."

"The wings are beautiful," I admit, fighting to keep a thoughtful frown off my face. I'm having a harder time with this whole thing than I thought I would, and I'm not sure why. Is it because I've been out of the fandom loop for the last six months, just reading fic and staying off Scroll? Two more contestants march across stage in homemade costumes, one completely unrecognizable and the other apparently some cracky, obscure fandom reference involving pizza that I don't get.

Then Kay takes the stage as Army John Watson and, if possible, gets even hotter.

"Next up is Archive author and Scroll user KayfortheWinnet!" the host announces. He tries to read the rest, but the audience explodes with cheers at the name, drowning him out. Wow, people really do know Kay in this fandom, for them to get that kind of reaction. They strut confidently to center stage, getting the Watson swagger down perfectly and carrying themself with a level of assurance I've never seen from them before. The host makes a faux-pouty face until things settle down then reads the rest of the intro.

"Fic author KayfortheWinnet is dressed in authentic uniform as John Watson from his British army years. They've requested to not be entered into the judging, but we can give them tons of love anyway, right, people?"

The crowd screams their approval again, and if anything, Kay walks even taller on the way offstage. Maybe it was getting the chance to use those they/them pronouns in a big, public venue that brought on that new glow or the clear appreciation from the crowd. Either way, when Kay makes their way back to our row, they're practically floating, all trace of their earlier gloom erased. They squeeze past me to sit back between me and Lady's empty seat, and without a second's hesitation, Kay turns to kiss me full on the mouth. My body leaps to respond to this strange, electric energy pouring off Kay, but they pull away before I can sink my fingers into their hair. They wink then lean back in their seat to cheer on the next contestants.

The more people who cross the stage, the quieter I get. Everyone looks so *different*. Not just from the rest of the world, but from each other. It's like everything you'd never see in a real pageant all poured into one place. There are fat people, really tall and short people, those sporting faded dye jobs or costumes that don't fit *at all*, and yet they're all walking across the stage with huge grins and boisterous gestures, like sovereigns of their own kingdoms, totally owning their power.

In my kind of pageant, you can practically hear the judges patting themselves on the back when they award a high score to a girl with a bigger frame, or short hair, or darker skin. When I tried to bring that up with someone once, they gave me some bull about how as a blond, white girl, it was harder to stand out from all the other blond, white girls. She clearly thought I was a safe person to say this to, since we're both white. I made it super clear that was *not* the case and called her the hell out on her garbage. The only way I managed to smile and walk away afterward was lots of practice, fear of the judges, and my pageant-bred self-esteem. It took me *years* to be able to walk across the stage with even a fraction of the confidence I see on this cosplay stage.

A fat girl goes up onstage next, cosplaying as Mrs. Hudson, walking daintily in kitten heels with a teacup and saucer in hand. She pauses at the center of the stage to toast the crowd with her teacup and toss a secretive wink, and the crowd goes wild.

"Ahhh, such a cute smile!" Cakes gushes from two seats down.

"I know, and that wink, ahhh, she's killing it!" Ami adds, flapping her hands excitedly with more enthusiasm than I've seen from her so far. Is this what she's like when her guard is totally down?

When Lady takes her walk as Violet Hunter, her reaction from the crowd is unparalleled. There's murmuring everywhere, and I catch little bits like "such detail" and "can't believe how accurate" and so on. She's got the most accurate category in the bag, I think. Kay and their friends loudly profess their love for Lady during her whole time onstage, until she takes her seat next to them. Everyone around us turns to shower Lady with compliments, until the next contestant strides onstage. Ami gives an audible squeak then leaps to her feet and shouts, "WORK IT, GORGEOUS!"

"I LOVE YOU, AMI!" they shout back, striding across the stage like they own it in what looks like a genderbent version of the villain Moriarty.

"I have never wanted to *be* a suit so bad in my life," Cakes groans, and someone in the row in front of us laughs her agreement.

"That's one of Ami's good Scroll friends," Kay whispers to me. "They haven't gotten to hang out much this weekend, but ze's probably her closest fandom friend after Lady and Cakes."

I hum an acknowledgment. Every person who walks onstage, no matter what they look like, gets some sort of compliment from Kay, Ami, and Cakes.

"That hair, I want to *bathe* in it! What brand of dye do you think she uses?"

"Can you believe those eyes? They're like . . . glowing!"

"Boobs." (A chorus of nods.)

"That stubble is *yum*."

"Oh my God, that costume must have taken *hours*, look at the stitching!"

Kay keeps up a running narration as people they know go across the stage, as if I'm not sitting here with my entire worldview shattered at my feet. I've never considered myself a judgmental person. I'm a lesbian, art nerd fangirl—I don't have much room to judge anyone for anything. And I've never judged anyone for their body or their clothing choices or anything. I do pageants, and I love the fashion and the fitness, but I'm not *shallow*.

At least, I didn't think I was.

And yet, it never occurred to me before that any of these

people could be considered truly *beautiful*. And there's a vast gulf between not judging someone for their appearance and actively appreciating their beauty.

When an utterly adorable boy dressed as a trash can with a John Watson wig rushes offstage, the music begins to wind down, and the green-haired guy smiles out at the crowd.

"Well, that was our last contestant! Did— Oh, what?" He pauses as a con staff member runs up to him with a final cue card, then he returns to the mic. "Never mind, apparently we have one more costume to see! Everyone, please give it up for . . ." He squints down at the card. "Miss North Carolina?"

My chest seizes up, panic stealing all the breath from my lungs as Miss North Carolina herself strides onstage, resplendent in her glittering evening gown and heels. Beside me, Kay goes absolutely rigid. A flurry of confused murmuring washes through the audience as Madison takes her first few steps to the edge of the stage, poses with her hands on her hips, then twirls and moves to the next position at center stage. Before long, though, the crowd begins to clap for her just like they did for everyone else. Embracing her, even though she's clearly not one of them. Miss North Carolina smiles like it's music to her ears, winking and popping her hips, soaking up the audience reaction. The murmurs continue even through the applause, though, all around me:

"Is that one of the girls from that Space Teen Whatever pageant?"

"What's she doing here? Pretty sure that's not TGG related. At all."

"Maybe she needed a practice walk in those heels? My ankles are breaking just looking at them."

One person is completely silent, though.

Beside me, Kay sits with their fingers clutched in the loose fabric of their cosplay army pants, seemingly unable to move or speak. In all the other close calls we've had with Madison, they've never looked this scared. I reach out to take their hand— then freeze. What am I *doing*? I have to get out of here! Madison can't see me here, or I'm absolutely ruined. But Kay lets out a high, thin whine that sounds so painfully familiar; it's the one I make when I'm having a nightmare and I need to scream but my throat won't work. I can't just leave them here. I take a steadying breath then grab their hand and tug.

"Come on, we have to get out of here," I say, trying to pry their fingers loose from the rough cloth. "It'll be so much worse if she—"

"Teagan, Kaylee! Oh my God, there you are!"

But I'm too late.

I close my eyes, and all the color drains from my face.

No, please, *no*.

I shrink down in my chair as if it'll make me invisible. *Go away, let it be some other Teagan, it's a trendy name, surely there's another one somewhere and*—

A thin, manicured hand lands on my shoulder. I look up into sharp, precisely lined eyes sparkling with intent, and my heart stops. Madison's time onstage was brief, but she only had one mission being here.

And I know what it is.

"It's so great to see you! Are you here to blow off a bit of steam with your girlfriend before the pageant finals tomorrow? Don't worry, you *totally* got into the top fifteen, I'm sure of it! You're *definitely* Miss Cosmic Teen USA material," she says, overemphasizing every bubbly word with a significant glance at the intently listening crowd around us.

I grit my teeth. "What are you doing here?"

Her face twists into a mockery of innocence. "Oh, you know I can never get enough of pageants, but I'm really here for a bit of practice, of course! One can never practice walking onstage in these shoes too much. You know how it is! Those heels you wore for the evening gown portion looked *so* challenging. Sorry again about your dress, by the way. I'm sure you'll look great in whatever you wear tomorrow."

I don't know what to say. For the first time in my entire life, I am 100 percent speechless. I cast about for some way I can play this off, to justify my presence at a con event to Madison, something I can do to salvage the situation. But before I can so much as take a breath, Madison changes targets—to Kay.

"Hi, Kaylee! Or should I say . . ." She pauses, squints at Kay's badge. "KayfortheWin net? So funny to bump into each other here, right? Lucky we did, because I got this amazing picture of you while you were up onstage. One should always keep a record of one's pageant performances to learn from, you know? But don't worry, I posted it on my private Posted account so you can save a copy later."

Madison flips her phone around, showing an unmistakable photo of Kay in their very masculine cosplay, looking happy and confident as they struck a wide-legged stance with folded arms. The caption below reads:

"Look who I ran into here in Florida! Apparently the convention for that TV show *The Great Game* is happening right here in the same hotel, and our very own Kaylee Beaumont is a well-known gay fan fiction author! Small world, right? Make sure you use they/them pronouns next time you see Kaylee. And you won't believe who their girlfriend is!"

She wears a sweet smile the whole time, but the threat is clear. "Come on, Tea, it's almost curfew! We need our beauty sleep before the finals tomorrow. See you at school, Kaylee. Say good night to your *girlfriend*."

Then she smiles at me, a hard, razor-edged thing that clearly states: *I win. Eat it, bitch.* She gives a cutesy wave to all the people staring at the train wreck she caused then pops her hip and walks away, a queen on her catwalk.

She made one mistake, though. I saw her private Posted username.

I manage to get my brain together just enough to snap a picture of her right in front of the heavily decorated entrance to the ballroom. The photo is a bit dark, but she's clearly recognizable against a sign advertising the TGG cosplay pageant, with rainbow flags and themed decorations all around. Maybe blackmail will keep her quiet. Or it'll be mutually assured destruction, at least.

But as soon as she's out the door, the rest of the world trickles back in—and with it, the sound of Kay openly weeping next to me. I feel the entire room staring at us, nearly silent at first, then humming with murmurs. I take a shaky, shallow breath and finally flick my eyes up to Kay's face . . . but their eyes are locked on their phone screen, which spills over with notifications. A call pops up on the screen from MOM'S CELL, and Kay lets out an audible sob.

"Kay—" I start, reaching for them, but they flinch away like my hand is made of spiders.

"Get away from me," they say, shaking their head like they've seen a ghost. "Get the ever-loving *fuck* away from me, Teagan."

My heart crumples in my chest. No. It can't end like this, not after—

"Kay, please, can we just—"

"No, we cannot *just* anything. This is over. *Everything* is over."

The tears burst over their cheeks, dripping onto their cosplay outfit, but the camouflage hides them perfectly as they push past me and run out of the room. I stumble to my feet and look around the room.

Everyone stares. All eyes are on me, but unlike at a pageant, I feel small and worthless. Like a freak. I press my lips together to hold back the anguish building in my chest.

But I fail at that, too.

I run from the room, Kay's friends right on my heels, the staring faces a blur through my tears.

Chapter Twenty-one

*

KAYLEE

I barely make it into the elevator before I start sobbing, huge, racking gasps that split my chest in two.

I can never go home again. Everyone knows now. They know *everything*. How can I possibly sit in a class with Madison ever again, knowing what she did to me? I've been too much of a chicken to pick up the phone or listen to my mom's three voice mails. I'm probably grounded until graduation. Or maybe she'll make me homeschool for the last year so I can't spread my "deviance" to other people. I wish I could be shocked at how quickly she found out, but it's actually the least surprising part of this whole thing. Gunnar Hudson almost certainly follows Madison's private Posted account, considering he's been trying to date her all year. His mom and my mom are best friends. He tells his mom, she tells my mom, and there you have it: small-town drama spread in mere minutes. It's a sick cycle I've seen play out a hundred times . . . though never before with me as the target.

And then there's Teagan.

What can I even say to her? She's a pageant girl like Madison. She'll be fine after this. Even if she gets in trouble and loses this pageant, she still has tons of scholarship money she's won in the past, and she's beautiful and confident and able to put up whatever front she wants. She's so good at being whoever she needs to be.

Do I even know the real her?

I feel sick.

When the elevator dings its fourteenth-floor arrival, I stumble out and down the hall toward the room, trying and surely failing to look like I haven't been bawling my eyes out. When I finally look up and see the scene at the end of the hall, I very nearly turn around and leave.

Teagan stands in the open doorway of the room next to ours, sobbing in the arms of a stunningly gorgeous Black girl who glares at me as I approach. My eyes cut to the little state cutouts on the door above them—this must be Miss Pennsylvania. My friends are clustered around them, all wearing worried expressions and looking vaguely out of breath. They must have sprinted up the stairs to beat me here.

"Kay," Cakes says, drawing everyone's attention. Teagan's head whips up, and her wet eyes find mine immediately. She drops her arms from around the other girl and sweeps gracefully down the hall toward me with a pleading expression. She even *walks* like Madison. My lip curls.

"Kay, I'm so sorry that happened. I have a plan to make sure she stays quiet, please let me show you," she says, reaching out for one of my hands. I snatch it away and take a step back as if she's on fire, averting my eyes from her tearstained face.

"It's too late. The whole school already knows everything about me. My mother has been blowing up my phone ever since that post went up, because *that's* the kind of town I live in," I snarl, beating back the small part of me that wants to give in.

"Besides, aren't you worried you'll get caught by the pageant moms?"

She cuts me off with a sharp gesture, her voice ragged and broken. "I don't care anymore. I really don't. If one of them walked up to me right now, I'd come out to their face. If they want to throw me out of the pageant, then fine, but I'm done hiding. I never wanted any of this to hurt you. This isn't just a weekend to me, Kay, I *really* like you and—"

I bark a harsh laugh. "*Of course* this is just a weekend. There was never going to be any kind of 'after.' You're here to win your little beauty pageant, and I'm here to drown myself in fandom and be queer while I can get away with it. Once this weekend is over, I'm marching right back into my North Carolina closet until college. Sure, maybe we'd message for a few weeks after, but that's all this would ever be. All it was *ever* going to be."

For the first time, Teagan's face hardens a bit, and she draws back a step. "What exactly is the huge problem you have with pageants, anyway? If I win tomorrow, it'll pay for an entire year at my dream college, and I'll get to spend a whole year doing sponsored charity work. Why is that a bad thing?"

"It's degrading," I spit back. "Parading around in a swimsuit for a bunch of old men—"

"This pageant doesn't even *have* a swimsuit category," she protests, but I'm on a roll now, and I can't stop myself. We're practically shouting, but everyone else has faded into the background, and all I can feel is the throbbing bullet of hurt forcing the air from my lungs.

"What you're doing is harmful for *all* women everywhere. You're only thinking of yourself, what *you* get out of it. What about the rest of us, who don't fit neatly into the unfair beauty standards you're perpetuating or into the gender binary at all? No one you saw onstage tonight would ever be accepted into one of your pageants because society thinks we're all *ugly*. *You* keep that shit going."

"But I *don't*! And in real pageants—"

"*Real* pageants?" I snarl. "Hate to break it to you, but what you saw tonight *was* a *real* pageant, with real people and their real beauty. Everything you do is fake."

Teagan shakes her head, her expression twisting as she holds back a sob.

"Well," she continues quietly, "looks like I'll get judged no matter where I go, so I guess I should at least get a free ride to college out of the deal."

Her eyes dry up instantly, as if on command, and her expression falls into blankness. Her spine straightens, and she lifts her chin.

"So glad I could be your 'checklist' for the weekend," Teagan says, quiet and firm.

It stings for just a second, with a flicker of something like guilt, but I shove it away. We don't even live in the same state, and we're only here for a weekend. How could anyone expect anything different? And look at her, just like that, like putting on a mask. She'll do anything to get what she wants, I guess. I won't be part of it.

"People like you make life hell for people like me every day," I say to her, just as Miss North Carolina opens her door to watch the proceedings. Case in point. I nod in her direction. "You're no better than her."

She flinches like she's been slapped, but the expression is gone as quickly as it appeared.

"We really do live in two different worlds, I guess," Teagan murmurs. Then she turns on her heel, takes Miss Pennsylvania by the arm, and disappears into their room, slamming the door behind her.

I feel Miss North Carolina's gaze on me as my friends herd me back into our room and press tissues into my hands. Not one of them tells me how ridiculous I've been, or how silly I was to let myself get so involved in such a short time. They just pile onto the bed with me, put on an episode of TGG, feed me cookies, and comfort me in one giant cuddle pile.

And if I cry more easily than usual at the sad parts of the episode, well. No one says anything.

This'll all make great emotional fuel for a story one day.

Part III

SUNDAY

Chapter
Twenty-two

TEAGAN

When I wake to the sight of Jess returning from the bathroom with my altered dress slung over her arms, I have to bury my face in the pillow to keep a fresh wave of tears from spilling over. I've been horrible to her this weekend. She's my best friend, and I've ignored her the entire weekend for a fling with someone I barely know who turned out to hate me anyway, whom I can't even be angry at anymore because I'm just so *tired*. Physically and mentally, because I was up until three in the morning finishing the alterations to my evening gown. And now Jess is taking care of me in the aftermath, thinking of the things I'll need today without even being asked.

I've never been so glad to have a friend like her, who knows me so completely and still likes me.

"You're a saint, Jess," I say as she hangs my dress up on the curtain rod.

She smiles softly at me. "Don't mention it. You've had a hell of a weekend. I've already showered, so get yourself woken up, and I'll make sure you get to breakfast on time. Don't forget to pack sunscreen."

My head falls back against the pillow, and I groan. "Oh God, today's the water park photo shoot. I've never felt less like having fake fun for a camera."

"So don't have fake fun," Jess says, grabbing my hands and dragging my dead weight into a sitting position. "Have *real* fun. You love waterslides. And dolphins and shit. Let it all go for the morning, okay?"

So I do.

Or at least I try.

I let Jess throw me into the shower, nurse me through break-fast, and drag me through the start of the event, smiling at cam-eras, ogling girls (non-pageant only) in their bathing suits and trying not to feel guilty about it. I have nothing to feel guilty about. No Kay, no problem. Kay doesn't exist.

I pet a dolphin, ride the waterslide four times in a row, and have staged competitions with my fellow beauty queens at a water obstacle course. I take every opportunity to boost Jess, too, talking her up in informal interviews and pushing her in front of me for photo ops. She deserves it. All in all, it's not a bad day. The Florida sunshine burns hot and bright on my heavily lotioned skin, and I reapply sunscreen after every single water exposure out of an excess of paranoia. It's a total trap, taking us somewhere that we could get badly sunburned right before the pageant finals, and I'm not about to fall into it. I keep my smile on, prance around for the judges with dollar signs in my eyes, and thank God all this is paid for by some sponsor who wants the photos and publicity.

And yet, when it's over and they drop us back at the hotel for a late lunch, my chest feels like an echo chamber.

I enjoyed the things I did, but it's almost like it all happened to someone else and I only read about it. I put on the mask, went through the motions. My friends were great. I hung out with Jess and Oregon who, it turns out, is just as awesome as Jess promised she would be, so now I have two friends I'm out to at this pageant. We bonded with another group of girls representing a bunch of the western states, laughed a ton, and actually—despite everything—managed to have a pretty good time.

My obsession with how fandom and the con made me feel completely overshadowed one of the things I love most about pageants: the sisterhood. People think we're at each other's throats all weekend, catty and bitchy or whatever. It's not like that at all, though. It's just a big group of ambitious, supersmart young women who are competing, yes, but also supporting each other and sharing a fun weekend together. I *like* pageants and the people who do them, and I really resent that Kay and the con almost made me forget that. Especially with how great Jess and Oregon were to me this morning. They even managed to keep Miss North Carolina away from me all day, though no amount of distance could dampen the radiant power of her smugness.

I honestly expected the entire pageant to know everything this morning. My giant lesbian secret. My fandom obsession. Hell, I half expected to have hundreds of Scroll notifications from pageant enemies across the world when I woke up this morning. The nothingness is almost worse. I'm waiting for the hammer to fall, for some final blow to come from Miss North Carolina. I sent her my blackmail, the photo I managed to snag of her yesterday, and I know she saw it. No word, though. No judges or group moms have come to give me a gentle talking-to about anything, either. But she still *knows*, and just that fact is enough to throw me off my game.

Maybe Madison knows it's already over for me. Maybe she

knows I didn't make it into the top fifteen, so she's let it go. Maybe she realizes she's done enough damage.

Except she hasn't.

I have a plan. It's probably a terrible one, probably one that will lose me the scholarship and get me banned from any future pageants. But I want to see the look on Madison's face. If I'm going out, I want to go out with a bang. I want to be the girl the judges see during my interviews, during my stage time. The wicked firestarter, unstoppable and driven. I lost sight of that somewhere, I think.

I'll get it back. Tonight.

If I'm in the top fifteen.

My hair is still dripping wet from my post–water park shower when my phone rings. I leap for it, scrabbling to unlock it with wet fingers, and—

"Hello?" I say in a rush.

"You aren't smiling."

My shoulders collapse. Just my pageant coach. I don't know what I was imagining—some terrible combination of Kay, of judges and chaperones, of my dad out on one of his endless business trips somehow getting wind of everything and calling to check on me. Instead:

". . . hi, Rhonda."

My dearly devoted pageant coach sighs on the other end of the line. "What's this I hear about a dress emergency?"

I groan internally but don't dare make a sound, lest I get a verbal slap on the wrist. The pageant community is frighteningly small, and I'm honestly surprised it took her this long to hear about it. And at the same time: so grateful it's this and not my *other* drama.

"Miss North Carolina stepped on my dress with her demon

hooves after the prelims. Intentionally. There was no saving it. I'm wearing my backup dress today."

"You don't *have* a backup dress," she snaps, audibly puffing up into full-blown scolding mode. "You should have called me right away! I could have overnighted something to you, and you could have had it steamed while you were at the water park, and you could have—"

"No!" I shout, the single word echoing back to me in the steamy bathroom. I look up at my own damp, bedraggled face in the fogged-up mirror, surprised at my audacity. I never talk back to Rhonda, and the sharpness of her silence is like a razor waiting to slice me open. But I push on.

"No. The overnight costs would have been outrageous, and you know I can't afford it. Not to mention the cost of a new dress. And it wouldn't be altered. I'm not willing to go into more debt for this. I already had to put the plane ticket on a credit card."

Rhonda's voice is deadly quiet when she responds. "You cannot wear that white monstrosity, especially not when your top competition is also wearing white. You have not gotten this far to waste your best chance in a terrible dress that the judges will hate."

"I've got a plan to make it work," I say, running a large-tooth comb through my hair with my other hand. I'm so done with this conversation already.

"Oh God, Teagan, I don't even want to know."

She huffs and puffs with indignation, working herself up into a truly stunning lecture. But despite her roughness, I know she likes me and honestly wants me to succeed. She's always supported me, wanted the best for me, and I don't want to take her down with me. So I make it easy for her.

"Rhonda," I interrupt. "Listen. I wouldn't be here without

you. You've done so much for me, and I'll always be grateful. That's why I think it's best if we don't work together anymore. You don't need to be part of this."

The line is silent for another minute.

"Teagan," she begins, voice dripping with reluctance. "Please let me order you a dress from a store near the venue and have it driven over to you. We can salvage this. You don't have to do . . . whatever you're planning."

"I do," I say. "I *do* have to do this."

"I can have a dress to you within the hour, your choice. You've worked so hard, and I don't want to see you—"

"No." I exhale, long and slow. No more crying. Done enough of that. I pinch the bridge of my nose and keep my eyes squeezed tightly shut. "Thank you, Rhonda. Sincerely. But no."

She's quiet for so long that I half think the line has gone dead. Then she clears her throat.

"I'll send the contract termination paperwork to your father. It's been a pleasure working with you, Teagan."

"Likewise. Thank you for everything."

A muffled sound, then the line goes silent.

And that's it. I'm on my own.

Win or lose, I'm going out on my own terms.

Chapter Twenty-three

KAYLEE

I slept through all the Sunday panels.

It wasn't deliberate. It's not like I'm trying to mope over Teagan or anything, but I woke up every five minutes last night, replaying everything, wondering what the hell I'm going to do when I get home. I still haven't listened to my mom's voice mails or read her texts. I'm going to be in more trouble than I've ever known in my whole life when I finally get home, but the idea of facing it right now makes me profoundly tired. I just want to live in this fantasy world for a little while longer. I can never get away from anything when I'm at home, never have any power or control over my situation. Here, though . . . for just a short while longer, I can still pretend.

When I finally woke up this morning, I picked up my phone to read through Scroll in bed for a bit (like you do) and found my DMs stuffed with messages from people at the con.

SuperSnogs:
Kay, are you alright? I saw you with that girl at the

cosplay pageant, and I think I saw you crying when you left. I'm sorry for whatever it was. <3 <3 <3

KayfortheWinnet:
I'm fine. Thanks for checking on me. <3

Anonymous:
Wtf was that? Why did you bring a beauty queen to a fandom event? Are you insane?

KayfortheWinnet:
I didn't bring her, she just showed up to torment me. Also, Nonny? You're an asshole.

Anonymous:
hope your ok. We never talk but I like your blog, and your fics always brighten my days. feel better soon

KayfortheWinnet:
Thanks, Nonny, appreciate it. Glad you enjoy my fics. More coming soon.

AnyaLovesSwoop: Don't let grouchy anons or pageant girls bring you down. You're beautiful and fantastic and you deserve everything

KayfortheWinnet:
ilu my dear. Thanks for this. <3

Anonymous:
Your a whore

KayfortheWinnet:
You're*

There are nineteen messages total, including no less than five asking for the whole story. They're only going to keep coming once everyone wakes up and sees the spillover from last night, so I finally give up and post a very brief summary to get everyone off my back.

> Look, I don't want to talk about this, but I also don't want my DMs overflowing with questions about it for the next forever, so here's your five-second summary. The beauty queen who walked the stage last night goes to my school. No one there knew that I write queer fanfic or that I'm queer myself. Now they do, because of her. The girl I was arguing with was also a pageant girl, but . . . different maybe? Or so I thought. She was the first girl I ever kissed. She respected my pronouns. But now it's over. I don't 100% know how to feel about it.
>
> I hope that answers all your questions, because I'd rather not get any more messages about it.

But of course, this is Scroll, so everyone ignores the last bit and has to immediately tell me all their opinions on everything.

Anonymous:
I didn't think you swung that way

KayfortheWinnet:
It's a bit of a recent discovery. Trying hard not to regret it.

Anonymous:
what is it with girls pretending they're bi for five seconds to get sympathy? not working here, sorry

KayfortheWinnet [draft]:
Honestly, screw you, nonny. What

[delete]

ConsultingMi221b:
Get off Scroll and get ready for your luncheon! You deserve that contract.

KayfortheWinnet [private reply]:
Thanks for taking care of me and kicking my ass all
weekend/year/lifetime. I'll get up in a few minutes. Hope
y'all are having fun at the panels.

TheGreatGamer:
I'm not at the con, so I don't really understand what's
going on. Message me? Wish I'd been able to come to
con and meet you. :(

KayfortheWinnet [private reply]:
Maybe later this week. Too exhausted by the whole
thing right now. Wish you were here.

LadiesLady:
Soooo, if you're identifying as queer now, maybe we
can chat sometime? ••

KayfortheWinnet [private reply]:
Sorry LL, but whole thing is still very new and I'm not
really eager to dive right into something else. Thanks for
your interest, I think?

Yikes.

Finally, 3:30 P.M. rolls around, and I can't avoid the rest of
the world anymore. The luncheon (and announcement of the
winner of the writing contest) is in half an hour, and I really
should muster up some enthusiasm for that. A vague stirring
of the excitement I felt yesterday flickers in my chest, pathetic
compared to how I should feel, but it's something. Maybe once
I get moving, I'll feel better.

I drag myself into the bathroom and take the fastest shower
possible, the raspy hotel showerhead pummeling me with stinging spray. I throw on whatever clothes are left in my bag, run a
comb through my hair, then take a look at my face in the mirror
and stop.

What am I *doing?*

This luncheon could be really important for me. I've never
thought writing could be a real career option, but what if this
is the start of something bigger? I could meet important people. They deserve a little effort, not this half-assed, empty-eyed
human who looks like they could be walking to their doom, not
one of the greatest opportunities of their life.

I slick my hands up with some product and shape my hair
into something a little less heartbroken-in-bed and a little more
possible-future-professional, then I swap out the ratty T-shirt
I'd grabbed for something with buttons. The buttons fight with
me at first (my ultimate nemeses, ugh), but a quick bra change
later, I'm finally dressed and looking like a semi-competent

human. Not up to Teagan's standards, I'm sure, but well enough for me.

It's not like her opinion matters, anyway.

I pull out my phone to double-check the time and location for the luncheon, ignoring the mountain of new Scroll messages waiting for me, and tug the last wrinkles out of my shirt.

Into battle.

I'm grateful for the buttons when I arrive at the luncheon to find it in the fancier of the two hotel restaurants, tucked away in a private room with a white tablecloth on the table and a centerpiece of fresh flowers. I'm not sure what I was expecting, but the luncheon is apparently going to be much smaller and more intimate than I thought, just one large table with six place settings. I recognize the three people already seated immediately: ImprobableEgg, the coordinator of the contest; Alyford, the founder and coordinator of GreatCon, and . . . Irishtea23.

Irishtea is here.

My heart leaps into my throat . . . then immediately crashes back down. I never really thought I had a chance at winning this contest, but there's no way I could ever win out over Irishtea. She's seated next to the contest coordinator and chatting easily, looking pretty and professional in a sundress and cardigan. I glance down at my semi-wrinkled trousers and button-down with a despairing look. It's bad enough that I'm the youngest person here by at least ten years. With this look going on? I must seem like an utter child to them.

Nonetheless, they look up and greet me with cheery smiles as I approach the table, directing me to a seat next to Irishtea. My full, real name is written in pretty looping script on a tiny card beside a sweating water glass, with my Scroll/Archive handle written just beneath like a serious job title. It's weird to see my online persona given so much weight in this context, placed next to gleaming, silver-rimmed plates and fancy, spiral-shaped chunks of butter.

I peek out of the corner of my eye to see if others have taken the artfully folded napkin off their plate to put in their lap yet, but no one else has, so I fold my hands in my lap instead to keep myself from accidentally touching the wrong thing. Am I allowed to drink the water yet? Will there be something with caffeine on order? Because damn, I would willingly rewatch the Episode That Must Not Be Named for a glass of sweet tea.

I glance up from my lap to find three sets of eyes fixed on me, soft with sympathy, and the worst realization of the morning hits me right in the chest. The fandom people at this table were probably all there last night to witness the whole awful confrontation with Miss NC, and if they follow me on Scroll, they probably saw my post about it this morning. I know Aiden, the contest coordinator, follows me, at least, and his eyes say he definitely knows. God, how embarrassing.

Then Irishtea smiles at me and gives my shoulder a gentle shove.

"It's good to see you again, Kay! I'm so excited you're the other person up for the anthology spot. How cool is this?"

It takes just a second too long to process that, yes, Irishtea both knows me from my writing and recognizes me from our meeting yesterday and is now speaking to me like an equal. Wild.

"Really cool," I say, then cringe. What a totally boring and meaningless thing to say. Move past it. "It's no surprise to see you here, honestly."

"You know, that never gets old," she says. "Every time someone talks to me about liking my writing, I'm as giddy as the very first time. It means a ton. Have you met Aiden and Aly?"

Irishtea gestures to the others at the table, a middle-aged, blond man with a rainbow flag pinned to his shirt collar, and a young woman in her late twenties with artsy clothes and black hair dye. I give them a little wave. "Only in email or on Scroll. Thank you both for putting all this together."

"So happy to do it," Aiden says. "I've read every Holmes adaptation out there and what feels like every fic in the fandom, so it's really more of a treat for myself if I'm honest."

His eyes flick to the doorway just then, and his expression smooths into something polite and professional, so I turn just in time to see a man and a woman in their forties enter the room, dressed in crisp, professional suits. The same ones who were at my panel yesterday. The editor and the agent.

It begins.

The others stand up when they approach, so I do, too, hastily scooting back from the table and sloshing a bit of water onto the pristine tablecloth. Are we supposed to stand for these people like they're judges or something? Is that etiquette I somehow missed out on in my life? But then everyone starts to shake hands for introductions, and I get it. When it's my turn, the man takes my hand in a firm grip and a sincere smile.

"Les Vanetti, editor with 221b Press at Waterhorse Publishing. And this is my wife," he says, stepping aside so she can take his place.

"Mariana Heimish," she says, her handshake just as commanding. "Literary agent with the Fairchild Agency. Pleasure to meet you."

"You too," I manage, a bit dazed and starstruck.

We all take our seats, and as soon as we do, a waiter sweeps in with a tray full of salads. And, thank the powers that be, a blessedly sweet and refreshingly cold pitcher of iced tea. A few sips and I'm feeling almost human enough to participate in the small talk around the table. I learn where everyone's from, how long they've been in fandom, what their past fandoms were, and, once the main course comes out, how GreatCon got started four years ago, and what goes into running it. (Answer: a lot. It's impressive.)

As we get toward the tail end of the main course (a fantastic vegetarian lasagna), the questions turn more toward Irishtea and me. What prompted us to post our first fanfic, how we feel about the level of reader-author interaction that comes with fandom, and why we decided to make the leap to writing our own original takes on Holmes for the contest. When they finally ask how long we've been writing in the TGG fandom, I feel like shrinking into my chair.

"Just over five years," Irishtea answers. "The hiatus between seasons one and two was killing me, and I had to do something. The characters and the world wouldn't let me go."

As soon as she finishes, all eyes swivel to me. I cough and shift in my seat.

"Um, I've only been posting for about a year. I wrote my first fic in the summer between my sophomore and junior years because of how much I loved her stories," I say, gesturing to Irishtea.

"That's one thing I'm proud to be at fault for!" Irishtea says with a laugh. "But honestly, what you said yesterday, Kay, when you were all surprised about me reading your stuff?"

I nod, and she continues, "The fact that you've been writing in this fandom for less time than I have doesn't have any impact on the quality of your work. Your fics have attracted the kind of following they have because you're talented and you write things people want to read. That has nothing to do with how long you've been writing fic. Or with age, because I know that's on your mind, too."

"Amen, couldn't have said it better myself," Ms. Heimish says. "In fact, your work reads like someone who's been writing for a lot longer than a year. Have you written in other fandoms?"

I blush and look down at my plate. "TGG is the first fandom I've ever written for, but I've been writing my own stories since fourth grade. I've written a few full-length novels since I started high school." My lips twist in a self-deprecating smile. "The early ones are all terrible, but I've learned a lot from them, and the more recent ones are getting better."

Ms. Heimish smiles and raises an eyebrow. "I was hoping you'd say that. Once either of you has a polished original novel ready to go, I'd be happy to see a query letter and sample pages."

She takes a stack of business cards from her wallet and passes one to each of us. "Just mention how we met, and I'll make sure my assistant requests your full manuscript right away. I can't promise I'll take you on as a client, but I'll be sure to read it and give you a personal reply."

I turn the card over in my hand, stunned. The typeface on it is slightly raised and almost shiny, and I run my thumb over it in awe.

"Thank you so much. This is . . . ," my mouth says without my input. A literary agent wants to read one of my books? My mind turns to my most recent one, just completed two months ago and badly in need of revising. Could it be good enough to actually share? Maybe . . . maybe I could let Lady, Ami, and Cakes read it and give me some feedback? The thought fills me with dread. But then I picture Ami standing over me months ago to make sure I actually submitted to the contest, doing her "be brave" flex every time I come close to chickening out of something. I *did* submit. I *did* come to the con. And even though it was disastrous, I *did* take a chance and complete my checklist for the weekend. It didn't have the best ending, but I accomplished the goal—figuring out my identity. And I'm here, a finalist for the contest.

A little bravery pays off.

The waiter comes by to clear our plates and passes out neat slices of cheesecake with delicate designs drawn on the plate in a bright-red sauce. I take mine automatically and peek up at the agent through my lashes. She catches me looking and smiles, her features softening. The offer is sincere, I guess. I will frame that business card and put it next to my favorite writing spot.

"And now, to the business of today," Mr. Vanetti says, and I sit up straight with a jolt of adrenaline. My heart kicks into gear, beating wildly at my ribs while the richly sweet scent of cheese-cake fills my nose and turns my stomach. The editor pulls out an envelope, withdraws a stack of papers, then clears his throat.

"This contest was incredibly difficult to judge. A panel of fan judges narrowed the playing field for me a bit, but I still had fifteen excellent short stories to read before this weekend. I narrowed it down to the two of you eventually, but then I spent all of Friday and Saturday agonizing over the decision. That's why you got the luncheon invitation so late, by the way. Completely my fault, not Aiden's at all.

"I finally asked him to invite both of you because, after reading your stories and spending so much time on this, I wanted to meet you and congratulate you personally on your accomplishment. It's hard to write something original enough to stand out in the wide world of Holmes pastiche, and you both managed to do it and do it well. That said, I spent yesterday afternoon on the phone with the publisher confirming my choice and got the final go-ahead to make my offer."

It's probably unprofessional of me, but I have to close my eyes and take several long, deep breaths to prepare myself for the disappointment. I know there's no way I can compete with a writer as experienced as Irishtea, so one by one, I force all of my wired muscles to uncoil, ridding them of the tension of expectation. There's nothing to expect. It's not going to happen.

"So, that said," the editor begins, leafing through the papers in his hands, "I'm pleased today to extend an offer of publication in our upcoming Holmes pastiche anthology . . . to both of you."

All the air leaves my lungs in a rush. Irishtea squeals and pulls me into a sideways hug, rocking me back and forth as she whispers fiercely in my ear, "I'm so *happy* for you!"

I manage to raise one hand and pat her on the arm and stutter a vague "congratulations" in return. I finally notice that the editor is holding a small stack of papers out to each of us and withdraw from Irishtea's embrace enough to take it.

A contract. With my name on it.

I'm getting published.

My words are getting *published*!

A grin breaks over my face, and I laugh, feeling it in a way I haven't felt anything all day. Like daylight breaking into the dark place my brain and heart have become. I didn't realize just how thoroughly I had convinced myself I wasn't good enough until suddenly . . . I *was*.

"Really?" I ask.

"Really," Mr. Vanetti replies. "I called the publisher and asked if we could add another sixteen pages to the book to accommodate two stories instead of one. He ran the numbers and agreed but said the stories had better be worth it. And they are. You are both incredibly talented, and I'm pleased to be able to offer you this opportunity."

"Though, Kaylee," Ms. Heimish cuts in, "since you're still under eighteen, you'll need to have a parent or guardian cosign that contract. Make sure you have someone read it with you."

"I will," I say, nodding like some kind of bobblehead doll. I have no idea how I'll get my mom to agree to signing it, but I'll figure it out. "I will, as soon as I get home. God, I can't believe this."

I turn to Irishtea, tears brimming, and manage a watery smile for her. "Thank you for inspiring me to start writing Sherlock and John. I wouldn't be here if not for you. And thank you for reading my fic, even though—"

"Even though *nothing*, Kay," she says, cutting me off with a fierce grip on my hand. "Did you really expect us all to judge your writing by your age or how long you've been in the fandom? That's out of your control. What *is* under your control is how hard you work and how seriously you take your writing. That's all you."

"Besides," Alyford says, "the whole point of fandom is the community of acceptance. We're here to support each other in our weird obsessions no matter where we come from or what we're like in real life."

Her words hit me like a punch in the gut, and all the thoughts of Teagan I've been holding back come rushing to the fore.

No matter where we come from or what we're like in real life.

My face heats as I recall the confrontation in the hallway last night, all the terrible things I said to Teagan rushing back at once. Awful, hurtful, judgmental words that were really about Madison, *meant* for Madison, but landed on her instead. I was so hurt, and scared, and overwhelmed . . . and I lashed out in the worst way.

God, she's probably been programmed to hide everything, being in the pageant world as a gay fangirl, just like I have been as a queer enby in Plainsborough. Can I really blame her for obeying that instinct again? Yes, okay, I still am not the world's biggest fan of pageants and everything they stand for. But everything

Cakes, Lady, and Ami said to me Friday night is still true. Feminism is supporting women in their choices. Choosing to play sports, or drown in fandom, or do pageants; whether to have sex or not, whether to have kids or not, whether to wear a hijab or not. I would never judge someone for choosing to play a sport, so why should I judge Teagan for her particular avenue to college and self-confidence?

And then I flash to the things she *did* say and do—bringing me flowers even though she didn't know me well enough . . . yet, talking about how close Virginia and North Carolina are. She wanted more. She thought I was worth more. I could have had more, if I hadn't pushed her away so thoroughly. Everyone back home knows about me now, so there's no point in denying myself anymore.

But now it's too late.

Right?

Is it?

No matter where we come from or what we're like in real life.

"You're absolutely right, both of you," I say, scrabbling for my phone. "And I've forgotten that this weekend. Thanks for reminding me."

I open Scroll and pull up a new message, the app automatically filling in Teagan's URL when I type the first letter.

I'm so sorry, Teagan. I shouldn't have reacted that way.
I was judgmental and terrible, and I want to see you
again one more time before we leave so I can apologize
to your face.

I hesitate then add: I know I can't expect anything more than that
from you, so don't worry about . . . any of that. No pressure. I just want

to make things right. Good luck at the pageant today. I hope you win. You deserve it.

I hit SEND and do my best to focus back in on the conversation at the table, but when five minutes pass and I don't get a reply, I feel like crawling up the walls in my impatience. With a suppressed scream of frustration, I open a new browser window and, through some Google detective work, find the website for the pageant and pull up the schedule.

And that explains why she's not answering.

The finals are starting *right now.* She's competing for her scholarship, trying to overcome all her setbacks from yesterday to win a chance at her dream school.

And I was one of those setbacks.

I taste bile in the back of my throat as I shove my chair back and stand suddenly, the conversation around me halting awkwardly.

"I'm sorry, everyone," I babble, pushing my chair in and folding up the contract. "I really appreciate this opportunity, and I hate to duck out early, but there's something I have to do. I hope you don't mind—"

"Go," Irishtea says, reaching over to squeeze my hand like she understands. And hell, maybe she saw my post this morning. Maybe she does.

Mr. Vanetti passes me one of his business cards and offers his hand for me to shake again. "Please email me if you have any questions at all. We'll be in touch with a digital version of the contract and some revision notes. Congratulations again, Kaylee."

I suffer through Ms. Heimish giving me similar reassurances, but I hardly hear a word of it. I need to go, or I won't make it in time. I race out the door as soon as I possibly can without being unforgivably rude and type another message to Teagan as I run to the lobby and out the front door.

I'm coming to the pageant, I type, pausing at the crosswalk that will take me to the theater. I'm coming to cheer you on while you win your big scholarship. You've got this. You're brilliant.

And, with any luck, she'll be generous in her forgiveness, too.

The light at the crosswalk changes.

I run the whole way to the theater, my new contract clutched tight in my hand.

Chapter
Twenty-four

TEAGAN

*T*he stage lights burn into my skin as all fifty-one of us stand onstage, awaiting judgment. The opening number went off without any disasters or diva moments, and I managed to say "Teagan Miller, Virginia!" with a suitable amount of pep, but I can already tell I'm not really feeling it the way I did yesterday. I can't seem to find my spark, my energy.

And now here I stand as the hosts blather on about some inane thing, their attempts at witty banter falling flat and awkward, waiting to find out whether I fail out of this competition now, or whether I make it into the top fifteen and fail later. At this point, I think I'd rather it be over sooner. With no drive, no confidence, and a second-choice dress for the gown portion, making Top Five is never going to happen. I'll never even get the chance to execute my grand plan.

Holding the smile and pretending to listen to the hosts with interest is just starting to make my face hurt when last year's Miss Cosmic USA finally brings us around to the point.

"Last night," she says, "these fifty-one women competed in

a preliminary exhibition to narrow down the contestants for tonight's finals to the top fifteen. The judges scored the fifteen
girls who will advance based on a personal interview from Saturday morning and the stage categories: Introduction, Casual
Fashion Wear, and Evening Gown."

Her cohost, a guy in a terrible, pale-blue suit, lowers his voice
dramatically. "Those fifteen young women will have a chance
to strut their stuff again tonight, competing for one of the final
five spots and a chance to answer an onstage interview question
to solidify their standing. The judges have tallied the preliminary results, so let's meet our Miss Cosmic Teen USA Top Fifteen contestants! In completely random order, they are . . ."

He opens the envelope, and I brace myself for the adrenaline surge and letdown cycle. Each name always brings a spike
of excitement, then a crush of disappointment, over and over
until your name is called . . . or not. On the outside, we all re-
main perfectly calm and collected, ready to applaud each decision. This is the part of the pageant that always feels the longest,
as fifteen states are called in a row. The host takes a breath to
call the first name, and I settle in for the long—

"Virginia!"

I blink. That was fast.

I let my smile widen in acknowledgment and strut to the
front, striking a pose with a hand on my hip. I feel weirdly
exposed—I've never been the first name called before. The next
few names pass in a blur, though I clap politely for each. Even
for Miss North Carolina, who stands directly in front of me after
her introduction, completely blocking the view.

It's fine, though, because the next name called is Pennsylvania, and I pour my heart into clapping as loud as I can for Jess
as she walks past me with a beaming smile. Even if I can't get
excited on my own behalf, I can at least get hyped for Jess, who

totally deserves this. Before long, the top fifteen are all assembled at the front of the stage, and the rest of the girls are filing offstage as we're congratulated on making it to the semifinals.

The hosts blather on for another minute, giving me the time I really don't need to start second-guessing everything about today. Despite all the time I poured into the changes to my dress, I really wasn't expecting to make Top Fifteen after the disaster of last night. Guess there's more riding on my last-minute fix than I thought—the fix brainstormed and helped along by Kay and their friends. I even still have the purple shoes Lady let me borrow to complement the altered dress. It feels so wrong, to still be benefiting from it all after our fight yesterday, with how angry I *should* be at Kay but can't seem to muster the energy for. My pulse flutters, and nervous sweat springs up on my forehead, hopefully not visible to the judges. I wonder if anyone has a spare Red Bull I could chug really quick. That 3:00 A.M. bedtime is really catching up with me.

We're finally sent offstage to change for the casual fashion wear segment, and Jess accosts me in the wings as soon as we're out of sight. She grabs my hand and gives a nearly silent squeal, prancing in her heels like an excited puppy.

"We did it! I'm so happy for us! Top Five, here we come."

I muster up a smile for her and wrap an arm around her waist for a quick hug before we separate for our individual dressing tables. I shed my opening outfit as quickly as I can without a single thought for modesty and pull on my soft, lacy dress and flannel shirt, wiping off my lips for a lipstick change as soon as I have a free hand. California passes me a Red Bull with a bright smile in response to my general plea, and I crack it open and chug half, all I can do before it's time to reapply my lipstick. When I glance down to find the right color, though, my eye catches on my phone, with two new notifications glowing on the screen.

Messages from Kay.

I really, *really* should not care. I shouldn't waste any time looking, not during the most important pageant I've ever competed in . . . but honestly my chances of advancing are gone anyway, and even though they were cruel to me yesterday, I can see without unlocking the screen that the first three words are I'm so sorry.

I tug the rest of my clothes on, put on my boots, and reapply my lipstick in record time, then unlock the phone to read the messages.

KayfortheWinnet:
I'm so sorry, Teagan. I shouldn't have reacted that way.
I was judgmental and terrible, and I want to see you
again one more time before we leave so I can apologize
to your face. I know I can't expect anything more than
that from you, so don't worry about . . . any of that. No
pressure. I just want to make things right. Good luck at
the pageant today. I hope you win. You deserve it.

And another:

KayfortheWinnet:
I'm coming to the pageant. I'm coming to cheer you
on while you win your big scholarship. You've got this.
You're brilliant.

And as I read, another one pops up:

KayfortheWinnet:
Okay, that ticket was shockingly expensive, even after
the "show has already started" discount and the "look
at my pathetic tears" discount.

A watery laugh slips past my freshly colored lips, and tears threaten to ruin my makeup. A carefully applied tissue saves the day, and another message pops up as the stage director calls the one-minute warning.

KayfortheWinnet:
. . . I may have told him my girlfriend was in the pageant. Don't worry, I didn't say who. And it doesn't have to mean anything. But he was intrigued enough that he let me buy a ticket for the $25 I had in my wallet instead of a FREAKING HUNDRED, WHAT.

I snort a very un-pageant-like laugh and let the complicated feelings bubble up inside my chest, let them fill me with energy and purpose. I should still be angry. The things they said last night, the way they reacted, it really hurt. Worse than I thought it might. It was cruel.

But after a whole weekend of hiding, a whole *lifetime* of hiding, I'm just exhausted.

And here's one person who knows everything about me. Finally, one person who knows every piece of who I am, and they're here to support me. Out there, in that audience, waiting to cheer me on. I never have *anyone* in the audience there just for me.

(*Girlfriend*, they said . . .)

It's time to let it go. Put down all the burdens, put down all the shame, put down every heavy thing I've been dragging along these past few years. I've let the judgment of others sap my confidence for the last time.

My gaze lingers on my second-choice evening gown, a final plan solidifying in my mind as I send off a quick one-emoji response then rush over to wait in line for my turn to walk the catwalk in my fashion wear. And when I go out there, when I lift my chin and strut my stuff, there's one familiar voice that cheers louder than all the rest.

When I smile for the judges, it's real, and wicked, and full of promise.

I'm a firestarter—and it's time to light some fires.

Chapter Twenty-five

KAYLEE

I slip in the door and take the first seat I can find near the back of the room, squinting at the stage to look for Teagan's face. All the girls are wearing identical pink outfits that mostly just look awkward. Crop tops and just-above-the-knee skirts, very summery, bright, and not exactly ideal on anyone. They're calling individual states at an excruciatingly slow pace and with lots of flair as the harsh stage lights gleam off shockingly white teeth and glowing blond hair.

"It's your turn now . . . Arizonaaaaa!"

The crowd goes wild, so I'm guessing this is more than a basic introduction. Maybe this is that Top Fifteen thing Miss North Carolina mentioned yesterday? I squint against the clashing stage lights and darkness and finally spot Teagan right near the front, one hand propped on her hip and beaming out at the crowd. She claps politely for each name that's called, but there's something off in her expression. It's perfectly polished, but she seems . . . sad. Or resigned or something. Miss Florida's hometown crowd goes wild, a group of people in matching shirts doing some kind of coordinated chant, so I use the delay to pull out my phone and send Teagan a quick message:

KayfortheWinnet:
Okay, that ticket was shockingly expensive, even after the "show has already started" discount and the "look at my pathetic tears" discount.

May as well let her know I'm here. I'm sure she won't see the message until after the show, but hopefully it'll keep her from running off before I get a chance to see her. Onstage, Teagan perks up a bit and claps faster when Pennsylvania is called to the front, and I recognize her friend from the hallway, the one she's rooming with. I hope Pennsylvania is willing to forgive me. I know how protective I am of my friends, and if anyone had spoken to them the way I spoke to Teagan last night, I would have been furious.

Speaking of protective, I should probably warn Teagan.

KayfortheWinnet:
. . . I may have told him my girlfriend was in the pageant. Don't worry, I didn't say who. And it doesn't have to mean anything. But he was intrigued enough that he let me buy a ticket for the $25 I had in my wallet instead of a FREAKING HUNDRED, WHAT.

It's ridiculous how much money people pay to come to these things. And there was a merch stand out front, too, selling replica tiaras and thirty-dollar tank tops. I hope all that money goes into the scholarship fund for the winner. For Teagan, honestly, because she's definitely the most beautiful girl up there. Not that I'm biased. And not that beauty is the only thing that goes into these pageants. I know that now.

Most of the girls begin to funnel offstage, leaving Teagan, Miss Pennsylvania, Miss North Carolina (ugh), and twelve other girls at the front as the hosts introduce the group as the top fifteen who will advance to the semifinals. Miss NC may be a vicious harpy, but at least she was right about Teagan making it this far. I only hope she doesn't have any more sabotage planned for tonight.

They finally send the girls offstage to get changed for the next category and launch into some incredibly boring and awkward small talk. When they bring out some past winner to add to the awkwardness, I give up on paying attention and retreat to the sanctuary of my phone to pass the time.

I pull up Scroll, and sure enough, the envelope icon at the top has a little number nineteen beside it. I'll regret it, I'm sure, but I skim through the messages anyway and find that, as expected, 80 percent of them are bashing Madison and Teagan or berating me for my part in the whole thing. I can let the anonymous trolls roll off my back, but this isn't fair to Teagan, and once again, it's my fault. I've gotta fix this.

I open a blank text post and write as quickly as I can before Teagan gets back onstage.

Hi everyone. You may have noticed that I've deleted my earlier post about what happened at the fandom pageant last night. I appreciate the support you've all shown me, but the truth is that I'm the one who's been a horrible ass here and needs to apologize. A very smart person mentioned to me today that the whole point of being in fandom is community, acceptance, and support for our weirdness, no matter what we're like IRL. That support and acceptance shouldn't automatically go away if someone happens to have some things going for them in the real world, like conventional beauty.

The hosts swap out last year's winner for some other former pageant-winning woman, this one in her mid-twenties and with a stage presence that dominates. The awkwardness of the forced banter hasn't diminished, though, so I keep writing:

And honestly, the girl who was with me last night, T, has to hide so much every day, from just about everyone, including her fandom involvement. She needs this fandom community just as much as the rest of us, and I shunned her and acted cruelly. Is that what we are? Is that what we want fandom to be?

I understand some of the feelings you might be having. After all, I had them myself yesterday, when I lashed out at T. I've been bullied by pretty pageant girls, by the one you saw onstage yesterday specifically, and similar people my whole life. It's in my nature to be automatically distrustful of them. But when we do that to them, we're doing exactly what we don't want them to do to us. And I know some of you will feel justified in doing so and will resent me for making this post and for choosing to apologize for the way I treated T. I'm sorry for whatever has happened in your life that has given you that mindset. I know it must have been hard. It was for me.

But in the end, I choose forgiveness. I choose acceptance. I choose compassion. And I choose to be a real feminist by embracing everyone's right to pursue what they love, whether it's pageants or fandom or both.

T, I'm sorry.

#personal #greatcon #state of the fandom

I post before I can change my mind, and I turn off the option to receive anonymous DMs. I know half the internet will have Opinions™ about this post, and I'm honestly not interested in seeing them. I've made up my mind and my heart. That's all I need. Now I just need to see if Teagan can forgive me.

My phone vibrates, demanding my attention, but I ignore it completely, because the announcers have finally shut up and turned the show back to the contestants for what they're calling *casual fashion wear*. It doesn't look all that casual to me, though I guess anything that isn't a ball gown is casual to these people.

With each girl's walk, the announcer rattles off a fact about their hobbies or aspirations. The girls are all aged sixteen through nineteen, and they span a whole range from college-freshman physics majors and prelaw students, to animal lovers and missionaries, to award-winning cheerleaders and debate champions. I never would have thought there'd be so much variety among a group of pageant girls, or so much . . . okay, yes, *intelligence*. That's a terrible thing to think. I have a lot of brain garbage to clean out, apparently.

When Teagan appears onstage, swinging her hips like a runway model in a gorgeous little lace dress and a yellow flannel shirt that looks touchably soft, my mouth goes dry at the vision of her confidence and beauty. She walks like she owns the stage, stalking from one corner to the next with a grin like she's got a wicked secret from the world, and it's a *good* one. Others are cheering, so I add my voice to the fray, whooping as loud as I can so she'll know I'm here for her.

It must work, because she adjusts her gaze so it casts out into the audience, hot and fiery, and her smile deepens into something true. When she pops her hip with a little more sass for her walk to the back, I know she heard me.

And better yet? I think she just might forgive me.

My phone vibrates again, and I glance down to check the message I ignored earlier.

> **paintmeinviolet:**
> 😼

> **paintmeinviolet:**
> What do I call YOU? Enbyfriend? Datemate?

I swallow hard as my eyes well up. I haven't even thought about terminology yet. I don't think I'm ready to, honestly. *Girlfriend* is something I'm used to, something I've been before. It doesn't squick me out the same way being called *young lady* and *good girl* does, which I suppose means it's good enough for now. I take a breath, hesitate to make sure it feels right, then message her back.

> **KayfortheWinnet:**
> Girlfriend is fine for now. We can figure it out for real
> later.

Because there'll *be* a later.

Because I have an amazing girlfriend who's about to rock this pageant.

Chapter
Twenty-six

✶

TEAGAN

*M*y blood pumps with a hot surge of adrenaline and want as I strip out of my fashion wear outfit, chucking the shirt under my station with all my pent-up energy. Maybe it's the Red Bull hitting my system, but I think it's more than that. God, it felt *great* out there. I rocked the stage, I could feel it, and the crowd reacted really well.

Kay reacted really well. They really are out there, cheering for me, waiting for me.

And this next bit? It's for both of us.

I slip into my formerly boring white evening gown, careful to make sure the side panels of the overskirt stay securely bustled to the sides of the dress until I'm ready to deploy them onstage. It's a mermaid silhouette gown, which does look great on my curves, and the white glows against my skin, but it's plain and lifeless and has no contrast.

Or at least, it didn't before. Now, from the front, the band of fabric accenting my waist shimmers the same purple color as the shoes. And that's just the start. There's so much more to show off out there.

I blot my sweat away, fix my lipstick and hair, swap out my boots for Lady's bright-purple heels, and rush back to the line as soon as I can so Miss North Carolina has zero time to mess with me. As if reading my mind, Jess slides into line behind me, guarding my back like a true best friend. We'll have to shuffle around into appropriate stage order eventually, but for the moment I'm glad I can take her hand and give it a squeeze.

"Congrats on Top Fifteen!" I say, bouncing on the balls of my feet as best I can in heels. "You've been so amazing this weekend. I'm so proud of us."

"What's gotten into you all of a sudden?" she asks, deftly side-stepping the compliment in favor of using our thirty seconds to grill me. "You were all Mopey McSadpants this morning and afternoon, and now you're on *fire*. What gives?"

I grin and waggle my eyebrows at her. "Part of it is Kay. They messaged me and apologized for last night, *really* apologized. And they're *here*, Jess. In the audience. You should have heard them cheering for me out there."

Her eyes narrow. "Love, are you sure you can let it go that easily? Last night was awful."

I tone down my scary, hyped-up smile and meet Jess's eyes directly, so she'll take me seriously. "I know. It was. And we'll have to talk about it. But I really do understand why they reacted how they did, considering the fact they got suddenly outed to their entire hometown. They were hurt and terrified. It doesn't make it right, but I do get that I was just a convenient target in the blast zone."

Jess purses her lips. "It really *doesn't* make it right."

"I know." I nod and lower my gaze. "But it also doesn't erase everything else from the whole weekend. I want to give Kay a chance to apologize and give us *both* the chance to do this right, with absolutely no secrets or holding back between us. To see if maybe we can be something once this weekend is over. And I'm just . . . tired. Of hiding, of denying, of being angry and . . . yeah, in some ways, *fake*. I just want to let it all go. Is that wrong?"

The producer calls out a thirty-second warning, and Jess takes my hand and squeezes. "It's not wrong. If you're sure, then you've got my support. But I'm still going to look out for you."

She pauses then raises an eyebrow, sticking one finger under my gown's overskirt to get a peek at the hidden alterations inside. "So, if Kay is here, then they're going to see . . ."

"Yeah." I grin, pride swelling in my chest. "Win or lose, this is going to be one for the history books."

Then the other girls start to join the line, and we're forced apart for our final walk onstage. I squeeze her hand one more time before we separate and whisper, "Break a leg." She smiles softly at me and waggles her fingers, and then we're moving, the line filtering one by one onto the stage for the gown pose and fun fact.

I hope the stage manager got my revised fact for tonight. I think it'll work out even if not, but it'll definitely add a bit of a "screw you" to the proceedings.

My heart starts racing long before it's my turn, but I reach back for some of the best advice Rhonda ever gave me: Tell yourself it's not nerves, it's *excitement*. I can't *wait* to debut this dress. This is going to be amazing.

I take a breath, lift my chin, and strut out onstage with the side panels of my dress gripped close to my hips. The initial crowd reaction is much less enthusiastic than for my fashion wear. Understandable; this dress is dull as dry cereal, even with the added purple flash. But the host reads off my fun fact—the new one—and I let my smile widen as I wait for my cue.

"Miss Virginia! Teagan loves to hand-paint clothing for friends and family, *and* for sale in her online shop. Following an unfortunate accident with the gown she wore for yesterday's preliminary competition, Teagan used her skills to create an intricate design on this plain gown."

And with a dramatic flip, I undo the bustles and snap the side panels of the overskirt out like a bird of prey spreading its wings. The audience audibly gasps, and suddenly the volume of the cheering quadruples as I take my first pose at stage right. I do a slow twirl for the photographers crowded around the front of the stage, letting the stage lights and camera flashes pour over the shimmery paint and holding the skirt panels open as I stride to the next spot.

Inside the panels, hidden from view unless they're allowed to flow open around the dress, I've painted a free-flowing design of waves and whorls, starting with red up near my hips, then fading into orange, into yellow, into green, down into a gradient of blue-indigo-violet at the hem. It took me hours last night, and more time for touch-up in between events today, but the result is exactly what I wanted. To the audience, and to the judges, it's probably a summery rainbow design of waves and sunrays, flowing with movement and rich, bleeding colors.

To me? It's a gigantic pride flag.

Kay's voice bolsters my courage for another pose and twirl at stage left, then I move up to center stage, directly in front of the judges. I turn in a slow circle, letting them see every intricate detail I managed to weave into the design with what little time I had. I worked especially hard to get the purple paint mixed to just the right shade to match the shoes, so it looks like the design flows down into them.

I can't see the judges through the stage lights, but judging from the murmuring I hear below me, I've made quite an impression. A good or bad one, who knows. But this will be memorable.

And, when I execute my final turn to walk backstage, I give the judges a view of the back. I wasn't able to do much, only paint the laces that tie up the back of the gown purple to match the shoes. But purple was my mother's favorite color, and it's the color of pride.

What they can't see? At the edge of each of the laces, in tiny, hand-painted letters, it reads *221b*. Jess didn't really understand that part, but then, she wasn't supposed to. That part is for fandom.

And the whole thing is for me.

This is probably my last pageant. My last chance to be on-stage like this. Word is going to get out about me after this weekend—Madison will make sure of it. But for the first and last time, for one glorious time, I am completely myself. A piece of every part of my life up there with me, for better or worse.

After the last of the fifteen girls finishes her walk, we do one last review walk before coming to a choreographed stop at the rear of the stage, leaving room at the front for the final five lineup. This is the moment where I find out if my gamble paid off. If the judges liked my gown stunt, I'll make Top Five and have a shot at this thing. If they thought it was too much, too distracting, or picked up on the pride aspect and decided to be homophobic douchebags, I'll be out, and the scholarship will go to someone else. Hopefully Jess.

Beside me, Miss North Carolina shifts her weight to her other hip. Beyond her, Jess stands still as a statue, betraying her nerves through her stiffness. I breathe slowly, in and out through my nose with my smile fixed in place. Sounds blur together as the hosts ramble on until they receive the envelope from the judges, the gold-edged paper gleaming under the blazing-hot lights.

The host glances down at the paper then out at the audience with a knowing smile.

"And now, without further ado, let's meet our top five finalists for this year's Miss Cosmic Teen USA! In random order, starting off with . . ."

The whole room is still, silent.

"Pennsylvania!"

I gasp as if it were my own state called and swing around to catch Jess's hand as she walks by, her face glowing with joy. This is one of the only parts where we're able to break our perfect poise and show genuine emotion for each other, so long as it's positive—and when it comes to Jess, I could not possibly have more joy in my heart for her. She squeezes my hand and lets out an excited squeak as she strides up to take her place at the front of the stage. I've never been so happy for someone who's not me to get into the top five of a pageant.

The crowd settles for the next candidate as soon as Jess is in her spot. The hosts pass the mic and read . . .

"New Mexico!"

I applaud with the other girls, but we're all thinking the same thing: Only three spots left. Then Colorado is called up with barely a breath between, and that makes two. Then the mic is passed to the cohost for . . .

"Come on down, North Carolina!"

It takes every ounce of my restraint to control my expression, when all my lip wants to do is curl in obvious disgust. It figures. North Carolina presses a perfectly manicured hand to her chest in exaggerated surprise and takes the fourth spot in the line, fanning herself like a fainting maiden.

Only one spot left, and I send all my mental energy toward that little piece of paper as if I could possibly affect the outcome. Come on, judges. Take a chance on me. Reward my creativity, reward my effort and resolve, go outside your usual box, and—

"Virginia!"

Chapter
Twenty-seven

*

TEAGAN

a shriek from the back of the audience covers my own un-controlled squeal as *Virginia* reverberates through the room.

The top five.

I made the top five!

With an internal fist pump of victory, I flip the panels of my gown open and make my walk to the front, my smile honest and real and half-laughing. I do the required congratulatory hand-hold with Miss North Carolina, since she's the one right next to me, unfortunately, but make sure to lean around and catch Jess's eye. Top Five together, just like baby Teagan and Jess dreamed of. There's no time for anything more than a quick grin, though, because the host plows right along the agenda.

"Let's learn a little bit more about each of our finalists! Each girl will be asked one personal question and one final interview question as part of their final score. First up, in random order is . . . ." He reaches into a fishbowl on the podium and withdraws a card. "Miss Pennsylvania!"

The crowd cheers for Jess as she glides across the stage, exuding a perfect aura of grace and calm. I know better, though. This is her ultimate fear. She can do her turns on the catwalk with the pros, all attitude and untouchable beauty, and she slays the interview portion when it's just a small panel of judges. Speaking in front of a huge crowd like this fills her with the worst kind of anxiety, though. I send her every spare bit of good energy I can muster as she gets through her personal question then forgets to repeat the question as part of the answer with the interview. Not an automatic loss, but definitely not in her favor. It's not looking good for her, and it shows in her posture as she takes her spot back in line.

Miss Colorado goes next and answers her questions brilliantly, though she speaks so fast, I almost can't catch her full answers. Definitely a knock to her score. Can't let the nerves get the best of you. Poor New Mexico gets screwed—her personal question answer is fantastic, but her interview question references current events that she obviously is not even slightly up on, and she has to stumble through a vague, bullshitted answer. I wince internally and smile encouragingly as she walks past me. We've all been there, and it's painful as hell. Then it's my turn.

"Miss Virginia! Come on over!" the host says with excessive pep. I flare the panels of my dress and make my way over with a smile, my heart fluttering against my ribs. I'm good at interviews, thanks to years of pageants, but no one is completely immune to being onstage like this. This round, more than anything else at the pageant, is completely unpredictable, difficult to prepare for, and contestants often sink or swim based on their answers. Once you're in the final five, the scores are close enough that any small word or gesture can make a huge difference.

I greet the host and the judges then turn to await my question, hoping it's not another dead mother stunt. They love to do that to me. And I don't mind talking about it, really, but I hate having it sprung on me suddenly or used like a gimmick. I listen attentively as the host reads from his cue card:

"Miss Virginia, one of your big hobbies is hand-painting clothes. How did you get into doing such an unusual craft?"

I smile, for once happy to answer one of their inane questions. This one is easy.

"I first discovered hand-painted clothing from a local artist in my hometown of Charlottesville, Virginia. Before she died, my mother used to take me to the craft fairs held on the downtown pedestrian mall, and I would be completely taken in by all the amazing things people made with their own two hands and creativity."

I let a bit of that nine-year-old fascination shine through in my voice and expression. It's not hard—those craft fairs are one of my most vivid memories, and I still go every year.

"I already loved to paint, but it wasn't until I was a few years older, after pageants had taught me a bit of confidence, that I felt like I could approach that artist at a show and ask questions about her technique. She was kind enough to teach me, and I've been practicing constantly ever since!" I finish with a smile and little flare of the painted skirt, as if to say, *See?*

Okay, I absolutely nailed that one. Repeated the question in the answer, slipped in a mention of my home state and town, referenced the benefits of participating in pageants, got to remember my mother, and told a cute anecdote that tied directly into the dress I'm currently wearing. They could not have asked me a better question, and the smattering of applause after I finish is more than just polite.

I hope with all my might that I get another easy one for my interview question as I reach into the fishbowl to draw the name of the judge who will ask it of me. I draw the woman with the kind eyes from yesterday's interview and turn to her with a patient smile.

She looks up at me with a mask of indifference, but the corners of her eyes are crinkled with a suppressed smile. "Miss Virginia," she begins, "what do you think are the three most important qualities a person should have to be a positive member of our society?"

Okay, don't go blank. Three qualities. Start repeating the question, use it to talk about qualities you possess. Do it now.

"I think the three most important qualities for being a positive member of our society are resilience, compassion, and drive," I say, summoning up as much of my fierce, powerful interview persona as I can. This is where I can clinch it, if I can actually connect those three qualities together into something coherent.

"We all experience many setbacks in life, and I believe we are defined by how we respond to those setbacks. Being resilient means always bouncing back from the bad things in life, learning from them, and letting them make you stronger. Drive is your momentum. It can be easy to fall into a rut, letting opportunities pass you by, especially after a setback. But if you can keep your momentum going, you can accomplish so much in your life."

Okay, that was less strong, but I can drive it home if I tie it all together. One last shot. "Once you are resilient and driven, the best thing a person can do is channel all that energy into compassion. If you treat your fellow humans with compassion in all you do, you make the world a better place with every word and action. It doesn't matter how great you are as an individual if you don't use your gifts to give back to others and leave the world better than you found it. Compassion also means treating *yourself* with kindness and respect, something that's easy to forget but absolutely critical. Self-compassion is the foundation for confidence, your ability to empathize with others, and the chance to learn from your mistakes and grow. I believe those three qualities are the best formula for a positive life."

There, a solid recovery that will likely wipe that fumbling in the middle from the judges' minds. I flash them a brilliant smile to stick the landing and catch two of them nodding to themselves as they scribble on their score sheets. A good sign, usually. This is going well.

I thank the host and walk back to my spot, passing Miss North Carolina on the way as she takes her place front and center. I did well on my questions, I know I did, and (unfortunately for the others) no one else came anywhere close. So, my final competition, as always, is Miss North Carolina.

And she nails it.

"Our biggest problem is child hunger," she says, and "On mission trips, healthy food is my top priority."

Her blond hair is dazzling under the lights, glowing with the force of her righteousness.

"My commitment to pageants and my deep faith keep me on the right track as a person," she says. "I'm so blessed to have Jesus in my life." I am so screwed.

My heart sinks.

There is no way I can win over that. Name-dropping Jesus and playing the good southern belle and feeding the hungry children, and *damn* it, she's got this in the bag. Unless she has lower scores in the rest of the pageant categories or a significantly lower interview score than me, I've just lost the title to Miss North Carolina, of all people. I came so close, overcame the sabotage and the spying, just to lose right here at the end.

"And now, ladies and gentlemen, we've come to the moment you've all been waiting for," the host says, his voice lowered dramatically, accompanied by a thrum of tense synth music. "It's time to crown this year's Miss Cosmic Teen USA! Our second, third, and fourth runners-up will all receive five-thousand-dollar scholarships to the university of their choice, and we're proud to award those scholarships starting with our fourth runner-up . . ."

The whole room grows still, and I hold my breath.

Please not me, please not me, please not me . . .

"Miss New Mexico!"

She steps forward to accept her bouquet and pose for the photo op with all the appropriate cheer, but her smile doesn't reach her eyes. Being the last of the top five is pretty great . . . but it's still last. The tinny synthesizers swell as the cohost takes the mic and announces the third runner-up as . . .

"Miss Colorado!"

Her smile is quite a bit less convincing than Miss New Mexico's. I applaud politely all the same, but my guts are in knots. Three spots left. North Carolina, Jess, and me. *Oh God oh God oh God oh God.* I exhale slowly out between my smiling teeth as the host takes the mic back.

"Our second runner-up, and the last five-thousand-dollar scholarship recipient is . . ."

Please not me, please not Jess, please, please, please—

"Miss Pennsylvania!"

My heart gives a painful throb as Jess leaves my side to accept her bouquet, radiant as ever. She deserves better. She's a powerful presence, a force to be reckoned with, and she would do incredible things with her year of service. I know this is more than she hoped for, more than she thought she'd get, but a cruel person like North Carolina shouldn't get more than Jess.

But that's exactly what's going to happen, because we're *it.* The final two. Me and Miss North Carolina. Runner-up . . . and Miss Cosmic Teen USA. But which of us will get the crown?

The cheering section chanting some coordinated song for North Carolina certainly has an opinion.

But so does my cheering section of one.

"Okay, this is it!" the cohost says, whipping the crowd into a frenzy. "Will the final two please step forward?"

We move to the front of the stage, turn toward each other, and join hands, clutching each other at heart level just like we're supposed to. But this feels anything other than sisterly and joyful, like it has every other time. Normally, I have immense respect for whoever is across from me. Often, it's someone I've hung out with and bonded with over the course of a pageant weekend, someone I could genuinely be happy for.

Not this time. North Carolina's nails bite into my skin, and she whispers without moving her lips, "You're going down."

There will be no excited hug after this announcement. One way or the other.

The music surges, a dramatic crescendo that grates at my already frayed nerves, then settles at a low, rumbling hum.

"Our first runner-up will receive a ten-thousand-dollar scholarship to the university of her choice. If, for any reason, tonight's winner cannot fulfill her Miss Cosmic Teen USA duties, the first runner-up will take over the crown and its responsibilities. The judges had a difficult decision on their hands, choosing between these two amazing young women, but this year they have chosen the first runner-up in this year's Miss Cosmic Teen USA to be . . ."

Please, universe. Let the gay nerd girl get a win. Let me make a stand. Let me do something with this. Please, let me, let me, let me—

"Miss North Carolina!"

I suck in a ragged gasp.

"Which makes this year's Miss Cosmic Teen USA winner Teagan Miller, Miss Virginia!"

Madison drops my hands like they're on fire, her mask of grace and poise wiping away like yesterday's makeup as I stumble back, eyes wide. I hear the words as if underwater, the roar of the crowd low and staticky, drowned out by the throb of my racing pulse. I'm supposed to be doing a practiced, photogenic reaction pose of surprised joy: hands pressed to my mouth, tears in my eyes, a little dip at the knees . . .

I gape like a frog catching flies.

Really?

Really?

Oh, here come the tears.

I press my fingertips into either side of my nose to keep them from spilling over as Kay's voice soars above the rest of the crowd, whooping and calling my name. Last year's Miss Cosmic USA steps forward with an enormous bouquet I can barely wrap an arm around as the host announces my prize package.

"Teagan will be flown to New York City for a jam-packed media week, followed by a year of community service and publicity events as the reigning Miss Cosmic Teen USA. She will also receive our grand prize, a twenty-five-thousand-dollar scholarship to the university of her choice. Congratulations, Miss Virginia!"

I barely remember to duck down in time to receive the crown, its weight both heavier and lighter than I expected as they settle it firmly on my head. When I stand back to my full height, the crowd roars its approval. For me, in my rainbow dress, crying openly before a packed theater.

"Teagan, it's time to take your first walk as Miss Cosmic Teen USA!" the cohost reminds me in a peppy voice, and I huff a small laugh at my own scattered brain. Right. Time to strut my stuff on the catwalk and pose for the cameras, crown and all. With the bouquet in my right hand, I can only hold one side of the gown open to reveal my rainbow design, but the bright flowers provide a brilliant pop of matching color. When I arrive back at the host's side, he smiles indulgently and leans close.

"So, Teagan, how does it feel to be Miss Cosmic Teen USA?"

I lean into the mic he tips toward me and smile my most brilliant smile. The dress would have been enough for me, but now that I have this opportunity . . .

I can do so much more.

"It feels amazing. I'm so grateful to the judges, to the Miss Cosmic organization, to my best friend, Jess, who is Miss Pennsylvania, to my father who couldn't be here today, and . . ." I swallow. Take a breath. ". . . to my girlfriend, whom you've heard cheering for me all evening. Thank you for coming to support me, Kay! It means the world."

I tip my head back just a fraction as fresh tears spill then lean back to the mic.

"This win is dedicated to my late mom and to all the other queer girls out there. You are beautiful, you are worthy, and you are perfect. Never forget it, ever."

A wave of scandalized murmurs washes over the theater like an angry swarm of bees, but the startled host recovers quickly enough to call for one more round of applause. It's a bit more tentative than before, a bit less raucous from certain corners, but I'll take it. Because for the first time—the first time *ever*—it's *me*, in all my honest glory, receiving their applause.

Another barrier broken. Another step toward pageants that celebrate *everyone*. I hope this is a push in the right direction, toward a future full of pageants that celebrate bigger bodies, darker skin, shorter hair, with winners who wear a hijab or are trans girls or use they/them pronouns. I want that so much. I hope this moment helps.

As the host rattles off thank-yous to all the pageant sponsors, I let one hand drift up to feel the jewels and spires of my new crown, tracing each curve with the tip of a finger. It's cool, and smooth, and surprisingly delicate.

I secretly hate tiaras.

But this one?

Well.

I guess this one's okay.

Chapter Twenty-eight

KAYLEE

The herd of pageant attendees parts for me easily, though that might have more to do with my newly discovered, super-queer force field than any actual skill at navigating crowds. The murmurs and stares certainly make it seem that way, but I can't bring myself to care. I'm here for Teagan. That's it.

When I reach the backstage door, a burly bouncer blocks my way with his massive forearms folded over his chest.

"Nobody through here without a pass," he grunts. With his message delivered, his eyes slide away, back to scanning the crowd. Obviously a person used to being obeyed without question.

"I need to see my girlfriend. She just won the pageant!" I say, emphasizing the word *girlfriend*. I don't know if it's totally accurate, but it worked before, so it might work again.

His brow furrows, and his eyes flick down to me then back out at the crowd. "No one goes in without a press or friends and family pass. I can't help you."

I blow out a tense breath. There's gotta be a way in. I can't not see her after that, after the rainbow and her proud announcement, the beautiful things she said. She's going to need support, and I need to be there to give it.

"Please," I say, summoning up some tears. It's not hard. "Do you really think they'd give *me* a friends and family pass? That would require them to admit that their pageant princess was . . . you know . . ."

I drop my gaze to my shoes and sniffle. The man heaves a thunderous sigh.

"They never let my boyfriend into anything, either. But I can't lose my job, so—"

"KAY!"

My head whips up. A girl with sleek, golden-brown hair in a bold green gown waves frantically in my direction. "Come on, she's asking for you!"

I have no idea who this girl is, but I'm not about to tell the bouncer that. I turn wide puppy eyes up at him.

"Come on, see, Miss"—I cut my gaze back to the girl's sash— "Oregon is personally inviting me back. Can I, please?"

Miss Oregon strides forward, graceful and confident, and lays a hand on the bouncer's bicep. "Come on, it's fine. They're with us."

The bouncer sighs again, but the corners of his eyes crinkle with a suppressed smile. "Fine, fine. I never saw you. I don't know how you got in."

I grin and toss him a wink. "I was never here, and I have no idea who you are. Have a great night!"

His lips twitch, but he definitely does *not* smile.

Backstage, Miss Oregon takes my hand and guides me through the mess of stage props, media representatives, and girls in gowns meeting their parents. Despite the crowd, it's easy to spot Teagan; she's the one lit by portable lighting equipment and surrounded by microphones, holding court with the reporters. She's radiant, posing for photos with the wings of her gown held open, smiling and answering questions with blunt honesty.

When her eyes land on me, all the noise fades to a dull roar. Her smile, so confident and powerful, softens into something gentler, a bit hesitant. I wave, shy but needing her to know I'm here for her.

And then I notice that all the cameras have turned toward me.

"Teagan, is this your girlfriend?" a reporter asks, shoving a microphone in her face.

"Can you confirm that?" another asks, shoving a microphone in *my* face.

Teagan and I lock eyes and burst out laughing. She shoulders her way past the crowd and throws her arms open, and I collapse into them, grateful, overwhelmed.

"Cameras away, please," Teagan says, her voice kind but firm. "They're under eighteen, and there's no one here to sign a photo release for them. Please give us a moment."

Most of the reporters lower their cameras, grumbling, but I hear a few stealth *clicks* behind me anyway. I should be terrified, consumed by obsession about whether and when the photos will make it back home and out me to the world. But Madison already did that, so there's not much more damage that can be done. In a way, she's freed me from the fear that has so dominated my life for the past few years. I guess in some ways, I can thank her for that. I run a hand over the laces up the back of Teagan's gown, searching for words.

"Oh my God, Tea, this is so *much!*" is all I can come up with, murmured into hair that smells sweet with the blend of products holding it in place. She squeezes me tighter.

"I know. Do you want to leave? You don't have to put up with this. I can meet you later, once the media junket is over."

"No," I say quickly. "It's fine. This is important. Finish what you need to do. I'll be waiting. I have so much I need to say."

"Me too," she says, pressing a kiss to my cheek.

I look down to hide my blush. "Any family members here I should be watching out for? Anyone you need to see tonight?"

She drops her forehead against my shoulders and groans. "What I need is the biggest, greasiest burrito you can find within walking distance of the hotel."

Oh my God, adorable. I wrap my arms around her and laugh. "Then let me take you out to dinner to celebrate when you're all done. I'm sure I can find you a burrito."

My phone buzzes in my pocket, and with a jolt, I remember—my friends. I texted them a garbled string of nonsense about getting the publishing contract and going to the pageant. I leave one arm around Teagan and pull my phone out with the other. Five unread texts.

Ami: Are you still at the pageant?

Ami: I saw your post on Scroll and it was so sweet I cried, you jerk.

Ami: I'm glad you worked it out, and I think you did the right thing by apologizing.

Ami: Are you okay? Are you going to see her?

Ami: We're planning to go to dinner tonight, are you coming?

Ah, there's a thought.

"I have an even better plan," I say. "You and me, and your friends, and my friends. Let's all go out together. I think you deserve that. A little fandom, a little pageant, and a little me holding your hand at the table all night. How's that?"

Teagan pulls away from my shoulder and looks up at me, smiling with tears in her eyes. "It sounds completely perfect."

I hug her again then freeze as Miss North Carolina walks by, scowling to herself and wrapped up in her own thoughts. Teagan looks up, curious, then her face twists into something I never expected. Sadness.

"Hey, Madison," she calls.

North Carolina stops but doesn't turn around. Teagan pulls away and lays a hand on Madison's arm. Their words are brief and murmured, and after a moment Madison jerks her arm away and storms off. Teagan's eyes follow her for a moment, then she sighs and returns to me.

"What was that about?" I ask.

Teagan shakes her head. "I don't want an enemy for life, but the bridge is pretty well burned, it seems."

I squeeze Teagan's hand.

"You're a good person to even try after what she's done to you," I say. "Are you going to be okay? Coming out like that, they're not going to take away your scholarship or your tour or anything, right?"

Teagan shoots me a sly smile. "Please, they're already writing the press releases." She spreads her hands in front of her, as if revealing the headlines. "First openly gay Miss Cosmic Teen USA! The Miss Cosmic organization is so forward-thinking and progressive! We totally knew the whole time! They'll milk it for all it's worth, because it's too late for them to do anything else without looking like tools."

She laughs, and her smile widens even more when Miss Pennsylvania breaks through the crowd—the best friend who saw what a jerk I was last night. I hope she doesn't hate me.

But if she does, she hides it well as she walks straight up into my space.

"Hey, I'm Jess," she says to me, holding her hand out for me to shake. "Nice to officially meet you."

I hesitate, my instincts still telling me even after all this that it's a pretty-popular-girl trap, but I fight it down and take her hand. "Kay. Nice to meet you."

"You too. I've heard a lot about you while I've been covering for Teagan's ass all weekend," she says with a smirk, then sticks out her tongue at Teagan. "A *lot* about you. Almost constantly. I swear, I was—"

"*Okay*, that's enough, thanks," Teagan says, throwing her arms around Jess in an enormous hug. "Jess is my closest friend in the pageant world. We've been best friends since we were thirteen, and she was one of the first people I came out to."

"Via text message because you were a *chicken*, loser," Jess shoots back, shoving Teagan gently aside. "Are we going out after or what?"

Teagan's smile dims just a fraction, taking on an edge of nervousness. "Actually, I was hoping we could all go out. Together. The three of us, Oregon, and Kay's friends. Is that okay?" she asks, hesitant.

Jess purses her lips. "Hey, OREGON!"

"WHAT?" Oregon shouts back from across the wing. She strides up, unaffected, a rolling suitcase behind her. Her green gown is gone, and she's dressed down in a pair of comfortable jeans and a plain black T-shirt.

"Come to dinner with us and a bunch of nerds?"

I bristle, ready to go on the defensive, but Oregon grins with something like relief. "Yes, please. I desperately need to sit at a table with someone who knows what a hobbit is."

I surprise myself with a laugh. "Yeah. You'll love my friends, I think."

Jess nods. "That's settled, then. Why don't you two go back to the room and find us a place to eat while we get changed and Teagan finishes her courtly duties? We'll meet you up there."

My heart doesn't want to leave Teagan, pulling at the inside of my chest like it wants to be inside hers instead. But I pull her close, and we kiss, long and lingering, until we're forced to separate with a squeeze of our hands. I follow Oregon in a daze, back across the street, into the hotel, into the elevator, floating on a cloud of Teagan's kisses and sparkling eyes. I hate being away from her, knowing we have so much to say and so little time left.

But now, at least, I know there will be more.

Dinner is surprisingly un-awkward. Ami and Jess hit it off immediately, seeming to sense each other's protective friend aura. The two of them end up in deep conversation with Lady for most of dinner, discussing some movie I've never seen and drawing comparisons to, of all things, *Wuthering Heights*. Nerds. Cakes and Oregon, on the other hand, end up making out in a bathroom at the restaurant and aren't heard from for most of the night.

And Teagan and I?

We sit pressed close from shoulder to knee through the whole meal, kissing frequently, touching constantly, and drawing plenty of annoyed stares from the Taco Stop's other clientele. Teagan's phone blows up throughout the entire meal with texts from friends, family, and the pageant coach she apparently dropped right before the finals. The coach, Rhonda, was gracious enough about it, apparently. The messages strike me as curt (you were right and congratulations), but Teagan assures me that coming from Rhonda, it's an effusive apology. Finally, Teagan gives up and turns off her phone so she can give 100 percent of her attention to me . . . and her burrito. After a long, lingering meal at which the three pageant girls delight in foods they haven't been allowed to touch for months, we all pile out into the street, clustered together under the streetlights in the humid Florida night.

"We're gonna go back to the room and watch a movie," Ami says, gesturing to Lady and Jess. A significant glance passes between Jess and Teagan, their lips twitching with barely suppressed humor. Cakes and Oregon glance at each other and link arms.

"I think we're going to hit the end-of-con pool party. I hear there will be dancing," Cakes says.

Pointedly, no one asks what Teagan and I have planned. We walk back to the hotel as a group, chatting easily until we reach the hotel lobby. As our party fractures into thirds, Teagan takes my hand, and we drift away from the others, into an elevator we have all to ourselves. As soon as the door closes, I wrap my arms around her waist and yank her to me, my mouth a hairsbreadth from hers.

"So, Fourth of July weekend?" I ask, my lips brushing hers with each syllable.

"Absolutely," she says. "My dad will be out of town."

"Oh no. Whatever will we do, all alone at your place?"

I trace my tongue along her lower lip then dip into her open mouth just as the elevator doors slide open.

We miss our chance and have to ride the elevator all the way back down again.

Part of me wants to hit the end-of-con party, wants to dance with Teagan again, knowing what we know and feeling what we feel. I want her to be there, to own it, to enjoy being out and proud in every way. Part of me wants her to have that experience and to have it myself, too.

But most of me wants to see her in my bed, that gorgeous dark hair spread out on a pillow, her body hot and moving against mine.

So we have our own private dance party.

No music necessary.

I don't think I'll ever have a problem writing kissing scenes ever again.

Epilogue

KAYLEE

*C*on drop is the worst. After spending a long weekend in a blissfully accepting, queer-positive space, going back to the heteronormative real world is like being doused with ice water and left to air-dry in winter. At least now I understand why it hits so hard.

By night, I write with a feverish intensity, motivated like never before by the signed contract tacked up next to my computer, my goals real and achievable and within my grasp. By day, I pass my volunteer shifts at the local library in a dreamlike state, shelving books as I replay my time with Teagan.

We talk on Scroll or via text every day and on the phone as often as we can. The Fourth of July weekend begins tomorrow, and I managed to talk my mom into letting me make the drive to Charlottesville alone. Theoretically I'm going to check out the campus of the University of Virginia, which I have no intention of applying to. I'm otherwise grounded for the rest of the summer, though, so whatever sells the trip, right?

Whatever gets me a long weekend with Teagan and her gorgeous *everything*.

"I know that smile," the teen services librarian says, jerking me out of my daydream. "Who's the lucky one? You and Mike aren't a thing anymore, right?"

I grin. Now's as good a time as any to start officially coming out to people around here, I suppose. It's all over the high school and my mom's social circles anyway.

"Her name is Teagan," I say with no hesitation. "You might know her from the news—she just won the Miss Cosmic Teen USA pageant."

"Oh, I did hear about that!" the librarian says without batting an eye. "I had no idea *you* were the girlfriend the article I read was talking about. That's so awesome, Kaylee. You're like . . . very mildly internet famous!"

The librarian gives me a high five then grabs a handful of books from my cart to help with the shelving. "How are you feeling about it? Are you okay with all the media attention? People are being good to you?"

I think for a moment. My mom was surprisingly indifferent, other than grounding me for ignoring her phone calls and texts, though it's clear she expects it to be a "phase" and otherwise refuses to engage with the topic at all. Ami snuck me her old Nintendo 2DS so we could play an old version of *Animal Crossing* together while I'm imprisoned at the house, being an amazing friend as always. Madison, for whatever reason, has left me completely alone since getting home. No internet harassment or anything. Hopefully she's given up and isn't just saving it all for the first day of school. Best of all, fandom nerds and queer kids from my school are coming out of the woodwork, reaching out to me to express quiet support or nerd out. I've been less alone than I thought all along. I was just too closed off to notice. So, overall?

"It's been . . . fine, actually. Good. No problems. Maybe . . . things are changing."

The librarian smiles.

"I hope so. Come to me if you need anything, okay? I've got your back."

"Thanks," I say, then hesitate for just a second before adding: "Actually, there is one other thing. I'm using they/them pronouns now."

The librarian nods then does a quick look around for coworkers before turning back to whisper, "Me too, actually."

And they hold their fist out for a bump of solidarity. Amazing.

I still can't really dress the way I want to dress or use my pronouns at school this year—I'm just not ready—but if I can take anything away from the GreatCon weekend, it's that I don't have to look a certain way to be who I am. If I feel nonbinary, I *am* nonbinary. There's no right way to dress or act to prove it. Even when I have to be in this town that doesn't welcome me, it doesn't make me any less who I am.

My phone buzzes as I slide the last of the books from the shelving cart into place, and I sneak my phone out of my pocket for a quick check.

Teagan: Okay, I just finished reading the manuscript you sent me, and YOU CANNOT END IT THERE. I'm dying. Tell me you have the ending written and you're just leaving me hanging to mess with me.

I snort and tap out a quick reply.

Kay: I was hoping you might have some feedback to help me figure out how to end it.

There's barely a two-second delay before Teagan's reply.

Teagan: Oh, I have FEEDBACK. Call me tonight?

I bite my bottom lip to keep in the ridiculous smile I can't help but wear these days, but it's horribly ineffective.

Kay: How about you tell me in person. Tomorrow.

Teagan: . . . tomorrow. 🖤

I'll spend the weekend wrapped up in her, breathing her in and hearing her voice without the dull interference of the phone. I'll feel her skin under my palms and her lips on mine, her hair sifting through my fingers and brushing against my shoulders. It'll be a glorious weekend, and it'll be too short, but it'll also be a much-needed reaffirmation. For us.

For me.

Since coming back from the con, it's like I walk taller. I've never felt so at ease in my own skin before. I'm more open to the people around me, to their struggles and secrets and wounds. I speak up more freely and take up more space.

I'm also more driven than ever. More confident. Brave, even.

I feel more *myself* than I ever have in my entire life.

Witness me.

ACKNOWLEDGMENTS

This book is intensely personal in a whole new way for me. All my books have big, raw, vulnerable parts of me in them, but this book is even closer to the truth of my heart than all the rest. I didn't have the language for being nonbinary as a teen. I barely understood that straight and gay weren't the only options. I loved fanfic, though, and I hated gender pressure, and I had feelings so intense that I thought I'd explode, and I poured all of that into this book. The fact that the world holds space for teens like Kay now is an immense source of relief and joy for me. It's still not a perfect or easy world, and there is so much fight left, especially for BIPOC queer folks. But for this kid, figuring things out in the '90s and early 2000s American South, it's a marvel to see the changes. I hope books like this one are a small balm for those who aren't quite there yet. It gets better. So very, very much better.

To the team at Wednesday Books: Working with you has been such a wonderful experience. Y'all are professional, dedicated, talented, and you really care. It shows in everything you do. Enormous thanks to Mara Delgado Sánchez (assistant editor), Brant Janeway (team leader), Rivka Holler (marketing), Sarah Schoof (publicity), Manu Velasco (copyeditor—sorry about the hyphens!), Eileen Rothschild (associate publisher),

Sara Goodman (editorial director), and the army of people I will probably never cross paths with in sales and production who are critical to making a book happen. Special thank-you to Olga Grlic (designer) and Katie Smith (illustrator) for the perfect, joyful explosion of color that is this cover! To my anonymous sensitivity reader: so grateful for your honesty and labor. And of course, to Alexandra Sehulster, my wonderful editor and this book's ultimate champion: Thank you for a truly delightful experience. Your kindness and enthusiasm are like writer catnip.

To my agent, Eric Smith: Look, it's our first book baby! Thank you for believing in this one and finding it such a wonderful home when I thought it would be in a drawer forever. You just get me. And a quick shout-out to my previous agent, Barbara: Thanks for sharing your pageant experiences with me!

To all the fandom friends who are slyly named in this book: You're here because you made an incredible impact on me. This book wouldn't exist without the good times we had, the fic we read and wrote together, the cons and watch-alongs and gay brunch and karaoke and so much more. I'm grateful for you.

To my non-fandom friends who nonetheless love me and put up with my babble: Thank you always for your support. Really, though, it's best to just not even bring up Sherlock Holmes, I've told you this. I was not kidding. Thanks most of all to Leigh and Jamie, who both read very early versions of this book and never gave up on it.

To my baby bug: I'm glad you get to grow up in a world like this. Whoever you turn out to be, I'll love you forever and ever.

These things will always end with words for N: Thank you for loving me, creating a life with me, and always accepting me just as I am. Being with you brings me such joy.